devoted

ALSO BY JENNIFER MATHIEU

The Truth About Alice

devoted

a novel

JENNIFER MATHIEU

ROARING BROOK PRESS · NEW YORK

Copyright © 2015 by Jennifer Mathieu
Published by Roaring Brook Press
Roaring Brook Press is a division of Holtzbrinck Publishing Holdings
Limited Partnership
175 Fifth Avenue, New York, New York 10010
macteenbooks.com

Library of Congress Cataloging-in-Publication Data

Mathieu, Jennifer.
  Devoted / Jennifer Mathieu. — First edition.
    pages cm
  Summary: Rachel Walker is devoted to God and her large family, but as
her curiosity about the world her parents turned from grows and she finds
that neither Calvary Christian Church nor her homeschool education has
the answer she craves, she considers leaving her sheltered life, as an older
sister did.
  ISBN 978-1-59643-911-5 (hardback) — ISBN 978-1-59643-912-2 (e-book)
  [1. Christian life—Fiction.   2. Family life—Texas—Fiction.   3. Home
schooling—Fiction.   4. Brothers and sisters—Fiction.   5. Texas—
Fiction.]   I. Title.
  PZ7.M4274Dev 2015
  [Fic]—dc23

                                                        2014047411

Roaring Brook Press books may be purchased for business or promotional
use. For information on bulk purchases please contact Macmillan
Corporate and Premium Sales Department at (800) 221-7945 x5442
or by email at specialmarkets@macmillan.com.

"The Summer Day" from *House of Light* by Mary Oliver,
Published by Beacon Press Boston
Copyright 1990 by Mary Oliver
Reprinted by permission of The Charlotte Sheedy Literary Agency Inc.

First edition 2015
Book design by Elizabeth H. Clark
Printed in the United States of America

1 3 5 7 9 10 8 6 4 2

For Hännah,
with enormous gratitude and respect

"Believing takes practice."
—*Madeleine L'Engle,* A Wind in the Door

1

James Fulton is sweating like a sinner in church.

Which, of course, is exactly what he is.

All of us—the older kids my age and the mothers and the fathers and even the little toddlers whose feet don't touch the floor yet—all of us congregants of Calvary Christian Church of Clayton watch wide-eyed and silent from our metal folding chairs as James shifts his weight from one barrel-thick leg to the other, his ruddy face covered in a slick coat of perspiration. He squeezes his hands together as he sways back and forth, and a little map of sweat starts to form on the front of his yellow polyester short-sleeved shirt. Pastor Garrett stands off to the side, clutching his enormous Bible and nodding along with everything James says.

"I'm here before you with a purified heart," James continues, looking at his feet. His white-blond hair is newly shorn, making his flushed face seem even more scarlet. "I know I need to live radically for the Lord again. And I'm asking you to help me walk with God again because I know the punishment for sin is separation from the Lord and eternity in hell." Exhaling shakily and squeezing his hands together again, he makes the briefest of eye contact with the congregation before gazing back down at his feet.

My four-year-old sister Sarah is sitting in my lap, and she turns her little head to look at me and whispers too loudly, "Rachel, what'd that boy do?"

People shift in their seats around us at her question, but nobody says anything. "Shh, Sarah," I whisper back. "He's talking about how much he loves Jesus."

What James Fulton did was gratify the desires of the flesh, but I can't say that to Sarah. And I can't tell her that he looked at pictures of naked women on a computer and he got caught, and I can't tell her that he just got back from two weeks at Journey of Faith, a camp in east Texas where he spent hours in prayer and physical labor and repentance. Sarah's too little to understand about Journey of Faith.

She won't be too little to understand for much longer, of course. But for now, at least, it doesn't take much to distract her.

It seems one or two of us are sent to Journey of Faith every few years. By us I mean the older kids at Calvary Christian. Some are as young as thirteen or fourteen when they're sent away, and they always leave suddenly, spirited off by Pastor Garrett or a church elder, leaving the rest of us to consider the rumors we've heard about what Journey of Faith is all about. Long, forced hikes, little sleep, and endless, backbreaking physical work, along with hours spent alone studying Scripture. Those of us who've never gone put the pieces together from testimonies like the one James is delivering now. We know that Journey of Faith is a place where life is hard, but the Lord is supposed to work on your heart and transform you.

Everyone comes back looking like James.

His cheeks are cherry red, and the shame he carries radiates off him. He hasn't come out and explicitly stated his sin, but he knows we must know about how he's strayed. He knows we know about his stumbling block. We've learned about the sins that send some of us to Journey of Faith in the same way we've learned about the camp itself. In whispers and bits of whispers. In requests for prayers during youth fellowship and at evening Bible studies.

In the Scripture used by those who've fallen upon their return to the flock.

"So in closing," James continues, "I want to say that the Lord is leading me to share with you this verse from Psalms, a verse that the pastor at Journey of Faith shared with me in one of our sweet fellowships." I can tell he has practiced this part many times from the way his voice picks up speed and volume. " 'Wherewithal shall a young man cleanse his way? By taking heed thereto, according to thy word. With my whole heart have I sought thee. O let me not wander from thy commandments.'" There's a ripple of nodding heads, and at last James makes his way back to his row to join his parents. His mother squeezes him around his broad, beefy shoulders and his father nods approvingly, and I see how James smiles at them, a quick upturned smile that disappears as quickly as it arrives.

Pastor Garrett makes a commanding motion toward the corner where Mrs. Carter sits at the upright piano, and as I hear the opening notes of "It's Through the Blood," I lift my little sister in my arms and stand up to get ready to sing.

⚜

After the service ends, all of us spill out onto the weedy patch of grass and gravel in front of the church. I put Sarah down and watch her speed off and start racing around with some of the countless other small kids her age.

I weave through the crowd, smiling back brightly at everyone who smiles at me as I try to keep watch on my younger siblings. When I was little like them I could climb back into the family van after services with my worn-out copy of *Anne of Green Gables*, but the last time I tried that, Dad said I wasn't showing a sweet spirit. I'm seventeen now, and not only am I supposed to watch out for my little brothers and sisters, I'm supposed to be their model of proper behavior.

"Rachel! Rachel!" Someone is yelling my name from across the parking lot. I turn and spot my older sister, Faith, waving me over with the one arm she isn't using to hold her infant son, Caleb. It's early May in Texas and five hundred billion degrees, but somehow Faith isn't sweating, and her lavender blouse and knee-length denim skirt don't have a spot of baby puke on them.

"Hi," I say, joining her and some of the other young mothers of the congregation, several just a few years older than me. They stand in a loose circle holding their little ones, and their carefully groomed appearances and enthusiastic smiles make me run my fingers through my long, dark curls so I don't look too disheveled. I wish not for the first time that my hair were straighter like Faith's, but almost immediately I hear my father's voice reminding me that *a sound heart* is *the life of the flesh: but envy the rottenness of the bones.* I imagine my bones strong and pure, constructed of nothing but molecules of good thoughts, absent of any vanity. I smile at everyone and wiggle my fingers at my little nephew Caleb, choosing to give him my full attention while the other girls chatter around me.

"I was just saying," Faith starts, shifting Caleb from one hip to another with ease, "that James's testimony really moved me, really moved us all, actually, and I think the Lord has laid it on our hearts to try and organize some time for fellowship, where some of us older girls get together with some of the younger girls and talk about, you know, modest dress. About helping the boys and the young men in their struggle to remain spiritually pure. Just, you know, recommitting to that idea of biblical femininity."

Faith's voice is filled with enthusiasm, each sentence practically spilling on top of the next one. The other girls are nodding. Faith has always been good at helping us think of others. When we were little, she taught me to flip over magazine covers in the grocery checkout line if they had immodest images of girls and women that might tempt the eyes of our brothers.

"That sounds like it would be nice," I say. Faith is talking on excitedly when my eyes spot James Fulton by the side of Calvary Christian. He's alone. The quick smile he shared with his parents at the end of the service is gone now, and he leans against the church wall, staring out at a cinder-block building in the lot next door. The building used to house a tractor-and-lawn-mower repair service, but it was abandoned a long time ago, and now it's just a crumbling mess of a place. It's not anything to look at, that's for sure, but James is watching it like it's something worth watching.

His cheeks still appear red—maybe this time from the heat outside—and he takes a big gulp of air and tips his head back against the side of the church, shifting his gaze to the blue, cloudless sky. I imagine myself stepping up in front of the entire congregation to admit my deepest sins, and I know that James feels an embarrassment so painful he can barely stand to look any of us in the eye.

We should show compassion toward sinners, and James looks so pitiful standing there all by himself that I want somebody to walk over to talk to him about the weather or where he got his yellow polyester shirt or something that doesn't have to do with his sinful behavior or Journey of Faith or how proud we are of how he's walking with Jesus. But nobody goes to him, least of all me.

"I mean, I think we would be really honoring James's testimony if we put his words into action, don't you think?" Faith continues, almost breathless in her excitement.

"Oh, definitely," I answer, offering a quick smile.

When my father finds me a few minutes later and tells me it's time to leave, James Fulton is still standing there alone.

"Rachel, are the beans almost ready?"

"Just about done," I answer, giving them a nudge with my fork.

My mother smiles at me and nods. "What were you looking at out there?" she asks, motioning toward the kitchen window.

I shrug my shoulders and mumble, "Nothing, really." I

don't want to admit I've been distracted from my work and staring at some hummingbirds darting back and forth at the shrub of yellow bells in the front yard. They love to swoop and swerve at one another to get the best flower, like little kamikaze pilots. Everyone thinks hummingbirds are these sweet little birds, but they're really hateful, actually.

"Are you feeling okay?" I ask her, pouring the beans into a serving dish. She looks paler than normal, and there's a parade of pimples marching up her normally clear complexion.

"Yes, praise God," she answers, touching her belly. Walker baby number eleven is just a couple weeks along, and the first few months are always the worst for my mom when it comes to being pregnant. With Sarah, she spent what felt like forever trapped in the bathroom, throwing up during what should have been school time at the kitchen table.

This baby surprised us. I mean, as much as babies can be a surprise in a family with ten children. But my mom is forty-four, and it was sort of understood that two-year-old Isaac would be the last addition. Then this spring during evening Bible study, Dad read those familiar verses from Psalms that always serve as an announcement that a new Walker baby is on the way: "'As arrows are in the hand of a mighty man, so are the children of the youth. Happy is the man that hath his quiver full of them!'" When Dad said it, everyone turned to look at Mom, and she nodded, smiling shyly.

I smiled, too, of course, but my stomach sank just a bit at the same time. Mom had more time for all of us now that Isaac was sleeping through the night and would soon be out of diapers. And how was I supposed to keep up with my chores and help teach the little ones with my mother pre-occupied with the new baby? I had to reprimand myself as soon as I had those thoughts. *In all things give thanks, Rachel,* I reminded myself.

With Sunday dinner finally ready, everyone sits down to eat at the three tables pushed together. There are so many of us that the end of the long table is practically in the hall-way leading to my parents' bedroom. I set down a platter of rolls.

"What a lovely meal, Rachel," says Paul in the same loud voice that he uses to say everything. Paul is my sister Faith's husband. They live with baby Caleb about thirty minutes away in the next town over, but that doesn't stop them from spending almost every Sunday afternoon with us. Paul is five years older than me, but he acts like it's fifty years instead of five. His face is always pinched up like a spider's, and he loves to quote Scripture like he's a pastor even though he's not. He gets on my nerves. No—that's unkind. Paul's a good Chris-tian husband and father, and Faith is blessed to be under his protection. And yet, I wish he would lower his voice just a little.

"Thank you, Paul," I respond, dishing out food for the

little ones before we all sit down to pray. I let myself wonder for a moment about my future husband and what he will be like, and I try to imagine myself returning here to my parents' house in just a few years with my own children. It's what's meant to be, but when I try to picture it, my head goes blank and my stomach twists.

My father sits at the head of the table, and we bow our heads as he thanks the Lord for food that will nourish our bodies so we can continue to spread His word. As Dad gets to the end of the prayer, he adds, "And Father God, we ask you to keep your child James Fulton under your careful watch, and that you renew a steadfast spirit within him and create in him a clean heart. In the name of Jesus, amen."

Everyone responds with an amen, but Paul's amen is the loudest.

I'm passing the butter to my younger sister Ruth when Paul brings up James again.

"It's so wonderful that you reminded us how much we need to pray for those who've strayed," he says to Dad.

"Well, we're all capable of straying from the love of Jesus," my father answers.

"Amen," Paul says, nodding vigorously. Faith is seated at his side trying to eat and feed baby Caleb at the same time. Her hand slips and she drops her napkin, but Paul is too busy talking to notice. I crawl under the table to reach for it.

"I was thinking of another person who has abandoned

Christ's path and who also desperately needs our prayers," he continues as I sit up. Faith looks over at him.

"Oh, yes," she says. "Paul's talking about Lauren Sullivan. She's back in town."

There's a shift in the room, and I realize I've stopped chewing.

"Really?" my older brother Andrew asks. "She left years ago. She moved to the city, right? I mean, that's what I heard."

"Yes, but someone saw her at the drugstore," Faith answers, holding back on her source. "And someone else saw her moving her things into that little apartment complex near the animal hospital. You know, the one on Rice Street? It looks like she's back for good. Or at least for a while, anyway."

Whispers. Bits of whispers. It's how we find out everything.

"Lauren Sullivan?" Ruth asks. "Something about that name sounds familiar. Who is she?" She tries to pry our little brother Isaac's fingers off the butter knife.

"Lauren is someone who needs our prayers, honey," my mom answers, and she smiles at Paul and Faith in a way that's clear this conversation is over. "Let's hope this move brings her back home to the Lord."

Ruth is thirteen now, which means she was barely seven when Lauren left, so it makes sense she wouldn't remember her clearly. But I do. I remember the morning she showed up at Calvary Christian with her long blond hair dyed candy-apple red. I remember prayer requests for her soul after the stories that she'd snuck out of the house, met boys, and drank alcohol. I remember the Bible verses the pastor would use during sermons that seemed to be directed straight at her: "'The eye that mocketh at his father and despiseth to obey his mother, the ravens of the valley shall pick it out, and the young eagles shall eat it.'"

I remember after that sermon how she stood up and calmly walked out.

She was like a grenade that had sat quietly for years and then, suddenly, exploded. But Lauren Sullivan didn't go to Journey of Faith.

She disappeared before anyone could make her.

2

In a family with ten kids, bedtime is nothing short of total chaos. We do it every night, so I think we should be a lot better at it than we are. But we're not. Trying to get all those bodies cleaned up, dressed in pajamas, and tucked into bed requires a formula I haven't perfected yet, try as I might.

Of course, Faith doesn't live with us anymore and my three older brothers—Matthew, Andrew, and David—can take care of themselves, but Ruth and I are responsible for Sarah, the twins Jeremiah and Gabriel, and Isaac. That's eight hands, eight feet, four faces, and four sets of baby teeth.

"Sarah, stand still, so I can get your molars," Ruth says, trying to manipulate Sarah's green and white toothbrush into our little sister's mouth. I'm sitting on the edge of the bathtub trying to wipe down Isaac's face and hands. Ruth is better at all of this than I was when I was her age. When I was thirteen and supposed to be helping at bedtime, my mom and Faith sometimes found me flipping through the encyclopedia or drawing pictures to go along with the stories I had written during school lessons. Faith would reprimand me and remind me I was supposed to be practicing to be a good helpmeet, and I'd guiltily shove my books and papers aside and start whatever task I was supposed to be doing. I'm grateful Ruth is so motivated to please others and to do what's right. I wouldn't have the heart to correct her if she misbehaved.

We lead the little ones downstairs to the family room where Dad is reading a devotional guide. He smiles as we walk in and find our places around the room for our nightly Bible study. Isaac snuggles into his place in our mother's lap. Not for long, I think to myself, picturing the new baby on its way.

"My children," Dad begins, taking his well-worn Bible in his hands and flipping through the onionskin pages, "I was thinking of a verse from Proverbs tonight that I wanted to share with you." His finger expertly traces the columns until he finds the verse he's looking for. "Here it is. Chapter 13, verse 20. 'He that walketh with wise men shall be wise, but a companion of fools shall be destroyed.'"

All of us nod, and my father asks if we know what the words might mean.

"That if we allow ourselves to be caught up in a God-hating culture with those who don't follow Christ, we will make poor choices," my older brother David answers immediately. "Choices that don't honor the Lord."

My father offers us a brief smile. "Yes," he says. "That doesn't mean that Father God doesn't want us to pray for those who are lost and who've strayed, but we must be careful not to be led from Christ. We must choose our company carefully."

I know the reason he's chosen this verse. I'm only curious if he'll mention her name.

"Earlier today Paul and Faith brought up a former member of our church family who has moved back to town," my father continues. "Lauren Sullivan. Some of you may be old enough to remember her." Little Sarah is sitting in my lap, and I've buried my nose into her still damp, freshly shampooed hair. But when Dad mentions those of us who might remember Lauren, I glance at him. His steady gaze is on me. Maybe it's because I'm around the same age Lauren was when she left, but his eyes make me feel like he can somehow read my mind from earlier in the day, when I thought unkindly about Paul and didn't trust in God's future plan for me.

"It's important to remember that we must pray for Lauren and for all those who have discarded the path Christ has set for them, but we must also remember what Scripture tells us about walking with the wise. We must remember that we should avoid speaking with or interacting with those who have left the flock."

"Amen," Mom whispers, her eyes pressed shut.

"Amen," we all echo.

Then the little ones form a line in front of Dad, and he stands up so he can lay his hands on them for a nightly blessing. His rough, callused palms are so large that one alone covers each small head.

"Lord, let salvation spring up within my children, that they may obtain the salvation that is in Christ Jesus, with eternal glory," he murmurs over and over as each little one approaches.

The younger ones kiss Mom good night, and, even though it will be hours before we'll finish our chores and go to bed ourselves, Ruth and I stand for a blessing from Dad. He stops in front of each of us individually, so he can lay both his hands on us. My dad's hands are so heavy on my head that sometimes I imagine myself sinking under their weight, folding in on myself straight into the house's foundation.

"Submit yourselves therefore to God," he says in his quiet, confident voice. "Resist the devil, and he will flee from you."

One night, after we had gone to bed in the room we shared with Sarah, Ruth whispered to me from her bed, asking why Dad always used the scarier verses with the two of us. The ones that mentioned hell and the devil.

"Because the devil is real," I whispered back. "And it's Dad's job to make sure we stay vigilant against temptation."

Tonight, after we read stories and tuck in little bodies and bring last minute glasses of water and kiss and kiss and kiss good night, I carefully shut my baby brothers' bedroom door behind me and step into the upstairs hallway, stretching my arms up over my head in an attempt to unwind. I want to curl up in bed with my favorite book, *A Wrinkle in Time*, but instead, I head downstairs to the family room, sit down at the desk in the corner, and start up our ancient computer. It whirs pitifully as it struggles to come to life, but eventually the log-in page pops up.

My dad is still sitting on one of our old, well-loved couches, reading his devotional. He glances toward me, watching as I carefully type in the log-in and password everyone in the family shares. Once I'm logged in, his eyes go back to his book.

A few years ago, I talked my parents into buying a how-to book for online businesses at the resale shop, and with its help I built a website and an online billing and appointment system for the landscape and tree trimming business Dad runs with my older brothers. I even set up a way to keep track of the books online with some simple accounting software I downloaded for free. It's a sin to be prideful, but I can't help but feel proud of myself for figuring it all out on my own.

When I got the idea to do this, there was a lot of concern from my dad about whether or not this was appropriate or even safe. After all, God's plan for me is to be a wife and mother, not a businessperson, and the Internet is a dangerous place full of temptation—I only need to remember

James Fulton's embarrassed face in front of the congregation to know as much. But after praying over it with Pastor Garrett, Dad decided to let me use the computer to work on the business as long as someone was always monitoring me. And anyway, I'm helping Dad, and I think that's practicing to be a good helpmeet.

My fingers have been clicking away for about twenty minutes when my father puts aside his devotional and gets up from the couch.

"Are you going to be much longer, Rachel?" he asks. We try not to do too much on the Sabbath besides church and family time, but if work has piled up, Dad allows me to spend a little time on the computer on Sunday evenings.

"Not much," I say. I have a few more appointments to set and that's it.

"I'm going to bed then," he says, walking over and patting me on the shoulder. "Don't stay up too late."

"Yes, Dad, of course," I answer.

It's been three years since I started working on the computer for the family business, and Dad is often so tired he dozes off while he's sitting up with me. Sometimes he's so exhausted he allows me to work alone. Tonight, although he's sleepy, I can still feel his watchful eyes on the screen as he stands over me, as if he's debating whether he should leave me alone. I let my fingers hover over the keys as though they're itching to get back to work. Finally, he nods and leaves, flipping off the light in the hallway as he makes his way down to his bedroom.

It's so rare that I find myself alone in my house that for a second I just sit there, listening to the sound of my own breathing and the air conditioner cycling on. I'm sure it's wrong to feel this way, but this moment of solitude feels pleasant. Delicious, even. The light from the computer screen shines onto my fingers, making them look like skeleton hands tapping on the keyboard.

I finish up the work I need to do, and I open up a search engine. I've done this before when Ruth or my mom or dad can't be sitting next to me watching me work. I usually look up questions that come up during school lessons or when I'm reading our ancient encyclopedias. I confess there was a not-so-small part of me that was hoping my dad would go to bed early this evening, and I look at the blank search screen and run my tongue back and forth on the back of my teeth. My father's words from a few hours before have been playing over in my brain. "'He that walketh with wise men shall be wise, but a companion of fools shall be destroyed.'"

James Fulton was a fool. That's why he had to go to Journey of Faith. Does that mean he's now wise? I know it didn't make him happy—at least he didn't seem happy this morning. But his happiness isn't the point. His submission to God is what's important. If you care about being happy, about pursuing pleasures of the flesh, maybe that makes you a fool. But I'm not looking for the same material James was caught looking at. I don't think I'm being a fool.

I stare at the long blank rectangle of the search engine and the blinking cursor sitting inside of it, winking at me. My heart outpaces the cursor three beats for every wink. I lean back and look over my shoulder and down the hall. No light shines out from under my parents' bedroom door. I peer up at the ceiling. No noises echo from the bedrooms upstairs.

With a touch so light I'm surprised it works, I type four words.

Lauren Sullivan Clayton Texas

3

I'm not just rereading A Wrinkle in Time, I realize, I'm breathing it. Breathing the familiar, comforting smell of the used paperback's yellowed pages, a scent more delicious than Ruth's from-scratch chocolate-chip cookies. I'm at one of my favorite parts, when Mrs. Whatsit announces that there is such a thing as a tesseract.

Ruth pokes at me with the eraser end of her pencil.

"I can't figure out this problem, Rachel," she says. "Can you help me?"

I hide *A Wrinkle in Time* under my notebook and lean over Ruth's math workbook. She's struggling with some basic multiplication problems.

"This isn't too tricky," I tell her, and I pick up her pencil and make a few marks. "See? Like this."

Ruth purses her lips at me. "You make it look easy."

"Rachel goes too fast," announces Jeremiah. He and his twin, Gabriel, are working at the other end of the table, quizzing each other on their spelling list for the week. Sarah and Isaac are on the floor of the family room playing with the ancient set of Legos that's been in our family since my older brothers did their lessons in this very room.

"I don't mean to," I answer. I hand the pencil back to Ruth. "I just do the problem how I do it."

But I do go fast. Faster than anyone else in my family, anyway. Mom's been our teacher since we were tiny, but even though she took algebra and even chemistry as a teenager, she's forgotten most of it. She focuses on the basics with us during our daily lessons—the stuff we'll really need to run homes and be good witnesses for the Lord—and she stopped teaching me around Ruth's age when there wasn't anything academic left for her to explain that I didn't already know. When I've asked her about ordering more advanced workbooks or worried about whether Ruth struggles too much with figures, she likes to quote Proverbs in order to remind me that the knowledge of the Lord is the real beginning of wisdom. I try to remember that when I'm sucked into an interesting encyclopedia entry or a difficult math problem.

Of course, Mom's latest pregnancy has her so tired she's resting in bed this morning, leaving me to run the lessons. I'm tired, too, I realize, probably from staying up too late the night before. I glance shamefully at the computer in the corner and wonder if there's any way my dad will be able to tell

I typed in Lauren Sullivan's name last night, even if I didn't hit Enter.

Stop being so paranoid, I tell myself in a different, sterner voice. It was nothing. You just hit a bunch of letters on a keyboard. You aren't a sinner. You're a good girl.

I go back to *A Wrinkle in Time*, which I convinced my mom to buy me on a trip to the resale shop last year even though she wasn't sure it was appropriate. Meg Murry is my favorite character of all time, even more than Anne Shirley. But as I turn the pages, I worry if I shouldn't put it away. Even though it's school hours and I like to use the time to read novels or interesting topics in some of our textbooks, I'm almost eighteen now, and my focus really should be on the little ones and learning how to be a wife and mother, a helpmeet with a cheerful countenance. To try and remind myself of what's most important, I rub the bracelet I wear on my wrist as I read—the bracelet my dad gave me on my twelfth birthday that's inscribed with a verse from the book of Titus: *To be discreet, chaste, keepers at home, good, obedient to their own husbands, that the word of God be not blasphemed.*

It doesn't say anything about loving to read or being really fast at math.

What might my future husband think about the fact that I've read *A Wrinkle in Time* three times in the past few months and that I taught myself algebra? My future husband. I've been hearing about him since I was nine or ten, a shadowy figure God will deliver to me one day. He'll want a woman who submits to his authority. A woman who is confident that God is working through his decisions. I discover I'm holding my breath like I always do when I dwell on my future for too long. Right now, I'm just a year younger than Faith was when she got married. I rub my bracelet a little more and manage to pull myself away from the book. I need to help Ruth with her math lessons before starting lunch.

But just as I pick up the pencil, I hear my mother's voice coming from the back bedroom.

"Rachel, come quick, I need you!"

My mother never yells. In fact, no one in our family ever yells—it's not godly behavior. I jump up, but the looks of confusion on the little ones' faces make me hesitate. Ruth doesn't stop. She starts for the bedroom and something about seeing her running shakes me awake, makes me run right after her.

My mother calls for me again, her voice shaking now, filled with fear. Ruth is bolting down the hallway with me close behind.

"I'm in here," Mom shouts, and we head through our parents' bedroom to their attached bathroom. The door is half open, and when we look inside, we see our mother sitting on the toilet, doubled over. Her long brown hair hangs all the way down to the white tiled floor. I can't see her face.

"Rachel," she gasps, "I'm cramping, and it hurts so much. Oh, Lord, Oh, God, I think I'm losing this baby. Lord Jesus, please be with my baby. Oh, Lord Jesus, save my baby."

Ruth's dark blue eyes are wide open. She moves past me and kneels down by Mom's feet.

"Lord, Father God, we ask you to be with us right now, Father God," she begins. I stand mute, trying to take in what's happening in front of me. A trail of bright red blood is snaking its way down my mother's inner thigh. The sight of it turns my stomach. I have to do something.

"You stay here with her, Ruth. I'm going to call Dad."

⁂

The baby is dead. My little brother or sister is gone, and I never even got to know him. Or her.

I feared the baby was dead this morning, the second I stared at my mom bent over in the bathroom, blood pooling at her feet. I feared it was dead when I was calling my dad at his work site and begging him to hurry home. But I knew it was dead the moment my parents came back from the doctor, my mom's face buried deep inside my father's shoulder. Only the loss of her child could make my mother so despondent.

"The Lord gave, and the Lord hath taken away," my

father tells all of us as we stand in the kitchen, the little ones looking at our mom, their faces covered in confusion. Our mother's body shakes with soft sobs.

Now the sun is setting, and I'm curled up on my parents' bed across from my mom, who's dressed in her white cotton nightgown with the tiny purple flowers all over it. I push her hair back as she stares out at nothing. My mom has such beautiful hair. There are tiny streaks of gray around the temples, but mostly it's still dark brown. Straight and thick like Faith's. She has fine, baby wrinkles around her big blue eyes, but even with those, a person would have to be blind not to realize my mother is beautiful.

"Rachel, I need your help."

It's my sister Faith. She came over with Caleb as soon as I called her, right after our parents left for the doctor's office.

"Mom, are you okay to be alone?" I ask. I can tell she's been crying, but now her face is just empty, her eyes staring at something I can't see. But she nods slightly at my question, and I slip out into the kitchen.

Faith is making tuna salad sandwiches for supper, and Ruth is setting the table. My older brothers aren't home yet. They're finishing up the job my dad had to leave when I called him this morning. My dad has gone to meet with our pastor so they can plan a memorial service for the baby. My parents will have to pick out a name, too.

I take my place next to Faith at the kitchen counter, just

like I used to when she wasn't married yet and still lived at home. As I scoop some of the tuna salad onto white bread, Faith places her hand over mine, closes her eyes, and prays loudly, "Our help is in the name of the Lord, who made Heaven and earth. Father God, be with our mother right now in this time of loss. We know our little one is with you now, Lord, safe in your arms for all eternity. Help us in this time of overwhelming grief. Amen."

I plop the tuna salad onto the bread. "Amen," I whisper.

I smush the tuna salad down with a fork. I haven't prayed for my mother or my unborn little baby brother or sister all day long, and the realization fills me with guilt. I'd been too busy cleaning up the bathroom and trying to read up on why miscarriages happen—first in the encyclopedia and then on the computer. But it wasn't just busyness that kept me from praying. I hadn't even stopped to call out to God like Ruth did when Mom first yelled for us—I'd just stood there until I thought to phone Dad. I shake my head a little, frustrated with myself.

"Are you okay?" Faith asks.

"It's just so awful," I say.

"This happened one time before," Faith tells me. "When you were tiny. Before Ruth was born. That's why there's that big gap between the two of you."

I put down my fork and look at Faith, my eyes wide. Four years is a pretty big gap between kids in my family, it's true.

We believe that it's up to God to decide how large our family will be, and with babies coming every year or two, that space between Ruth and me stands out. But I thought that was just how God worked things out. I never knew about a miscarriage.

"She was further along that time," Faith says, not looking at me as she continues to make supper, her movements quick and precise. "And she stayed in bed for almost a month after. All the women from church helped, but it was so bad Dad even had to call Aunt Marjorie to come help us out."

I stare at Faith. "Aunt Marjorie? Dad's sister who lives in Dallas? I've never even met her." Dad rarely communicates with his family because they aren't believers.

"Yes," Faith answers. "She came down for a few days, but it was a disaster. She showed up and started insisting that Dad take Mom to a mental doctor or something. I don't remember all of it. I was really little at the time."

"Why did she want Dad to take Mom to a . . ."—I search for the word—"psychiatrist?"

"Because Aunt Marjorie doesn't know the healing power of the Lord," Faith responds, stacking the finished sandwiches on a plate and heading for the table. "She said Mom had depression." Faith rolls her eyes just slightly. "Of course she was sad. Of course she was depressed. Her baby went to Heaven before she'd even had a chance to hold him. But he went to Heaven." Faith pauses and looks at me before continuing. "And that's what helped Mom, eventually. I think that's what helped her get up out of bed. She realized by living her own life in a manner that glorifies God, she knew that one day she'd see her baby again. And then she had Ruth, and eventually she got pregnant with twins. I believe it was God's gift to her for enduring so much."

Faith nods definitively and puts down the plate, then crosses the kitchen to peek out the window.

"Dad's late at Pastor Garrett's house," she says. "I would stay, but I have to get home with Caleb before Paul makes it back. He's up in Huntsville with his father ministering to prisoners this afternoon."

"I can handle things," I say. But my stomach knots up at the idea of having to handle supper and bedtime with just Ruth helping me.

"Well, call me if you need me, all right?" Faith untucks the blue-and-white-checked dishtowel she's been using as an apron and folds it neatly into thirds before laying it on the kitchen counter. She gives it a quick double pat like she's reminding it to stay put.

"I'll call you if I really have to, but I'm sure we'll be okay," I answer. "Thanks for coming over."

I really want her to stay. To reassure me that Mom will be all right. That everything will go back to normal. But I'm too ashamed to talk to Faith like that. Faith doesn't doubt God's will. Faith is a living embodiment of her name. Steadfast and resolute, unlike me who flounders.

In the Bible, Rachel was always jealous of her older sister. I wonder if I'd have been different if my parents had chosen to call me something else.

After Faith collects Caleb in her arms and we exchange a quick hug, she walks out the back door, and I slip into my parents' bedroom to check on my mother. She's asleep, huddled in a ball under the covers. I watch her quietly for a moment, my heart hurting for her. And then I turn around and head back into the kitchen, so I can make sure the little ones are washed up and ready to eat.

"*Rachel, are you asleep?*" Ruth's voice whispers to me from across the room.

I sit up on my elbows and shake my head no, then hold my finger up to my mouth. Ruth throws her covers back and waits for me to nod, giving her permission to tiptoe across the room and crawl into my twin bed with me.

"Don't wake Sarah," I whisper. Our little sister is passed out on her tummy, her arm dangling off the edge of her bed and her sad, little stuffed sheep named Sheepie wedged under her face.

Ruth slips into the bed next to me, and we both turn on our sides to face each other. Ruth and me, we're the snugglers and the cuddlers in my family. My dad gives us pats on the head, and my mom doles out brief hugs and fast kisses in quick succession—after all, there are so many of us to hug and kiss. But when Ruth was around two or three and I was six or seven, she'd have a bad dream or couldn't drift off and

I'd roll over in the middle of the night to find her sweet face peering up at me from the side of my bed, her hands gripping the edge of the mattress in hopes that I'd invite her in. I always did, and I didn't even mind when her ice-cold toddler feet bumped into my shins as she slid under the covers in the middle of winter.

But tonight, Ruth doesn't slide under the covers; she kicks them off. It's hot. The air conditioner in our house doesn't work too well, but the borrower is slave to the lender, Pastor Garrett likes to remind us. Money has been extra tight lately, and my mind has already jumped ahead to worry about what I'm sure will be Mom's expensive medical bills. Until we can save up for a new air conditioner, we need to be grateful for what we have, but Texas summers are so brutal it's hard not to feel at least a little miserable. And frustrated.

"It's so sad about the baby, isn't it?" Ruth whispers. Her mouth smells of mint toothpaste and ChapStick.

"So sad," I whisper back. I give her a hug, and we press our foreheads together for a moment.

"Mom looks terrible," she continues. "I don't think I've ever seen her like that. It scared me."

"I know," I answer. "It scared me, too. You know what Faith said?" In a hushed voice, I tell Ruth about Mom's first miscarriage. I want to share it with someone, to get it off my chest, but I leave out the part about Aunt Marjorie coming to help because I'm not sure Dad would like it if I told Ruth about that. I don't think Ruth even knows Aunt Marjorie exists.

"So we have another brother or sister waiting for us in Heaven," Ruth says, her forehead wrinkling in curiosity. "But Mom never told us that. Don't you think that's strange?"

"Kind of," I say. "Maybe it was too sad for Mom to talk about. But we know we'll see him again. Or her. I just hope that Mom doesn't need a whole month to recover this time." That's selfish, I realize. Whatever the Lord needs us to do as Mom gets better, we'll do it. And we'll do it with grace, I promise myself.

"Rachel, will Mom be okay?" Ruth whispers, her eyes worried.

"Yes, Ruth," I answer, even though I'm not entirely sure. "Mom will be okay. Everything will be okay."

"Do you think we should pray?" Ruth asks.

"Yes, that's a good idea," I tell her. Ruth squeezes her eyes tight and says, "'And the prayer of faith shall save the sick, and the Lord shall raise him up.'" She opens her eyes, and I smile at her, grateful for a little sister whose righteousness is an example to me.

It's the Sunday after my mother's miscarriage, and she's spent all week in bed. After she had a dream the baby was a boy,

Mom and Dad decided on the name Joshua, but she still didn't get up. As my own duties around the house mount in her absence, I check on her regularly, and she's always the same; a lump on the bed, sometimes weeping a little, but more often than not staring out into space. One morning after Sarah spilled her orange juice twice and the twins fussed about starting their schoolwork, I found myself questioning why my mother would even want to be in charge of so many of us all the time, day after day. Then I found myself holding my breath out of anxiety again as I thought about my future children. I gave my forearm a firm smack to snap myself out of it.

As my brothers and sisters finish getting ready for church, I find myself standing by the kitchen counter, dish towel in hand, staring at the peeling green and white linoleum of the kitchen floor. Mom and Dad are talking to each other in their bedroom, and I know I shouldn't be listening but I'm not able to stop. What if Mom doesn't get better? What if this is worse than the time Faith told me about? My parents' voices slip from behind the cracked-open bedroom door into the kitchen where I'm cleaning up after breakfast.

"It's time to go now, Elizabeth," Dad says. Quiet but urgent. Soft but insistent. "We have to leave now."

"Jacob, I can't," Mom answers in a sharp, still voice I've never heard her use before. "I honestly cannot go."

"Yes, you can. You will."

"Please don't make me go." I can't see her, but I can hear her. She can barely get the words out.

"'Be strong and of a good courage; be not afraid, neither be thou dismayed: For the Lord thy God is with thee whithersoever thou goest.'"

"Jacob, talk to me," my mother begs, her voice on the verge of breaking. "Please talk to me. Please don't preach to me. Not now. Just talk to me. Talk to me, please."

I'm holding my breath, shocked at what I'm hearing. Mom's always taught us that a woman's role is to submit to her husband because the husband is the head of the family just like Christ is the head of the church. I don't think I've ever heard her ask my father for something she didn't already know he wanted to give.

And Dad doesn't want to give her the chance to stay home from Sunday services at Calvary Christian.

The bedroom door shuts, and my parents' voices are too muffled to make out. I finish up in the kitchen, and a few moments later Dad walks out, his face more stern than normal.

"Your mother is still recovering," he says, "and she'll be staying behind today. We need to make sure we really pray for her and for Joshua today at church. They need us to lift them up to the Lord."

"Of course," I respond, unable to remember the last time my mother didn't come to services at Calvary Christian.

In our ancient, fifteen-person van on the way to church, Dad asks us what the Bible tells us about Joshua.

"God let Joshua approach Mount Sinai when all the other Israelites weren't allowed," Ruth answers. "Joshua was special."

"And that's why we chose that name for such a special soul as our baby," Dad tells us. "So special God called him home early."

"So special," Ruth repeats, nodding.

"Special!" Sarah mimics, clapping her hands.

I scan the faces of my siblings, but everyone wears the same neutral expression. The same soft half smiles we always wear to show a cheerful countenance. Besides Dad, I'm the only one who really knows how much Mom resisted coming to church. Dad just explained to the rest of my brothers and sisters that God needed her to heal at home today, so they don't seem worried. But I picture Mom all alone, crying in bed with no one to sit with her. I swallow hard and try to ignore the image. Am I the only one who's thinking of Mom? The only one who's really worried?

At church, the service goes on as it normally does until Pastor Garrett asks Dad to come stand with him, at the same place James Fulton stood the week before. Pastor Garrett lays his hands on Dad's head, just like Dad does to us when he blesses us before bedtime.

The pastor's voice booms from the front of the church. It's a loud, sure voice that doesn't seem to match the reed-thin body that carries it, but when Pastor Garrett preaches, he doesn't even have to use a microphone. The first time he preached a Sunday sermon I was ten years old and jumped half an inch in my seat when he opened his mouth. Dad says Pastor Garrett was born knowing how to proclaim Christ.

"Proverbs reminds us to trust in the Lord with all your heart, and do not lean on your own understanding!" he bellows. "And how we must lean now, Lord. How hard it is to understand the loss of a child, Father God. But by faith we receive the unending peace of your presence, Lord, knowing that while Joshua's life on Earth was brief, he dwells forever in your light as you once promised Abraham. Let us pray for this father and for Joshua's mother, your servant Elizabeth, who is still recovering at home and who by the power of your command can have strength restored to her body and joy to her spirit."

The pastor and Dad are a little huddle at the front of the church. Pastor Garrett's hands press into Dad's skull as he faces the congregation. Dad is stoic, firmly planted into the floor, nodding along with everything Pastor Garrett says.

I hear Faith's muffled crying from the row behind me. "Father God, give us your peace," she whispers, loudly enough that I can hear it. I want to turn around to comfort her, but I'm not sure what to say. I shift in my seat, waiting for my tears to fall, but they don't.

All around me women are wiping away tears and pressing napkins dug out of their purses to the corners of their eyes. I should be crying, too, and I worry that people won't think I've been moved by the pastor's message. I am touched by his words, of course, but I just want to go home and check on Mom and make sure she's all right.

Lord, let my mother be all right, I pray, but I'm frustrated that I can't come up with better words to reach out to God. Long, elaborate phrases full of just-right Scripture that sound like something Faith or Pastor Garrett might say. But since it's all I have, I repeat my prayer in my mind over and over again, letting the words flow along with my breathing.

Lord, let my mother be all right.

Finally Pastor Garrett is finished, and Dad moves back down the aisle to a chorus of "Amens" and "Yes, Lords." We sing "How Great Thou Art" to close the service. Clutching Sarah's hand in mine, I exit the church, but in the gaggle of people, we get separated from my dad and the rest of my brothers and sisters. All the women who were crying before now smile brightly at Sarah and me. *A merry heart maketh a cheerful countenance*, Proverbs tells us, and our hearts should be merry all the time because we've been saved and born again. But how I wish people wouldn't smile right now. I know they're all smiling because Joshua is with the Lord, but I wish my family could have a few minutes to feel sad about it, at least. Would that have been too selfish?

As I gaze out over the crowd searching for Ruth and the other little ones, I lose my footing and run smack into the person in front of me.

"Oh, I'm so sorry," I manage, gripping Sarah's hand to make sure she doesn't trip.

"It's all right," says a woman's voice. The figure turns, and it's Mrs. Sullivan, standing there with her husband.

Mr. and Mrs. Sullivan. The parents of Lauren Sullivan. The girl we're not supposed to talk about.

I quickly glance behind them, almost expecting to see Lauren's dyed red hair and the firm, set expression she always wore to church. Lauren Sullivan never smiled unless she really wanted to. And toward the end of her days with us, she never seemed to want to.

But of course Lauren isn't with them. She's moved back to town, but not to Calvary. It's ridiculous to expect her to be here, absurd to even be looking.

"Rachel, that was a beautiful laying on of hands for your father and a wonderful way to give thanks for the homecoming of your baby brother's soul," Mr. Sullivan says.

"Thank you, yes, it was," I answer.

Mrs. Sullivan is older than Mom and looks it, her long, waist-length hair gone totally gray, the space between her light eyes etched with deep lines. "We have several babies we never got the chance to hold who are waiting for us in Heaven, too," she adds, her smile fixed, and I remember that Lauren was an only child.

"Well," I say, searching my brain for the right response, "the Lord's steadfast love always endures." Like the rest of us, the Sullivans don't mention Lauren. It's as if she's been erased.

"Yes, the Lord's steadfast love always endures," Mr. Sullivan repeats, his voice flat, the skin covering his long face turned into a thick leather from hours of working outside in the torturous Texas sun. The Sullivans make a motion to go, promising to pray for us.

As I follow the flow of the crowd outside, I remember how we prayed for Lauren Sullivan years before. Pastor Garrett laid hands on her and proclaimed, "Your adversary the devil prowls around like a roaring lion, seeking someone to devour. Be vigilant! Your adversary the devil prowls around like a roaring lion, seeking someone to devour! Be vigilant!"

Although I was eleven and knew better, I expected a lion to stalk up the aisle, baring bloodstained teeth. Some of the little children started crying at Pastor Garrett's repetitive, forceful shouts of Scripture, but the moms didn't make a move to leave like they sometimes did when babies started fussing. No, we all stayed and watched as Mr. Sullivan, Pastor Garrett, and some of the other men of the church, including my dad, circled Lauren as she sat in a folding chair at the front of the church, her hands folded in the middle of her lap, her eyes staring straight ahead. We all watched as Pastor Garrett and her father laid hands. We all watched as Lauren kept staring at us like she could see through us, unmoved.

The devil already has her, I thought to myself. *It's too late.*

"Rachel? Rachel, are you listening?" I feel an arm touch me. It's Faith, standing with the other girls her age, Caleb drifting to sleep in her arms. "Are you all right? You look like you can't catch your breath."

"I'm okay," I answer. "It's nothing." Little Sarah spots Ruth and the twins and drops my hand, running off to join them.

Faith nods, continuing eagerly. "The girls and I were just saying that Mrs. Garrett wants to help us with that modesty workshop we talked about last Sunday. Focusing on biblical femininity? We set the date for next Wednesday."

"Oh, that's good," I say. "I'm looking forward to it." It's what Faith wants to hear.

Faith smiles, the tears she cried during the service all gone now. Her trust in the Lord must be so strong. She glides easily from correct emotion to correct emotion, where I always have the wrong ones.

I search for the words to pray to God for guidance, but my mind's as blank as the cloudless sky. I give up, shading my eyes with my hand and looking out toward where the vehicles are parked. I watch as Mr. and Mrs. Sullivan climb into their pickup and drive away.

5

It's difficult to read and knead meatloaf at the same time, but I'm attempting both when Ruth comes downstairs and finds me in the kitchen.

"Rachel, can you help me? Sarah just threw up."

"Like throw up or spit up?" I ask.

"Throw up," Ruth announces. "All over the floor of our bedroom."

I exhale louder than I should and pick my hands out of the meatloaf, reluctantly taking my eyes off *A Wrinkle in Time.* I'm just at the part where Charles Wallace and Calvin and Meg meet Mrs. Who for the first time. Just before Meg helps Calvin with his math homework and they take a walk under the light of the moon. That part always makes my heart thump. I wipe my hands on the dishtowel I've tied around my waist. Pulling my gaze away from my book is much harder than giving up on the meatloaf.

"I'm sorry," Ruth says. "Should I have helped her?"

"No, Ruth, it's all right," I say, managing a smile. "It's just that some days it's . . ." I exhale again.

No. Stop it, Rachel, you're being selfish. You can do all things through Him who strengthens you.

I try to draw something out of the verse, even visualizing the words running through my muscles, forcing them to move. It helps a little.

I head up the steps to clean the mess and get Sarah into bed, placing a trash can next to her just in case. I whisper a silent prayer that her stomach is upset from something she ate and not anything contagious. Then I give her the little bell we always use when one of us is sick, so she can ring for me if she needs to.

"Ray Ray, I love you," Sarah says, using her nickname for me. Her eyes flutter just a bit, and I can tell she's drifting off to sleep, but I stop to kneel down and kiss her toes.

"I love you, too," I tell her. She's such a peanut, really. It's hard to get upset even when she throws up. I take the clothes she's vomited on to add to the ever-growing pile of laundry that I should have tackled yesterday.

After I make it back downstairs, I peer through the cracked door into my parents' room and watch my mother shift a bit under the covers, then settle into another round of sleep. She's barely gotten out of bed since she lost Joshua—not for evening Bible study or supper or Wednesday night fellowship. What if Aunt Marjorie was right? Maybe a psychiatrist could help Mom get better faster. But Dad would never let us call one.

Ruth and I have to alternate checking on Sarah, but we manage to get a slightly overcooked meatloaf on the table by the time my dad and brothers are home. Ruth brings a plate in to Mom's room even though I know when I go to collect it, it will have only been picked at a little.

Ruth and I get the little ones washed and ready for bed—Sarah is still asleep—but when we walk into the family room for Bible time, my stomach sinks. My older brothers and father are seated in their usual spots, but instead of holding his Bible in his hands like he usually does, my dad is holding something else.

My copy of *A Wrinkle in Time*.

How stupid I've been. How careless.

I left it on the counter amid rolls of paper towels and school books and dirty dishes and a dozen other pieces of evidence that I've been struggling with my job of running the household as I should.

But the book is the worst piece of evidence. The most damning thing. Because it proves not only that I am not a young woman of God, but that I've been distracted by something my father is sure to believe is sinister. And he's sure to believe that my soul is in danger.

"Come sit down, everyone," my dad says. Dad never gets mad in an obvious way. He always keeps the same serious tone in his voice that manages to sound reassuring when things are moving smoothly and frightening when things are not.

Ruth glances at me, her eyes nervous. She's seen me reading the book before and knows it's mine. I offer a quick forced smile then sit down on the couch next to my older brother Matthew. Isaac toddles over to climb in my lap, but Ruth takes him into hers at the last moment.

"Rachel, Scripture tells us that the testing of faith produces steadfastness," my father begins. "With that in mind, I want you to tell us what you're doing with this book."

I swallow. Even the little ones aren't squirming. They can tell from Dad's tone, from the way my cheeks are flushing, that this is serious.

"I asked Mom to get it for me at the resale shop a few months ago," I say, my voice steady, like I've known this moment would come. Maybe I have. And I wish for a moment that Mom was here, though I know she wouldn't defend me. She might try to take some of the blame, but she would defer to Dad. "It was a busy day, and we were buying so many things," I continue, "and I think I—I know I took advantage of that and at the last moment I asked her to buy this book for me." With Dad's eyes on me, I can't hold anything back. Every word I'm speaking is the truth.

"Did you wonder if that was a godly decision?" Dad asks. He's staring at me, his brow furrowed with concern.

"Yes," I manage, not able to look back at his eyes, just at the space between them. "I did wonder. But I've read about the author. And she was a Christian, Dad. I looked her up in the encyclopedia. I thought she sounded like a godly person."

My father nods like he expected this kind of answer from me. "There are many who call themselves Christian and don't follow the word of the Lord," he says. "I looked through this book, Rachel, and it troubles me. It involves magic and time travel, among other questionable things." I feel Ruth's eyes on me, and when I glance at her, I see her mouth has dropped into a perfect little *O* of surprise.

"You know full well that Galatians warns us that those who are involved with sorcery and idolatry will not inherit the kingdom of God," my father continues.

"Yes, Dad, I know," I say, my cheeks so hot they hurt. I can't decide where to look, so I choose my feet and stare at my worn-out, black lace-up boots that once belonged to Faith. Perfect Faith who feels and thinks and does everything right. Shame courses through me, and I feel my eyes start to glaze over with tears. I can sense everyone's eyes looking at me, and Lauren Sullivan's resolute stare flashes through my mind. I wonder if this was how she felt when she was admonished in front of the entire congregation. That I even think of Lauren in this moment makes me feel more ashamed, and I drop my gaze even lower.

But there's another, deeper part of me that wants to jump up and cry out. To tell Dad that in the book, Mrs. Who quotes Scripture, telling the children that *the light shineth in darkness; and the darkness comprehended it not.* And that Meg saves her brother because she loves him and light wins over darkness, and isn't that something? Doesn't love of family count as good? As godly? And doesn't Proverbs say that the heart of the righteous studieth how to answer? Doesn't that mean that pondering, wondering, questioning is all right? That books that make us think should be allowed?

But Dad can't read my thoughts, and there is no point in expressing them. We must honor and obey our father at all times. And anyway, expressing any other thoughts would only get me into more trouble.

"Rachel, I don't believe this book honors the Lord, and you must destroy it," he says. "Now." He motions to the kitchen.

Numbly, I walk to the trash can as my father and siblings follow. Dad hands me the book, and as I rip the pages out and throw them into the garbage, I think about Meg and Charles Wallace and Aunt Beast and Calvin and how I'll never get to be with them again. I think about how delicious it felt to read the book under my blanket with the flashlight I took from the garage, and how good it felt to absorb its words for the first time. How it didn't feel evil at all. I think about how even after I'd read the book once, I could read it again and again and always find some new word or phrase or have some new understanding about it.

I try not to cry as the pages slip into the garbage can like dead leaves.

And the light shineth in darkness; and the darkness comprehended it not.

It runs through my mind on a loop.

⁕

After I destroy the book, Dad tells me I need to sit down at the kitchen table with the Bible and find five verses that speak about witchcraft and sorcery and copy them each down ten times. Several of us have had to do this before, like when Matthew was caught looking at swimsuit magazines in the grocery store. Dad even made him eat alone in the garage for three nights after that. The last time I had to copy Scriptures as punishment was a few years ago, when Dad found me watching television at an appliance store downtown. I feel trapped in the kitchen alone while the rest of my family hums along with its usual bedtime activities. Ruth has been left to tend to all the little ones, and I work as quickly as I can to find the verses because I don't want her to be overwhelmed with so much to do. Sometimes being part of a big family feels suffocating, but when you're purposely kept out of it, it feels terribly lonely.

Finally, I find one more verse and scribble it down on the piece of paper Dad's given me. I go back into the family room and hand it to him.

"I'm so sorry, Dad, that I've disobeyed you and the word of God," I say. I squeeze my fists tight as I say this. I want to believe it so very much. But I can't ignore the other part of me that wonders just why my behavior is so disobedient.

Dad takes the paper and gives me my nightly blessing, then looks at me and says, "Rachel, I love you so much, and it's my duty to make sure you don't stray from the word of the Lord. You understand, don't you?" He frowns slightly, perhaps worried he hasn't made his point.

"Yes, Dad, I do understand," I say. I know his attention to our protection and salvation is foremost in his mind at all times. I should be grateful.

As I pass my parents' bedroom on my way to my room, I see the light is off. I wonder if Dad will tell Mom what's happened. I wonder if she'll have the energy to care.

The little ones are asleep, and I quickly brush my teeth and wash my face before slipping into my nightgown and crawling into bed. I think Ruth's sleeping, but as soon as I curl up with my pillow, I hear her voice.

"Rachel, can I come over?"

"Sure," I whisper.

She tiptoes over and slides in next to me, and I realize it

won't be much longer before we'll be just about the same height.

"I thought you might be frustrated with me," I say. "I'm sorry you had to put everyone to bed without my help."

"No, it's all right," Ruth says. "I'm just worried. For you."

I freeze. We're laying so close, but I feel a silence growing between us.

"You're worried for me?" I ask.

Ruth nods seriously. "Yes. For reading that book, Rachel. Shouldn't . . . I mean, didn't you think it wasn't a godly book?"

I can't look at Ruth when I answer. "No," I say. "I mean, I thought Dad would be upset, yes. I knew he wouldn't think it was godly. But honestly, Ruth, it's a really good book. I just don't understand how it can be evil when it quotes the Bible and talks about Jesus and the characters aren't bad at all. I don't."

Ruth frowns. "Really? You mean you really don't know how a book with magic and time travel can be bad?"

"Yes," I say. "I mean yes and no. I know that Dad doesn't like it. I know the Bible speaks out against it. But the Bible also speaks about pondering things and loving your family and . . . fighting the darkness. And all of that is in the book, too. So which is right?"

Ruth frowns. "Dad is right. I think we have to trust him."

Suddenly, little Sarah shifts in her bed and cries out. Ruth and I pause, holding our breaths, worried she might be getting sick again. But soon our little sister settles back down to sleep.

"Rachel, you promise you won't read something like that again, right?" Ruth asks, turning her attention back to me.

I nod. I've been caught, and I know there's no chance that I'll ever be able to read about Meg and Charles Wallace or anyone like them again.

"I promise I won't," I say.

"Really promise?" Ruth asks. "Never again?"

"Ruth," I say, "I wouldn't lie to you."

Ruth smiles, reassured. "Good, Rachel. That makes me feel better."

"I'm glad," I say. "Now go to sleep."

"Mmm hmmm," Ruth manages, and soon she's lightly snoring while I stare up at the ceiling, remembering how Meg Murry called herself the oddball of her family and wondering if I know just how she felt.

Mom is still frozen inside of her bedroom, hardly eating and barely talking. The shut bedroom door stares at me blankly each time I walk past it, as empty of expression as my mother's face. And each time I creep inside her bedroom to check on her throughout the day, I half expect to find that she's disappeared somehow, totally eaten up by sadness.

She doesn't go to church the Sunday after I have to destroy *A Wrinkle in Time,* which makes two Sundays in a row. I'm not sure what she says to Dad or what Dad says to her because this time their bedroom door is firmly closed before we leave for services.

"Children," my dad says as he walks into the family room where Ruth and I are struggling to get shoes on the little ones, "your mother needs to rest a little this morning. She still isn't feeling well and won't be coming with us."

"Does she have a fever?" Gabriel asks. A fever is the only kind of sick that keeps you home from Calvary Christian.

"Not exactly," Dad answers. "But we need to pray very hard for her to get well."

At services, Faith walks up to me and asks why Mom hasn't come back to church.

"Dad said she still wasn't feeling well, and we need to pray for her," I answer.

Faith nods and says, "'The prayer of faith shall save the sick, and the Lord shall raise him up.'"

"Yes, I know," I answer.

"You mean, 'amen,'" Faith responds.

"Yes, amen," I answer, turning my attention to baby Caleb.

That night, after Ruth and I put the little ones to bed, I head toward my parents' bedroom door to check on Mom again, if only to watch her breathing or to see if she'll at least have a glass of milk. But Dad stops me and insists she needs her rest.

"Better to leave her alone right now," he says, and my heart breaks a bit because I so want to see my mother.

Instead, I sit down at the computer to balance the books and do a little more work on the Walker Family Landscaping and Tree Trimming website. I frown as I work through this month's latest expenses. Business has been slow, and even though Dad always reminds us we should owe no one anything but love, we still haven't received all of Mom's medical bills, and I have no idea how we'll figure out how to pay them.

Dad is in the bedroom with Mom—the two are talking in low tones, and I can't make out what they're saying. Ruth is in the kitchen writing out a list of groceries for the next week. One of my older brothers is showering upstairs, and I can hear the hot water chugging through the pipes like a train. My brothers don't help with bedtime for the little ones, and their lack of evening chores affords them the luxury of a long shower at the end of the day.

My fingers flutter over the keyboard like hummingbird wings, and as I work, I try to ignore the little itch that's been building in the back of my brain for days now.

An itch that began when I spoke to Lauren's mother at church last Sunday. That intensified when I had to throw away my book.

Suddenly I see the words *Lauren Sullivan Texas Calvary Christian* sitting in the search box, looking me right in the eye. My heart pounds so hard it aches.

I hit Enter.

Pressing that key feels like a release. Like when I water the plants in the front yard and push my thumb against the garden hose for a minute, letting the water pressure build up and tickle me before I move it just a little and let the water explode all around me, the spray kissing my bare feet.

Maybe nothing will happen, I think, but in a millisecond my eyes focus on the very first link.

BUTTERFLY GIRL—About Me—Links—My Very Favorite Things—The Great Escape

Hi! Thanks for finding me on the Interwebs. My name's Lauren, and when I was a teenager, I escaped from a scary situation that involved abuse and . . .

That's all I can read unless I click on the link. What are the Interwebs? I'm not even sure this is Lauren Sullivan, but the word *abuse* stands out. Lauren didn't like what happened at Calvary Christian, I know that. But it wasn't abuse. Abuse is hard smacks and kicks, not the kinds of swats my parents have given all of us since we were little. Abuse is someone touching you inappropriately in your private areas. Mom was careful to explain that to us when we were little, and I know she took it seriously from the way she almost always got tears in her eyes when she talked to us about others imposing their sexual immorality on innocent children. Touching in the wrong way is abuse. What happened to Lauren made her run away, but how can she call it abuse? Weren't we just trying to bring her closer to Jesus?

My eyes shift down and there are links to results from track meets and spelling bees at other schools and districts with names involving Lauren or Sullivan or Calvary or Christian, but none of the other links that pop up seem to be even close to belonging to the mysterious, redheaded Lauren Sullivan from years ago.

I take a deep breath and listen some more. The shower upstairs has stopped running. If I strain, I can still hear Mom and Dad's muffled voices. Even though I don't know what they're saying, something about the sound pricks at my heart.

But every man is tempted, when he is drawn away of his own lust, and enticed, I think, remembering the book of James. I tug hard at the ends of my long hair in an effort to wake myself out of this daze I've sunk into. I pull so hard I wince, and the skin on my scalp fights my pulling. A sharp sting travels over my skull. I yank hard one more time for good measure. To make sure I don't click on that first link.

Quickly, I clear my history and double-check to make sure there's no trace of my searches.

"What are you doing?"

I turn around wearing a face that has to give me away, I'm sure of it. It's Ruth, the memory of *A Wrinkle in Time* and my promise to never read it again no doubt burned in her brain. She's holding a piece of paper in her hand.

"Nothing," I answer. "I'm just finishing up work for Dad."

"Okay," she answers, a long, wary pause sitting awkwardly between the word's two syllables. *Oh-kay.*

"I thought if you had a chance you could go over the grocery list with me, just to see if I've missed anything," she continues.

"Sure," I say, burying the realization that despite all of my promises about how I won't read certain things and how I will listen to our father, I'm now lying to Ruth for real.

6

I stare at myself in the bathroom mirror and rub away the crust lining my red-rimmed eyes. A blemish is peeking out on my chin, a painful one that will soon erupt into an ugly face-volcano. I remind myself not to be vain—it's not godly behavior—but in the same breath I can't help but think that I wouldn't look so worn out if I could sleep at least six hours a night. Either Isaac wakes up coughing or Sarah has a nightmare or my own guilty thoughts creep into my brain and won't let me drift off. After I found the Butterfly Girl link last night, I shifted positions so many times in my twin bed Ruth finally muttered that I might want to try sleeping on the couch.

For a moment the idea seemed appealing because I would be so close to the computer and might be able to get on it again. As soon as the thought slipped into my brain, I pinched myself on the upper thigh. Hard. *No, Rachel.* Finally, I managed to fall asleep, only to be woken up by my alarm what felt like five minutes later.

And now there's a pounding on the bathroom door.

"Rachel, I hafta use the bathroom!" Gabriel cries. "And Dad said you gotta get downstairs and help."

"All right!" I answer back. My brain searches for the right words or Scripture to ask God for strength, but the words won't come, and I give up and scowl at myself in the mirror. It's not something I do often, and we never scowl in front of each other—a merry heart maketh a cheerful countenance, and being born again means we should always be merry— but something about scowling in private feels like releasing just a bit of steam out of a boiling pot.

When I head down to the kitchen, I discover Faith standing there, wiping down the counters and buttering toast and cleaning sticky faces. Faith always seems to have twenty arms when it comes to housework, and all of them work faster than mine.

" 'To be discreet, chaste, keepers at home, good, obedient to their husbands, that the word of God be not blasphemed,' " my father says, standing with his arms crossed, smiling broadly at Faith.

"Let all your things be done with charity," Faith responds, blushing slightly.

"Hi, Faith," I say, walking over to start washing the first round of dirty breakfast dishes, quickly, so my father witnesses my efforts. "What are you doing here?"

"I thought you might use the help of your big sister today," my father says, answering for Faith as he sits down at the kitchen table to lace up his work boots. "As your mother continues to recover, so much is on your shoulders, Rachel, and I want to make sure you're able to keep things running smoothly here at home."

I don't know if it's because of the mountain ranges of dirty laundry collecting in the family room and the hallways or the overcooked meatloaf or my copy of *A Wrinkle in Time*, but my heart sinks. I touch my Titus 2 bracelet and for a brief moment I feel sorry for my future husband, stuck with a girl who's more interested in books than in being a good help-meet. With a girl who looked up Lauren Sullivan's blog.

As I approach my older sister, she looks at me carefully. "Rachel," she says in a whisper that's still loud enough for everyone to hear, "I need to speak with you." She guides me out of the kitchen and around the corner into the hallway leading to Mom and Dad's bedroom.

"Rachel, have you examined your outfit carefully in the mirror this morning?" she says, her hands planted firmly around my shoulders. She's an inch or two shorter than me, but her grip is solid. Sure of itself.

I glance down, anxiously searching for my offense. I'm wearing one of my ankle-length denim skirts, but it's clean with no obvious stains. I have my black boots laced tight— the ones that used to belong to Faith—so I know they can't be my error.

"What is it?" I ask, panicking.

"Look at your shirt," Faith says, speaking slowly and deliberately.

"It's a white shirt," I say, and it is. A simple white button down with three-quarter sleeves. Clean. No stains.

"Rachel, your undergarments are clearly visible through this shirt," Faith answers, the sweet tone of her voice cut with a firmness Faith has used with me since I was young and got distracted when I should have been helping during bedtime. "And you know that's not appropriate. Remember Timothy. 'In like manner also, that women adorn themselves in modest apparel, with shamefacedness and sobriety; not with adorned hair, or gold, or pearls, or costly array.'"

I look down. Faith's right. My white button down has been washed so many times it's more transparent than I noticed, and the outlines of my tan resale shop bra are easy to spot. My cheeks flare up, and I'm grateful at least that Faith maneuvered me out into the hallway where my father wouldn't overhear yet another one of my stupid mistakes.

"I'm sorry, Faith," I start. "I've just been so exhausted lately, and I didn't realize . . ." I trail off. There's no excuse for this, so I shouldn't even try. "I'm going to run upstairs and change right away."

"Yes, I think you should," Faith answers.

"Of course," I say, my cheeks reddening so much I think I might melt right there in the hallway.

Faith lets go, and I race upstairs and into my bedroom where I shut the door to change. It's rare that I'm in my bedroom without Ruth or Sarah there, too, asking me to help them find a missing sock or wiggling in front of me while I try to braid their hair. I open the closet we share and start pushing hangers aside, looking for something appropriate and clean, but I feel the ache in my throat about to crack open. Before I can stop myself, I sink to the floor of the closet and collapse into tears. I can't do anything right. I can't control my temptations not to think about Lauren, and I can't run the house properly. I'm not godly, I'm not good, I'm not like Faith, and my future husband won't ever appear if I keep being the mess of a girl that I am right now.

"Lord, please be with me," I beg, hot tears sliding down my cheeks, frustrated that minutes before I could only scowl instead of finding the right words to ask God for guidance. I can't even pray as well as Faith, who remembers the right Scripture to use at the right time. I clutch the hem of one of Ruth's dresses and scream into it as loud as I can, muffling the noise so no one hears me. Just as we don't scowl in front of each other, we don't raise our voices in anger in this house. Ever. But for a moment, I feel lighter.

I wait, worried someone will come up the stairs to find out what's wrong. But no one does, and I take a few deep breaths and get up, forcing myself to focus on the clothing hanging in front of me until I find a dark blue button-down shirt that I can wear. I ball the white shirt up and shove it to the back of my closet. My mom always has us cut up old clothes to use for cleaning rags—it's cheaper than paper towels—but right now I just want this shirt out of sight until it doesn't remind me of all the ways I can't stop stumbling.

Finally, I manage to calm myself and head downstairs to continue the morning routine. I catch up on laundry while Faith goes over lessons with the little ones. When lunchtime comes, I carry a ham sandwich on wheat bread and a glass of milk into my mother's room. Even though I offer her food several times a day, I have the best luck trying to get her to eat something in the middle of the day.

My mother is sitting up in bed, propped up on some pillows and staring out the bedroom window to her left. I washed the windows carefully late last week and the sun is streaming in, but my mother looks past the sun somehow. Her hands are folded in her lap like they've been sculpted there. Like they can't move for anything. When she hears me come in she turns to look at me and smiles, but it's a practiced smile. Just her cheeks pulling up on the sides, and only barely.

"Hi, Mom," I say in a soft, low voice. I can't stand to see her this way. Once when I was younger, Mom burned her hand on the oven rack, and it left a welt as thick and long as a number two pencil. But when she burned her hand she exclaimed, "The joy of the Lord is my strength!" and kept going. That's the mother I know.

But this mother is propped up on her bed, halfway here and halfway somewhere else. Since the day Mom lost Joshua, I've managed to read about miscarriages a few more times on the computer, and some websites mention a condition called postpartum depression and medications that might help. Dad would just say that God is the great physician. But why do Mom and Dad believe in doctors for our bodies and not for our minds? After all, our brains are part of our bodies. But my questions are irrelevant because there's no one to give me the answers.

"I have your lunch," I say, placing the plate on the bed next to my mother and the glass of milk on her nightstand. She makes no effort to touch them, but she manages a quiet, "Thank you."

"Can't you take one bite?" I ask, sitting gingerly on the edge of the bed.

"I'm really not hungry, Rachel. Maybe later."

"It's important you get your strength back," I say, feeling the lump in my throat threaten to split open again for the second time in one day. But I don't want to cry in front of my mother—that will only make her feel worse.

"Yes, I know," my mom answers. "I'll eat something later, I promise."

"Take just one bite, so I can see," I say. "Please?"

For the tiniest second, my mother smiles a real smile, but it's gone so quickly I'm not sure if I imagined it or not. She reaches out, takes a small bite of the sandwich, and puts it back on the plate.

"That wasn't so bad, was it?"

My mother exhales and starts crying. My mother cries during church services when she seems moved by a particular Scripture or song, and she cried out of joy when Faith told her she was pregnant with Caleb, but I'm not used to seeing her cry like this. Out of sadness.

"Mom, I'm sorry," I start, moving over to be closer to her. "I'm sorry. I shouldn't have made you eat when you're not hungry."

"No, Rachel, it's not that. It's just that I miss Joshua. I miss my baby boy. Did you know I had a dream where God spoke to me and told me it was a little boy? Did I tell you that?"

"Yes, Mom, you did," I say. What I don't say is I know you miss Joshua, but you have ten babies. Right here. Ten babies who need you. I need you. If you were here, I wouldn't be getting a handful of hours of sleep a night trying to raise my brothers and sisters. If you were here, you would have let me know about my immodest shirt without making my cheeks burn. If you were here, you would have pretended not to see how much I loved that book, and I wouldn't have had to rip it to shreds.

If you were here.

But I can't say that. I shouldn't even be thinking it.

"I miss him," my mother continues, "and I know he's

waiting for me in Heaven, but I think he needs me now. I'm his mother, and he needs to be with me." She wipes her tears off the bridge of her nose with both hands. "It's wrong to question the Lord's plan, but Joshua may have been my last chance for babies."

Her last chance. I know my mother sees her childbearing as her gift to the Lord, as her way to praise Him. I wonder if she worries she won't be able to praise Him enough if she doesn't have any more children. My mind seizes on an image of myself pregnant, my stomach swollen tight, and my chest contracts and I try to find my breath. I think of the years stretched out before me, and know I could have a dozen children, maybe more. The thought of it, of ending up like my mother, crying alone in a bed while her other children wait for her, makes me want to scream, not sing God's praises. And Mom is crying so hard now I'm scared Faith will hear and come in to see what I've done wrong.

I grab some toilet paper from her bathroom and give it to her. I pat her shoulder and try to comfort her, but I don't have the words. I want to hug her, but my mother's hugs have always been so measured. So careful. Parceled out in even pieces. I'm not even sure how to hug her right now, just the two of us.

My mother always told us she wanted lots of kids—from the day Dad met her working at a Stop N' Go when she was nineteen and he was twenty, and they started talking and Dad asked her if she had a personal relationship with Jesus Christ.

"I was on the wrong path, and it wasn't the path Jesus wanted me to walk," Mom would tell us. This was the part of the story we always loved best when we were little. How God timed everything just right, and then all of us came along. We've heard the story so many times, but that still doesn't make picturing my mother working at a Stop N' Go any easier. It's like trying to picture her flying through space. In the earliest photo I've ever seen of Mom, she's pregnant with her first child, my oldest brother. It's like she didn't exist before that. And we've been everything to her, but now it feels like we're not enough.

Not even ten of us are enough.

"Rachel, I need some time alone now," my mother says, slipping down under the covers. "Thank you for bringing me the sandwich."

"Okay," I say, leaving the meal she won't eat on the nightstand.

As I walk out, I stand by the door and look at the lump under the covers.

"Mom, I love you," I whisper.

She doesn't hear me. She doesn't answer back.

That night after Faith has gone home and everyone heads to bed, I creep downstairs. Standing by my parents' bedroom door, I count to one thousand to make sure they're asleep. The day is already lost—a big black mark on the calendar. A messy scribble. An ink stain. I can't start over until I fall asleep and the sun rises.

I might as well take advantage of my mistakes. My immodest clothing. My inability to run a house or make my mother feel better. My unnatural fear of the idea of getting married and having babies of my own.

I tiptoe down the hallway and sit down at the computer.

My heart is bumping up against my ribs—out of excitement or nervousness or both—and I find the link to Lauren's blog easily. Once I click, there's no going back. I know that. If I click, I'll read the blog.

And I want to read it.

My index finger rests on the mouse. I hold my breath and squeeze my eyes shut.

I click the link.

Lauren's blog pops up. There's a cartoon drawing of a blue and green butterfly at the top left, next to a loopy black font.

BUTTERFLY GIRL—A blog about being born again from being born again.

There's a picture, and it's Lauren. It's Lauren Sullivan without a doubt, and she's sitting on a bed with her legs crossed, wearing black shorts and a dark blue top—the kind that doesn't have any sleeves, just thin strips of fabric running over her shoulders. I can see her bra straps peeking out from underneath, too. Black bra straps.

Lauren's red hair is blond now, with green streaks in it the color of lime popsicles or Palmolive soap. She's six years older, but I don't think she looks it. Weirdly, it's almost like she looks younger somehow. That's impossible, I know, but that's how it seems to me.

She's smiling so big. She's smiling with her entire face. Even her dark brown eyes are smiling.

Then I'm struck by the realization that I'm smiling, too. Smiling right at her. So big and so wide my cheeks hurt. I put my hands up to my cheeks to make sure. Yes. I'm smiling. Hard.

I lean back a little in my chair and peek down the hallway toward my parents' bedroom. I glance up at the ceiling to listen for noises. Nothing. I wait for the right verse to burrow its way into my brain, reminding me I shouldn't be doing this.

I can't hear one single piece of Scripture, just the hum of the computer building up and down over and over again like a heartbeat.

I shift a bit in the folding chair and lean in toward the light of the screen. I start reading.

Lauren Sullivan is currently working at Clayton Animal Hospital as a vet tech—a job she got since moving back to town. She has two cats named Mitzi and Frankie, and she is a vegan. A vegan, I've learned, is someone who doesn't eat any animals or animal products—not even cheese or eggs.

Lauren is learning about meditation, which means sitting and emptying your mind of thoughts, but she says she's not very good at it even though she likes the idea of it. Her favorite singer is a woman named Loretta Lynn and her favorite book is called *The Handmaid's Tale*, which, she wrote in one post, "totally and completely and seriously blew my mind."

She has two tattoos, one of a butterfly on her shoulder and one of a rainbow on her ankle.

Since getting these tattoos, I've determined they're sort of cliché, but at the time I swear to you I got them

in earnest, I really did. They meant something to me.
They meant rebirth in the most earnest, honest way
possible and I guess they still do, even though
now I think they're corny.

That's what Lauren wrote about her tattoos on her blog,
which I sit here reading even though it's well past midnight.
I stare in fascination at the illustrations, amazed that Lauren
would choose to do something so permanent to her body.
Amazed that she can. She writes so much about her tattoos
and her food habits and her favorite things that my eyes dry
out trying to read about all of them.

Hello hello hello dear readers—all fifteen of you—in
this post I am going to talk about my very favorite
Manic Panic hair colors so get ready because there
will be pictures . . . lots and lots of pictures.

Okay, so I've been wondering a lot about what it means
to make the leap from vegetarianism to veganism, and
sometimes I feel kind of flipped out that my food issues
are just the old part of me looking for some legalistic
lifestyle where I feel safe following a Set Of Rules
which is sort of why I think sometimes I still eat bacon.
To prove to myself that I'm still in charge of me.

Sometimes I miss the city . . . I miss the openness and the differences and the way no one knew about my past. But I needed to clear my head and I needed to move on from some of the crap I got sucked into living there so I'm back in my childhood hometown and that is kind of Freaking Me Out and everything because I'm afraid I'll run into Them or people from the cult who hurt me, but it's cheap as dirt here and I love my job and Mitzi and Frankie love it, too.

Every set of words Lauren writes sounds like an explosion—like she has so much she wants to say she can't even stop to use periods or commas. Her pictures are like little explosions, too. In each one she has different hair, each picture starring some new, unusual color that can't possibly be natural. Lime green. Lemon yellow. Sky blue. Like fireworks. I'm stunned at what she looks like. I suppose I thought she would still look like I remember her from her days at Calvary before she began to rebel. I instinctively touch my hair. The thought of even cutting it seems sinful.

Back in my old life, I couldn't do anything to my hair. My hair was my crown of glory—or that's what I was told—so I wasn't supposed to cut it at all. But now my hair is mine to do with what I want, so I want to do the most extreme things I can think of with it. Dye it, shave it, gel it, whatever it. I keep wondering if I'll get sick of doing these things and just let it grow out normal again, but it's been six years since The Great Escape, and I'm still doing them so I don't know.

Sitting in the family room, I blink my eyes over and over, trying to keep them comfortable as I race through Lauren's blog. Each little story she writes has links to some other story, and my fingers slip over the keyboard and grip the mouse, clicking and pointing, stopping only to read as fast as I possibly can. I can't stop. I can't get enough of finding out what happened to Lauren Sullivan.

What would I look like to one of my family members if they found me now, like this? Hunched over the dim light of the computer in the middle of the night, my gaze focused and intent, my mouth slightly open, my mind anywhere but with God? Is this how James Fulton's parents found him before they sent him to Journey of Faith for looking with lust at women on the computer?

But this isn't immodest images. Not really. It's just like reading a book. A story.

One where I happen to know the main character personally.

I force myself to take a breath and listen for creaking on the steps or Sarah crying out or my dad getting up to go get a drink of water—he's not the heaviest sleeper. But there's just the tick of the clock coming from the kitchen and the sound of rain lightly drumming on the plants and bushes outside.

There's one link I haven't clicked on yet. If I don't click on that, what I'm doing isn't wrong. If I don't click on that, all of this is research, really. Learning. Just like reading the encyclopedia. It's okay as long as I don't click on that one link. The one at the top right hand corner of Lauren's blog that stares at me like it can hear me thinking.

The Great Escape: How I Left My Fundie, Homeschooling, Woman-Hating Past Behind

I don't know what *fundie* means. Lauren was homeschooled like the rest of us, that's true. But if Scripture tells us that an excellent wife is more precious than jewels, how can she say we hate women?

But it doesn't matter because I'll never click on that link. If I don't click on that link, I haven't done anything that wrong. That's what I tell myself.

Suddenly, there's the sound of coughing coming from down the hall. Gruff and deep. My dad's cough.

I leap up, shutting down the computer with a few quick clicks. There's the cough again. I can either make an excuse for why I'm down here or I can make a break for it up the stairs. But maybe he won't even come out into the kitchen?

The computer is sighing shut, evidence of its recent use.

Please be quiet now, I will it.

There's the cough again.

I could race to one of the family room couches and hide under a blanket. The lights are off, and he might not even see me on his way to the kitchen. Or I could race into the kitchen and get myself a glass of water, too, and if Dad walked in I could act like it was a strange coincidence. But if I were thirsty, wouldn't I have gotten a glass of water upstairs?

My body trumps my brain, and I run down the hallway and tiptoe up the stairs by my parents' bedroom. There hasn't been another cough. Once I reach the top landing, I take a breath. My heart is hammering away, but I've made it. Mostly. Only there's the problem of the computer browser. I didn't get a chance to clear the history.

At this thought I hug my arms to myself and run my fingernails down my forearms as hard as I can, digging into my skin. I wince, and as fast as I scratch myself I begin rubbing my hands up and down the marks I'm sure I've left behind, trying to make the pain go away.

I listen, still trying to catch my breath. There's no more coughing.

But it's too risky to go back downstairs to try and fix my mistake. I can't do anything except check on Sarah and Ruth briefly before I slide into my own bed. My two little sisters are asleep, blissfully blanked out. Heads empty.

Mine is anything but. I lie in bed, unable to sleep.

Lord, I . . .

Father God, please . . .

Jesus, my heart calls out . . .

I can't finish any of the prayers I start. By the time I fall asleep, the bedroom clock reads 3:00 a.m.

<hr />

The next morning I find a surprise in the kitchen. Mom is sitting at the kitchen table holding a dozing Isaac as my dad and brothers pour the coffee Ruth's already started. Yesterday my mother wouldn't even eat lunch.

"Mom?" I ask, hopeful. Is it possible our prayers are finally starting to work? At least, is it possible Dad's prayers and Faith's prayers and Ruth's prayers are starting to work? I doubt mine have done much good, especially after last night.

But when Mom looks at me, her face still seems blank. Hollow. She tries to smile, but it's forced.

"Good morning, Rachel," she says, her voice soft.

I doubt she's much better but still, she's out of bed. At least we should be grateful for that small blessing.

I get to making breakfast, and all of us—my dad, my older brothers, the little ones—move around one another tentatively, carefully, as if one wrong motion or word will send Mom back to her bedroom cave. Eventually, Dad kisses Mom goodbye and whispers something into her ear. She smiles faintly.

After the breakfast dishes are done, we move into the family room and settle into schoolwork. Mom sits on the couch while Isaac, who's finally woken up, scoots his toy trains around her feet. Everything feels awkward and strange. Like at any minute my mother might break. I'm not sure if I'm the only one who senses this or if my siblings feel it, too.

"Dad told me there will be the girls' fellowship about modesty at the church tonight," she says after a while. I'm in the middle of showing the twins how to multiply fractions, and her voice makes me jump a bit. She's barely spoken since she wished me good morning.

"Yes," Ruth says, looking up from her own work. "Faith and Pastor Garrett's wife are helping organize it."

Mom nods. "He wants you both to attend. I can watch the twins and Sarah and Isaac this evening if you can help get supper ready before you leave."

Is this the reason Mom got up this morning? Dad takes his role of protector seriously, but I didn't realize having Ruth and I go to church this evening would be so important to him. I figured Mom's illness took the meeting off the table, and in fact, I secretly hoped it would, even though I knew I shouldn't. Going back to fractions with my brothers, my stomach turns like it does whenever I think about women's fellowship at the church. Sitting in the circle of metal folding chairs, I worry I won't be filled with Christ's inspired word and will instead say something that will have everyone's corrective gaze on me—in the same way that we all once stared at Lauren Sullivan, taking note of every flaw. My mind jumps back to last night. To Lauren's words. To that one forbidden link I've promised to ignore.

"Rachel, will you look this over for me?" Jeremiah asks, breaking me out of my thoughts.

"Of course," I tell him.

I take his math worksheet and tick through the problems, trying to see if his work makes sense. After I hand Jeremiah's worksheet back to him with his mistakes circled, I ask Ruth for her paper, determined to keep busy.

By supper Mom's pale face seems paler, and her short answers even briefer. Leaving her with all the little ones could be too much for her, but then Dad is home by supper—a simple salad and sandwiches with cold cuts is enough for today—and he says we should head to Calvary.

As we get ready to leave, Dad stops Ruth and me by the back door for a prayer. His hands press on our heads, and once again I imagine sinking into the ground under the weight.

"'Favour is deceitful, and beauty is vain, but a woman that feareth the Lord, she shall be praised,'" he says, and I think for a moment about Lauren Sullivan's tattoos and dyed hair.

"Amen," we respond. When we open our eyes, Dad is smiling at us. The careful, half smile I've come to prize because he gives it so rarely. Like Mom's kisses and hugs, there aren't ever enough of Dad's smiles to go around. But not every girl has a protector like Dad. I need to be more grateful for what God's given me. As I climb into the van, I wave to Dad's figure standing in the doorway, watching us drive away.

I can tell from the way Ruth keeps straightening her skirt and checking her reflection in the broken mirror on the back of the van's sun visor that's she nervous but also excited for this evening. This is the first time she's been considered old enough to attend an event like this. She hasn't begun her monthly cycle yet, but she's started wearing a bra.

"Are you all right?" I ask, turning down the van's radio. It's set to the classical radio station, the only music Dad lets us listen to when we're driving anywhere.

"Yes," Ruth says. "But I'm wondering if I'll be the youngest one there tonight."

"Maybe," I answer, "but probably not. I bet Donna Lufkin and Margaret Pierce will bring their little sisters, too. They're about your age."

Ruth nods thoughtfully as we pull into the open space of grass that serves as Calvary's parking lot. When we walk into the meeting room, Faith is busy moving the chairs into place, and one of the other older girls, who got married last summer and is pregnant with her first child, is setting out cookies and cartons of store-brand fruit punch.

"Hi!" Faith waves. "I'm so glad you were able to come this evening. We're going to have such a sweet fellowship, I'm sure."

"Yes, we're glad we were able to come, too," Ruth says, her words carefully chosen. Then, when we're close enough so not everyone can hear, her voice drops and she adds, "Faith, did you know that Mom got out of bed today?"

"God is so good," Faith says, smiling and not at all surprised. "Now let me go check on Caleb, and when I come back we'll get started." The older girls take turns watching the babies and toddlers during women's fellowship, but it's not my turn for a while. God has purposed that I be here, in the meeting. It must be why He's helped Mom gain enough strength to leave her bedroom today.

We all take our seats, adjusting our skirts and crossing our legs at the ankles. Donna Lufkin is seated next to me. She recently started courting a boy whose family lives outside Healy, about an hour away. I'm sure we'll be celebrating her wedding day soon and witnessing their very first kiss, which they're saving for marriage. My future husband looms in my mind again, a masculine figure roaming the planet somewhere, seeking me out. I can never picture a face, just a body that's bigger than mine and a voice that reminds me of my father's.

"Let's pray, shall we?" says Mrs. Garrett, the pastor's wife. Her voice is like honey, smooth and comforting. "Father God, we thank you for everyone gathered here this evening, and we surrender ourselves and ask you to come by your Holy Spirit and inspire our hearts tonight. Come fill our fellowship with your truth and grace, and fill this meeting with your presence. In Christ's name, we pray."

"Amen," we all say in unison.

Faith and Mrs. Garrett lead the meeting. Donna talks about how courting instead of dating helps her remain modest because she and the boy she is courting are always with a chaperone.

"It helps me remember that everything I do needs to be for the glory of God and not the praises of man," Donna says. We all nod.

Another girl talks about how she posts a checklist on the bedroom mirror she shares with her sisters so they can help each other dress modestly each morning. Does a loose-fitting blouse show too much if she bends over? Does a purse strap cut into her chest and accentuate her body in a way that might be a stumbling block for a man who sees her? If arms are raised is too much midriff revealed?

Mrs. Garrett nods her head approvingly as each item on the checklist is discussed. She even asks if copies could be made of the checklist so we could each have one. "We must remember that it is up to us to help men resist temptation," she reminds us. "We want our clothing to reveal a humble heart that loves the Lord and nothing more."

It must be so hard to be a man. Whenever we go to the grocery store, worldly women are everywhere, their tight shorts cutting into flesh and low-cut tops revealing too much. My mind flashes on the picture of Lauren Sullivan and her black bra straps peeking out in the picture on her blog. I squeeze my eyes shut, trying to unsee it.

So much of a man's godly path is dependent on me and what I choose to wear, and the responsibility terrifies me sometimes. I know the men in the congregation sometimes have workshops where they talk about how to overcome what Pastor Garrett calls a prison of lust. I wonder what that kind of lust feels like. At the women's workshops, we never talk about controlling our lust—I guess because women don't really feel lust. But then I remember the way my heart beat quickly when I read the scene in *A Wrinkle in Time* where Meg and Calvin take a nighttime walk. Was I feeling lust? How do I control it? I feel my brow furrowing with worry.

"Rachel?"

I blink, aware that someone is talking to me.

"Yes?"

A few of the other girls grin just slightly, and Ruth shuffles her feet and looks down. Clearly, I've missed something.

"Rachel," Faith says, smile even, her voice coated in practiced patience. "I asked you to tell us about the other morning when I was at your house? I thought it would be a wonderful way to illustrate how important vigilance is when it comes to biblical femininity."

So many eyes are on me. Curious eyes. Eyes that are already judging me even though I haven't opened my mouth. My ears start buzzing, and my cheeks are so hot they hurt.

"Oh," I say, curling my fingers around the bottom of my chair. *Lord, help me speak.* "Yes. Um. The other morning, Faith helped me to realize that my, um, undergarments could be seen through my blouse, and I . . ."

I'm crying. Tears are spilling out and down my cheeks and running into my closed mouth. The salty taste is sharp on my tongue.

"Rachel?" Mrs. Garrett's face is full of compassion, and she leaves her seat and comes toward me and kneels down at my feet. She takes my hands in hers, and I grab on to them because I need something to hold. Desperately.

"I'm sorry," I say. My tears keep sliding down my cheeks, driven by so many reasons. Because I read Lauren's blog. Because I'm probably filled with lust, even when I shouldn't be. Because I wasn't aware enough of being modest and wore the wrong shirt. Because Faith brought up my mistake to all the other girls my age at church and now the shame running through my veins cuts so sharp I want to disappear. I want to crawl out of my skin or sink into the floor or vaporize myself into nothingness. Anything so I don't have to be here anymore. My crying turns to outright sobs.

Faith looks stunned by my behavior. She comes over, and Donna gets out of her chair so Faith can sit next to me.

"Rachel, it's all right. Your message tonight helped all of us move one step closer to always walking with modesty and self-control." She reaches out, hesitates, and then pats my shoulder lightly. Faith didn't bring up my mistake to embarrass me. She sincerely wants all of us to walk with Christ. And she's right. We should be modest women. So why am I so upset?

Mrs. Garrett excuses me to the restroom. I splash some cold water on myself and blot my red face with paper towels. When I come out, Ruth is leaning against the wall outside the restroom.

"Rachel, are you all right?"

"I'm okay," I sniff. "It's just . . . I'm not sure. I just don't like being the center of attention like that, I guess." That's true, but I know this can't be the only reason I'm crying.

"I know," she says, her eyes concerned. "But they're still meeting out there."

"I know they are," I say.

"We should go back, I think?" She chews a bit at her bottom lip. I just want to leave and go home, but I know Ruth is right. We need to go back. I follow her to the circle of chairs, and the other girls act like nothing has happened. I try to follow along. I nod when I think I should nod and smile when I think I should smile. When Mrs. Garrett closes the meeting with a prayer, I tip my head and shut my eyes. But my head feels blank. Empty. My cheeks still feel like they're burning.

In the van on the ride home, Ruth stares out the window. We don't talk.

When I pull up to the house, I see my older brothers in the garage, fixing some of the equipment they use for the family business. My older brother Matthew walks up to the driver's side window.

"I think Mom needs your help," he tells me. "The little ones are still awake."

I nod, and when Ruth and I go in, I hear Mom upstairs, still trying to cajole my younger brothers and sisters to get ready for bed. My dad is sitting in his chair in the family room, his eyes intent on the Bible in his lap. He's holding a pen to make notes in the margins.

I take a deep breath and head upstairs. Mom is trying to get Isaac to put on his pajamas. Sarah is pulling out several of her books, and I hear the twins in the boys' bedroom doing anything but getting ready to fall asleep.

"Mom, why don't you go rest?" I say, and she sees me and nods, grateful. She kisses Sarah and Isaac goodnight and as she walks past me, she gives Ruth and me quick pecks on the cheeks.

"I love you, girls," she says.

Her words are enough to keep me going until everyone is asleep and Ruth and I can finally brush our own teeth and slide into our own beds. But once I'm in bed, I shift repeatedly, unable to get comfortable.

"Rachel, can I come over?" Ruth whispers.

"Sure," I say.

Ruth snuggles up next to me. She pushes my bangs out of my eyes and offers a hopeful smile.

"Rachel, why were you crying tonight?" Ruth says. "You seemed so upset."

"Oh, Ruth," I start, my voice on the verge of cracking again. There are too many reasons to name. And none I can identify clearly. "I'm not sure. I'm just . . . I'm tired. I'm worried about Mom, I guess. I don't know."

"But Mom got up today," Ruth says. She always sees the bright side of things.

"Yes. But . . . I don't know. I don't know what's wrong with me."

"I feel like . . . do you think maybe we should pray?" Ruth asks. "That always helps me feel better."

"Maybe it would help," I say, willing to try.

Ruth clasps my hands in hers and whispers, "I'm thinking of that verse in Jeremiah that I like. The one that says, 'Call unto me, and I will answer thee, and show thee great and mighty things, which thou knowest not.'"

I smile in spite of myself. I've always liked that verse, too. I think it's because of the phrase, "great and mighty things, which thou knowest not." I'm pretty sure God isn't referring to the entries I like to read in the encyclopedia about what animals swim in the deepest part of the ocean and how electricity works, but still, I like the idea of knowledge as some sort of gift from the Lord.

"Ruth," I ask, "is this how you pray sometimes? You just think about your favorite Scripture?" It seems silly that I've never asked her this question before.

Ruth shrugs. "Well, sort of. I mean, I guess. I just think about the verses I like and I try to figure out why my brain has come up with them in that moment. It's like they're secret messages from God."

"And when you pray, the words make you feel better, right?"

"Yes," Ruth says, frowning. "You mean, they don't for you?"

"Mostly," I say. Not usually. But I can't say that to Ruth. It would trouble her too much.

"So Father God," Ruth continues, "please help Rachel. Please guide her with your love and grace. Call to her and she will answer you, and you will show her great and mighty things which she knowest not. Amen."

Ruth grins at me, and I kiss her forehead, and soon she's drifted off. I watch her sleep for a little while, counting the freckles on her little turned-up nose. When I'm sure she's in a deep sleep, I carefully crawl out of bed and head for the bathroom, and once inside, I lock the bathroom door and start the hot water. I slip my nightgown up over my head and step out of my underwear.

With my feet planted firmly on the ancient yellow bath mat, I stare at my naked upper half in the mirror on the medicine cabinet. My face looks like a deflated balloon. Shriveled. Empty. I look at my chest, spotted with a few dark moles. My breasts aren't as big as Faith's, but I've had to wear a bra since I was twelve, just before I started my cycle. That's when my father gave me my Titus 2 bracelet to serve as a reminder that my future husband was waiting for me and expected a woman of virtue on his wedding day.

But reading Lauren's blog and forgetting to be modest when I should have makes me as bad as Eve, naked in the garden. If my father had found me on the computer, he'd have had every right to send me to Journey of Faith, just like James Fulton's parents sent him. There's nothing different between what he's done and what I've done. And the thought of going to Journey of Faith terrifies me because it marks you. Shames you. Everyone looks at you differently after you return, no matter how much you promise that you've been redeemed.

I press my fingers into my bare thighs hard, leaving red marks.

I'm sinful. Dirty. I shouldn't even be staring at my own body like this when I'm not wearing any clothes. It's vain.

Climbing in the shower, I let the water pour over me and think about Ruth's sweet prayer for me. I've got to do better. I've got to be better.

Warm water pours over me, and it feels good. "Cleanse me from all unrighteousness," I whisper. This is a fresh start. I'm not ever going to use the computer again for something against the Lord. Tomorrow I'll be as good as Faith. As sweet as Ruth. My father won't be disappointed in me again. I'm pure of heart now. And this time for good.

8

The next morning I head downstairs early, eager to start the coffee for Dad and my brothers before they're awake, ready to show off what a godly girl I am.

I enjoy about fifteen minutes of perfect calm before the younger ones join me and everything falls apart. Isaac spills milk all over the clean laundry, Sarah goes missing, and Ruth and I are in a panic until the twins find her chasing bugs in the garage. And when my father and brothers get ready to head out to work, I realize I forgot to print out that day's invoices like I usually do—I've so committed to avoiding the computer that I forgot I was actually supposed to use it this morning.

And my mother is in her room, her one-day escape forgotten.

"Dad, I'm sorry," I say, as I race to the computer, searching for the files I need to print the invoices.

"The Book of James reminds us to be patient," my father

says, "and to establish our hearts as the coming of the Lord draweth nigh." I search his face for a half smile to go along with his recitation of Scripture, but there isn't one. He just nods, waiting for me to do what I should have already done.

I can feel my resolve from last night vanishing, slipping from my soul. My mind flashes on Lauren's smiling picture from her blog and how it made me smile back. It flashes on my humiliation the night before and the way I cried in front of all the women and girls at church. It flashes on the countless tasks piling up in front of me like a tower of Isaac's wooden blocks, about to collapse at any moment. And it flashes on Journey of Faith, looming in front of me like the real threat it is. I grit my teeth and print out the invoices.

The day keeps on. I fake my way through lessons with the little ones, too tired and mixed up to keep focus. When suppertime approaches and I realize I have to start planning a meal, I head for the kitchen. As I pass my parents' bedroom door, I pause. Slowly I push it open just enough to peek in. The lights are off and the blinds are pulled.

"Mom?" I say.

Nothing.

I wait for some piece of Scripture to come to me, like Ruth's secret messages from God, but my mind blanks. I try to use my own words—*Lord Jesus, I ask you to come and . . .* but I can't find the right ones. I need to begin again. *Lord Jesus, please restore your servant, our mother . . .* But I've tried that before, and it's not working. *Father God, I come to you with a servant's heart . . .*

I squeeze my eyes tight and give up. Either my late night baptism wasn't enough for God or He's still trying to test me. I can't decide which, and I just want to go upstairs and scream in the closet again, like I did after Faith reprimanded me. But I don't.

When Dad gets home, he heads into his bedroom and shuts the door. I hear some muffled conversation but can't make out what's being said. But Mom joins us for supper like she did the night before.

"This all looks so nice, girls," Mom says, running her fingers over the small white flowers that dot the edge of her plate, but her voice sounds hollow. Her skin is pale, and she's noticeably thinner.

After Dad says grace, we pass the bread basket and the bowls of macaroni and cheese, the easiest thing to whip up without much time. Normally during supper, Dad and my brothers talk about difficult jobs or unusual clients, or Mom shares the silly things Isaac or Sarah said during the day. But Mom's absence and presence are equal forces that loom over us and seem to shape everything. So none of us talk much.

Tonight, Mom tries to smile at us and instead tears up, wordlessly pressing a napkin to her eyes to dry them. Isaac pats her hand, which only makes her tear up more. My dad shifts in his seat and serves himself a second helping. My older brothers chew their food. The twins sip their milk. Everything happens like it's in slow motion. Everyone moves like we're stuck in molasses together.

I push my food around on my plate. I don't have any appetite, and my mind is full of questions. If Dad took Mom to a psychiatrist, would everything go back to being normal? If Mom hadn't gotten sick, would I have looked up Lauren's blog? If I prayed in the right way, would I be sitting here, coming up with unanswerable questions?

I'm tired of asking myself questions. I want answers. The Bible says it is not for us to know times or seasons that God has fixed by his own authority. So wouldn't it be easier for God to stop letting me have so many questions he won't answer for me?

I've just asked myself another question. I put my fork down and give up on supper.

After Bible time and nightly prayers and getting the little ones to sleep, I crawl into bed.

"Rachel?" Ruth says, her voice barely audible.

"Yes?"

"Do you want to snuggle up tonight?"

"Sure."

Ruth crawls into bed with me, and I kiss her forehead.

"I'm so tired, but it's like I can't fall asleep," she says. Her voice comes out in whispers. I can feel the warmth of her breath on my face.

"I can't sleep lately either," I answer.

"Rachel?"

"Yes?"

"When will God heal Mom? I thought yesterday she was getting better, but now I don't know. She went right back to bed after supper."

I feel the tug of two answers battling it out inside of me.

"Well," I begin, "Scripture tells us that whatever you ask in prayer, believe that you have received it, and it will be yours."

Ruth smiles. "You're right. I guess we just have to keep praying."

I nod and smile back. Soon, Ruth drifts off. Her face is placid. At peace. I prop myself up on my elbow and look at her.

"Ruth," I whisper. There's no response, so I keep talking, my voice so low I can barely hear it with my own ears. "Ruth, the truth is, I don't know. I don't know when God will heal Mom. I don't know if God will heal Mom. That's what I wanted to tell you, but I didn't want to break your heart."

Ruth doesn't move. I wriggle down under the covers and wait for sleep to come.

"And so, my brothers in sisters in Christ, I ask that as you walk out those doors today and confront all that is worldly, that you not forget what Scripture tells us about following the will of God," says Pastor Garrett from the pulpit, his voice like thunder. "'Therefore to him that knoweth to do good and doeth it not, to him it is sin.' 'For the wages of sin *is* death, but the gift of God *is* eternal life through Jesus' Christ our Lord.'"

There's a chorus of amens, and we stand to sing our closing hymn. I join in, trying to say the words without thinking about them.

Yield not to temptation, for yielding is sin
Each victory will help you some other to win
Fight manfully onward, dark passions subdue
Look ever to Jesus, He'll carry you through

The part about yielding not to temptation makes me think about The Great Escape—the one link on Lauren's blog that I never clicked on. The one I promised myself I never would. As I mull over this, I catch James Fulton out of the corner of my eye, standing with his parents and mumbling over the lyrics, his face down. His hair has started to grow in a bit more since he left for Journey of Faith, but he still seems marked to me.

I look over at Mom, little Isaac clutched to her chest. Her eyes are shut tight, and she's swaying back and forth to the music. It's the first time she's come to church since losing

Joshua. She's been eating supper at the table with us these past few days, too, and I think she's trying, but it's still as if every smile she offers has to be found somewhere deep inside her.

When services are over, we make our way out. Mrs. Garrett comes over and lightly touches my shoulder. "Thank you again for attending our fellowship on modesty, Rachel."

"Oh, thank you," I answer, managing a smile. "It was such an encouragement." We don't mention my crying. It would only make us both uncomfortable, and anyway, my careful smile hopefully suggests to her that my episode that evening was just a silly moment of feminine insecurity.

My family loads itself back into the van, and I strap Isaac into his seat. Faith, Paul, and Caleb come over shortly after we arrive home. It's the first time they've joined us for Sunday dinner since Mom lost the baby, and Faith rushes in all energy and good cheer. The kitchen is instantly her domain again, and I'm grateful to just follow her orders.

"Rachel, will you . . . ?"

"Rachel, can you . . . ?"

"Rachel, might you . . . ?"

Mom wanders in, and Faith doesn't skip a beat, doesn't coddle or question—she just hands her a bowl of strawberries to wash and slice. Mom follows Faith's commands, and I think I even see a little smile on her face as she joins in.

I can hear Paul in the family room, relating to my

brothers how he spent hours with an inmate at a correctional facility in Houston the week before and brought him to Christ.

"As Matthew 28:19 tells us, go ye therefore, and teach all nations," Paul intones, as if he's saved the entire continent of Africa and not just one man in Houston.

Finally, the food is ready. Dad prays over the meal. "Father God," he says, "it's so wonderful to feel your presence as we sit down to eat this good food. Let us live to please you, and give glory to your name."

As we begin to pass around platters of sliced ham and turkey, of buttered bread and fresh fruit, Paul clears his throat loudly. "Dear family," he says, "may I have your attention?" His smile is so broad I can see his gums.

He waits until he has all our eyes on him, and then he makes us wait a beat longer before he finally speaks.

"The Lord God has given us many blessings," he begins. Faith has Caleb in her lap, and she kisses him on the head, smiling like she has a secret she can't hold in.

"Yes, God is so good," Dad says, nodding, not understanding Faith's expression or Paul's words.

"We have one special blessing we are very grateful for," Paul continues. My mother stops and gasps. My eyes meet Ruth's across the table. She's guessed, too.

"The Lord has blessed us with another child," Paul announces, proudly. "Faith is due just after Christmas."

"Praise God!" my father says, beaming. He jumps up from the head of the table to shake hands with Paul and give Faith a kiss on the cheek. My brothers do the same, and the younger children immediately begin guessing if it's a girl or a boy.

Mom breaks out into a huge smile.

"Yes, praise God!" she says, clasping her hands together, tears finally sparked by joy instead of sadness. "This is God's work. This is His hand helping us recover from the loss of Joshua."

Everyone nods and smiles and hugs and praises the Lord, but I just sit there like a lump.

"You haven't said anything, Rachel," Faith says, her eyes searching mine, bemused. "Did you even hear what Paul said, little sister?"

I smile carefully. "I'm so happy for you both," I say. To my own ears, I sound like I did when I thanked Mrs. Garrett after church. Practiced and robotic. An expert faker.

"Soon, little sister, you will know the joy of being a mother," Faith says, tickling baby Caleb's chin. "Even as we sit here, our Lord is preparing your future husband. And He is preparing you to be his future wife and mother of his children."

I blush hard as my family turns to look at me. Only Ruth looks away. She knows I hate having everyone's eyes on me like this. But what she can't know is that Faith's news sends me into a panic as I picture myself in just a few years delivering a similar announcement at this very table.

Suddenly, my throat starts to close up, and I can't breathe very well. I try to focus on the drops of condensation forming on the pitcher of orange juice.

"Excuse me, just for a moment," I say, pushing my chair back and heading to the hall bathroom.

"Rachel, are you all right?" someone calls out after me.

Please don't let anyone follow me.

I shut the door behind me and force myself to take deep breaths. I count the tiles on the floor and then I count the rings on the shower curtain. I flush the toilet and make the water run in case anyone is listening out for me. Last night I gave Ruth the answer I knew she wanted when she asked about Mom getting better. I told her everything we asked for in prayer we would receive. Now I want to pray, but as usual I can't find the right words. And what would I pray for? *Please, Father God, don't find my future husband, not now. Please, Father God, don't give me so many babies I can't find a moment's peace to read or think or watch the sunset.* But even as I pray the words I know they're the wrong things to pray for.

I struggle to take a breath but manage it. Then I take another one, inhaling more deeply this time. *Breathe, Rachel. Breathe.*

It helps, and when I come back out to the table, I get a collective worried look.

"I'm fine, just not . . . feeling one hundred percent," I say. My family members glance at one another quizzically, but soon we're acting as if nothing ever happened.

I'm not the only one in my family good at faking.

⁂

Even though I was worried that Faith's news would make Mom sad, she seems anything but. During nightly prayers and Bible time, she keeps smiling and talking about how good God is to send a new baby to the family when we desperately needed such a blessing. Dad keeps smiling and nodding and saying, "Amen" to everything Mom says. Instead of his usual half grin, he's wearing a smile so full I think his cheeks must be hurting.

No one says anything to me about running to the bathroom.

That night when I get on the computer, I work on the Walker Family Landscaping and Tree Trimming site while Dad reads his Bible in the living room. When he turns off his reading light, he stops by the computer desk and puts his hand on my shoulder.

"Almost done, Rachel?"

"Yes, Dad."

"Good. Make sure you turn in early."

"Of course, Dad."

I wait until his bedroom light is off and I hear his light snoring before I pull up Lauren's blog.

It's still there. Her picture is still smiling at me.

I don't even pause. I just do it. I click on *The Great Escape*. My eyes swallow up the words, greedy for them.

Some of my friends tell me my life before I met them sounds like I made it up. Like it's something from a bad fairy tale where a princess is held kidnapped in a tower until she's rescued. Like Rapunzel.

Only, no knight in shining armor saved me. I saved myself.

From birth I was part of an extreme religious community—some might call it a cult . . . when I'm having a bad day, I call it a cult—where women were marginalized, shamed, humiliated, and not given one ounce of autonomy. And why? Because the Lord dictates this is how it should be.

I never went to regular school until I was old enough to go to vet tech school as a legal adult. I didn't cut my hair or wear pants until I was 18 and I didn't have a boyfriend until I was 19 and for a long time I didn't even think it was possible to exist outside of this weird, tightly-controlled world with my dad in charge of everything I did. When I say my dad was in charge of everything, I don't mean everything like where I went and who I hung out with, although he was in charge of that for sure. I mean he was in charge of what I wore, what I read, what I said, and even what I thought.

I hate my dad for so much, but do you know what I hate him for the most? I can't even pray to God anymore without hearing my father's voice in my head.

I was told that my only possible future was acting the way my future husband would want me to act, and I was told that my dreams of becoming a vet were just that. Dreams. That I had to maintain a cheerful countenance and practice to be a good helpmeet. Mother and wife. My only options.

When I was a teenager, I started rebelling. I met some kids hanging out near the local gas station when I went to fill up my dad's car—one of the few things I was allowed to do outside my house. The rest sounds like a bad teen movie (note:—I didn't even get to WATCH bad teen movies until I wasn't a teenager anymore, but anyway . . .). I started sneaking out of the house, meeting (jerky) guys, drinking cheap vodka in the backs of trucks. Yes, cheap vodka in the backs of trucks. I told you. Teen movie.

The cult didn't like it. They prayed over me, they preached about me. They threatened to send me away to this camp where they force you to do hard labor and barely let you sleep and brainwash you.

One day I just literally walked out. I'd made some friends from the outside by then, and when I thought the preacher was talking about me during one of the Sunday services, I'd had enough. I just got up and walked out. No one came after me, not even my parents. I didn't have a car. I hitchhiked into town and called one of my new friends from the only pay phone still standing. She said I could come move with her to the city where she was going to start taking classes at a community college.

That night, I went back home to my parents' house to get a few things. My ID, a few of my clothes, the little bit of money I'd saved from taking care of our neighbor's dog. And I really wanted to say goodbye to my two cats, Fluff and Stuff. I knew I wouldn't be able to take them with me even though I desperately wanted to. I'd bottle-fed them from birth after their mom abandoned them in the flower garden outside the house.

So I walked in and my friend was waiting for me in the car outside the house. I walked in and my mom was on her knees praying out loud in the living room. She had to have heard me come in but she just kept praying. It hurt my heart, it's true. But my mom hadn't defended me or herself in so long I wasn't surprised.

I was sobbing at this point, and I ran upstairs with a paper bag for my things when my dad came down the hall and stopped me when I got down to the foot of the stairs. He was so furious I thought he was going to explode right there in the middle of the kitchen. His face was so red.

"Dad, I'm leaving," I said. It was like I was watching myself from someplace else. Now that I've seen movies, I can say it was like I was a character in a movie, but the movie was real. The movie was my life. But at the time I just knew it was like I was outside of my body somehow.

That's when my dad hit me hard. Right across the face. It stung like a million fire ants bit my face all at once.

My dad had beaten me and my mom in the name of God many times before, but never like this. He was pummeling me. Hard. I was down on the ground crouching into a little ball and my dad even kicked me while I was down there. I was screaming, trying to protect my head with my hands. I heard my mom crying and praying, but it was like she was doing it in some other language, not English. My dad was screaming something but I couldn't understand him either.

I crawled far enough away that I was able to scramble up to my feet and dart out the front door. I raced to my friend's car.

When I got to my friend's car she screamed that I was bleeding from my nose. I said my dad did it.

I never saw my parents again after that.

There's more to the story. How I moved to the city and how I transformed my life and why I left the city after some pretty dumb stuff and how I moved back to my hometown even though I run the risk of running into my mom and dad again.

But I'm dead to them, I think. My mom and dad, I mean.
I'm dead to them and I don't exist. I'm dead to
everyone else that I knew before. All of them. It's like I
don't exist to them. My salvation, if ever I really earned
it, I've given up through my bad behavior. I'm a
nothing. A mistake. But it's taken me six years to know
that if salvation means giving up every human thing
about myself and becoming some robot with no real
emotions, then I don't want it anymore.

I want to write more about what happened after that
day I ran away, but as I type this, my eyes are full of
tears. I need to take a break from this.

If anyone is reading this, thank you. I'm still here. It
feels so good to type that.

I'm still here.

I stopped breathing halfway through the post and only
after I've read the last word can I exhale. I'm scared someone will hear me, the breath is so loud. I picture Mr. Sullivan
at church after the laying of hands on my father, telling me
the Lord's steadfast love always endures. Telling me about
his babies waiting for him and Mrs. Sullivan in Heaven when

his living daughter hasn't seen him in years. I think of Lauren bleeding from the nose, crouched helpless like a wounded animal on the floor. Yes, the Lord has granted parents the right to discipline their children, but that isn't what God intended.

I'm squeezing my fists so hard my arms are vibrating. I want to scream, yell, shout. A flash of Scripture flies through my mind, trying to correct me.

The discretion of a man deferreth his anger, and it is his glory to pass over a transgression.

But if that were true, then why did God let Mr. Sullivan get so mad?

For the wrath of man worketh not the righteousness of God.

Then that means that Mr. Sullivan isn't a real man of God, right?

A fool uttereth all his mind, but a wise man keepeth it in till afterwards.

Then am I a fool to be so angry right now? Am I as bad as Mr. Sullivan?

Nervous energy charges through my veins. So many missing pieces of Lauren's story are a part of my mind, fixed there forever. After all these years, I know the truth about what happened to her, and it makes me so sad, even though I'm shocked that she was able to get away with so much forbidden behavior while still part of our community.

When Lauren Sullivan was younger, around Ruth's age,

she sang in the Calvary Christian Church choir, belting out the songs so loud it was like she thought the words could float up to Heaven itself. She set up games in the parking lot after services to see which of us kids could run around the church building the fastest. She could memorize Bible verses faster than some of the adults, and she read them confidently, her voice booming, almost like a little pastor.

And this Lauren with the dyed hair and the strange tattoos seems different, even frightening, but isn't the Lauren of my childhood still this Lauren? And isn't this Lauren still someone we should love? Someone who should know we haven't forgotten her?

I want to tell her somehow. Tell her I think about her. I care about her.

But if I get caught.

I remember Dad's warnings about mixing with those who've abandoned Christ.

I remember my punishment for getting caught with *A Wrinkle in Time*. Copying Scripture.

If I get caught doing this, the punishment will be so great, copying Scripture for bad behavior will seem like a laughable consequence. I picture James Fulton paraded in front of us after being sent away to Journey of Faith. I consider Lauren's words about what happened to him and to everyone who is sent there. Brainwashed. I'm not one hundred percent sure what that means, but the word makes me shiver.

And then I think about sitting at my parents' dining room table in a few years, responsible for a baby in my belly and a baby in my arms.

And I can't breathe.

I stare at my hands, like they belong to someone else. Someone I don't know but who lately seems intent on making herself known to me, whether I like it or not. They move over the keyboard and open up the email program for my dad's work—the only email any of us are allowed to use.

FROM: Walker Family Landscape and Tree Trimming
TO: butterflygirl@mailservice.com

Lauren,

You probably don't remember me. But I remember you from Calvary Christian. I found your blog, and I want you to know that I'm really sorry about what your dad did to you. And you're not dead to me. You never were.

"He healeth the broken in heart, and bindeth up their wounds." Psalm 147:3

Sincerely,
Rachel Walker

I hit Send. I look up and out the family room windows and imagine the message traveling through the ether and across the night sky, slipping around the twinkling stars on its way to its destination. I picture it floating through darkness until it finds Lauren Sullivan, who opens it and reads what I've written.

9

The next morning when I head downstairs to start breakfast, I see my dad on the computer.

Dad hardly ever gets on the computer. He doesn't like it, and he only agreed to get one when it became clear that running a family business profitable enough to feed a family as big as ours depended on one.

The sight of him hunching over, his beefy fingers gigantic against the keyboard, makes my body go cold. Even though I cleared the history and erased my sent message to Lauren, my dad could be checking the company email. He lets me do it most of the time, but he could be checking it. He could be.

What have I done?

"Dad?"

He turns to look at me, and I catch a glimpse of what's on the screen.

It's his list of appointments for the week. Nothing else.

"Rachel, I'm looking for the address of that new client? The one over in Dove Lake? I've misplaced the printout of the schedule you gave me last night."

I dart over to the computer, anxious to take control of the keyboard. Still in the chair, my father slides to the side, and I tap away, searching for the information he needs. My heart is still racing, my cheeks still pink. Forcing myself to focus, I print out what my father needs and hand it to him.

"Good morning."

I'm still so on edge I jump at the voice and turn to see my mother walking down the hallway from her bedroom. For the first time in almost a month she has her hair styled carefully and pulled up away from her face. Her skin is still pale, but there's a slight spark in her eyes that's been missing these past few weeks.

"Mom!" I manage. "You're feeling better?"

"A little, yes," my mother answers, nodding. "God's wonderful gift of a new baby for this family has made my spirit joyful. He understands the pain of my loss, and he's healed us with this child. God is so good."

"Yes, he certainly is," agrees Dad, a smile stretching across his face.

"Yes, of course," I say, nodding, almost afraid to step away from the computer as if an email from Lauren might pop up the moment I do. Only when Dad gets up from the chair and follows Mom into the kitchen do I finally manage to fill my lungs with air. *Relax, Rachel. You didn't get caught.* I head into the kitchen to start breakfast, serving my mom a cup of coffee first.

Finally, after the frenzy of the morning is over and Dad and my brothers are gone, we settle into the family room for schoolwork, and Mom joins us on the couch so she can watch over the little ones.

"I need to check something on the computer," I tell Ruth and the twins after an hour or so. "For Dad." I say it loudly, just in case Mom is listening, too.

"Okay," says Ruth, barely looking up from her workbook.

There are a few messages from some of Dad's clients and a company that sells us equipment, but nothing from butterflygirl. I frown and then catch myself, correcting my face into a neutral expression that hides what I'm really feeling.

I don't just want Lauren to write back because I want to catch the email before someone else sees it. I want her to write back so I can read what she has to say to me. But what if she doesn't write back? What if she doesn't remember me? Why would she want anything to do with me after what her father did and after the way we made her feel?

All afternoon I check for a response as often as I can, hopefully without drawing suspicion, but there's nothing from Lauren.

"Rachel, what are you doing?" Ruth says from the kitchen

table as I quickly click refresh on the computer for the fifth time that day. "Are you sure everything's all right?"

"Yes. I'm waiting on an important email for this payroll software update." Again I say it loudly for Mom's benefit. Neither one has any idea what I mean, but Ruth nods, and I force myself not to check the email again for another hour.

It's getting so easy to lie to Ruth. So easy to lie and so easy to keep breaking rules I never thought I'd break. That night, long after everyone is asleep, I creep downstairs, pausing every few steps to listen for any sounds that others are awake. When I turn on the computer and bring up the email program, I see a new message. It's in bold text, marked as unread.

It's from butterflygirl.

I reach my fingers to the screen and touch it, like I can read it through osmosis. Then I quickly click it open.

Rachel,

Hi. Thanks for your email. As I type this I keep picturing all these situations where you're not reading these words and someone else is and then you get into trouble. I really don't want that, so I suggest if you want to email me again, you never email me from this address. Can you set up an email address that's just for you? Do you know how to do

that? If you don't, let me know and I can help you. Also, I ask that you not tell my parents you've communicated with me. That's very important to me.

I didn't respond to your email right away because I was so stunned when I received it, to be totally honest. It's the first time anyone from Calvary has contacted me since I left. And, so . . . I started thinking about myself when I was back where you are . . . not that I don't do that a lot, of course, in this sort of abstract way. But now I was thinking of another girl—you—right where I was six years ago. And it kind of flipped me out. Since you've read my blog, I think you know what I mean.

So I wasn't sure I could write you back, but then I started thinking about all the things I wish I could have told myself back then. That I was a human being. A whole person with a brain and a body that are mine. Not anyone else's. Not my dad's and not Pastor Garrett's.

Why did God give me a body if he didn't want me to run, jump, laugh, dance, and swim in a yellow, two-piece swimsuit?

Why did God give me a brain if he didn't want me to use it to learn about anything I wanted to learn about?

Well, I'm blabbing on like I sometimes do, and I don't want to overwhelm you. Mostly, I want to say that I appreciate your words. I'm glad you remember me. I remember your family and I remember you as a little girl. You didn't talk much but you always seemed so kind. Sensitive. You were a girl with faraway eyes. That's a title to a song you don't know, but trust me, it's a great song.

This is enough for now. I'm doing really well, and thank you for thinking about me. If I never hear from you again, I want you to know I wish you well. But if I can help you somehow, let me know.

xoxo Lauren

I read her words over and over. I can't get enough of them. But soon, I'm hearing Pastor Garrett's voice as he debates her points. I'm hearing my own father's voice as he argues against her.

Wherefore be ye not unwise, but understanding what the will of the Lord is.

I delight to do thy will, O my God, yea, thy law is within my heart.

There are many devices in a man's heart, nevertheless the counsel of the Lord, that shall stand.

But then I realize that the voices in my head aren't mine. They don't belong to me. They belong to other people.

I read Lauren's post one more time and tip my chair back to look down the hall to make sure my parents' bedroom light is still off. Opening up a free email service, I create a new address for myself. It's mine. Just mine and no one else's. My toes curl up at the thought.

I click on the button that says compose message. As I type, it's almost as if I'm typing to myself as much as I am to Lauren. The click clack of my fingers on the keyboard sounds like a pleasant little song that belongs only to me. The words spilling out of me take a weight off my shoulders.

FROM: rachelwalker123@freemail.com
TO: butterflygirl@mailservice.com

Lauren,

I'm not sure what to say, but first of all, I want you to know that I won't say anything to your parents about you. I promise. And please don't say anything to anyone about me writing to you, okay? Of course you wouldn't, but I know you understand what could happen to me if I get caught.

The first question that comes to mind might make you laugh, I guess. But have you really gone swimming in a yellow bikini? Really?

I can't quite put my finger on why I'm writing to you. It's a risk, like I said. An enormous risk. But lately, I feel like something is building inside of me, and I can't stop it. I don't even know if I want to anymore.

After church last Sunday, my older sister Faith told us she is pregnant with her second baby. She's almost twenty, just a few years younger than you. You probably remember her, too. I'm the quiet one and she's the opposite.

For some reason after she told us, I got really anxious. I had to go into the bathroom to compose myself. I know everyone expects me to be next—to get married and have babies just like Faith. And I really love kids. I love my little sister Ruth, especially. Even though she's not that little anymore. But the thought of having babies of my own in just a few years—I know it's what I should want. But it just isn't.

And it's not only about having babies. It's about . . . everything. About wondering why I can't find the right words to pray to God. And trying to understand why I keep having all these questions inside of me that no one can answer. About wanting to learn and know things that everyone around me doesn't seem to think I have a need to know.

I feel like I'm failing here. Like I'm doing everything wrong even as I try to do everything right.

I feel like I can't breathe in this place anymore.

I'm not sure exactly what I'm doing writing you this email, but for some reason writing it makes me feel a lot better. I'm going to hit send before I chicken out.

Sincerely,
Rachel Walker

And just like I promised I would, I hit send before I can stop myself. Before any voices in my head tell me I'm making a mistake.

Tuesday morning I'm groggy from staying up too late. Mom comes out of her room again, and this time she even helps feed the little ones. I want to believe she's getting better, but I still wonder how real her recovery is if it's only secured by the idea that Faith is having a baby. I force myself through the motions of breakfast and school, but all I can think about is Lauren's email to me and what I've written back to her. I think about her dancing. And swimming.

My family went to Galveston once, years ago, for a family picnic. We found an isolated part of the beach and put down old quilts, and my brothers and sisters and I ran down to the shoreline and dipped our feet in the Gulf of Mexico. Then my older brothers waded in wearing T-shirts and old denim cutoffs down to their knees, but Faith and Ruth and I just huddled by the shore, waving to them from the edge of the water. There are some Christian-run websites that sell special modest swimsuits, but they're very expensive. Much too expensive for our family. So my brothers jumped in the surf, dunking themselves and one another while the rest of us laughed and cheered them on.

Even though my sisters and I could only get our feet wet, I remember wondering what the ocean floor felt like and what it would be like to be underwater. Maybe it's like time slowing down. Or stopping altogether.

"Rachel, you just finished my entire problem for me."

I blink. Gabriel is wearing a small smirk on his face, and

I realize as I've been letting my mind wander, I've also completed one of Gabriel's math problems instead of letting him finish it.

"Oh," I say. "I'm sorry."

"I'm not," Gabriel mutters. "I don't like math anyway."

I hand my younger brother his pencil and head toward the kitchen for lunch, pausing by the computer. I've already checked it twice this morning. After yesterday, I sense Ruth and Mom are even more aware of my checks. And with Mom feeling even better, it's just too risky to try and see if Lauren's emailed me back.

My mother's light touch on my shoulder interrupts my thoughts.

"Rachel, help me with lunch?"

"Sure, Mom," I answer, my eyes glancing back at the computer once more before heading into the kitchen.

We bow our heads in prayer before eating our lunch of hot dogs, pretzels, and cut-up fruit. Instead of thanking God, my mind swims with thoughts of Lauren.

After lunch, I make an excuse to print out Dad's appointments for the next day. It's not something I usually do until later in the evening—and often when Dad is sitting next to me in the living room—but I can't help it. The urge to reread Lauren's words consumes me.

"This will only take a second," I tell Mom, quickly clicking around to find Dad's files but opening up a second window to check my email.

"All right," my mom answers from the couch where she's going through infant clothes for Faith's new baby. I think her gaze lingers on me for a moment before she goes back to folding a tiny newborn onesie into a neat square. But maybe I'm just imagining it.

I check and there's nothing. Disappointment washes over me. Did I say something to Lauren that bothered her? Did she think I was being judgmental when I asked her if she went swimming in a bikini? Has she just decided she wants nothing to do with anyone from Calvary Christian Church?

That night during Bible time and nightly prayers, my mind buzzes, and my father's words slip over me. I don't even try to grasp them. I'm just waiting until I can get online again. But once Ruth and I have finished putting the little ones to bed and I head to the computer, Dad stops me.

"Rachel, there's no need to worry about working on that tonight," my father says. "You need your rest."

"Yes, Dad, of course," I answer automatically. But I curl up my fists and dig my thumbnails into my palms in frustration. Dad never worried about my need for rest during the time that Mom was sick.

Ruth is fast asleep when I crawl into bed, and as much as

I love our snuggle-ups, right now I'm glad to be alone. I slide my head under my pillow.

I wait for Scripture to come to me, like Ruth's secret messages. Nothing. I try to speak in the careful, practiced language Dad uses. Nothing. When I was tiny, not much older than Sarah, I pictured God as a bigger version of my father, sitting on a chair high up in the clouds. Then later, I pictured Him as described in Revelation, with the hairs of his head white like wool, like snow. Eyes like a flame of fire. Lately, when I try to visualize God, I keep imagining a desert landscape, open and vast and never ending.

It's not very comforting.

"God, what's wrong with me?" I whisper into my threadbare sheets that have been washed more times than could ever be counted. "I don't even know how to pray to you. I want to, but I can't." I wait for tears, but there aren't any. "I'm sorry," I add, halfheartedly.

I curl up and wait for sleep to come, finally dozing. When I wake up in the early morning hours before the sun is up, I decide to take advantage of the opportunity. Creeping downstairs I turn on the computer and pull up my email. I don't even stop to listen for the sounds of anyone else who also might be getting up early. I don't even wince when my foot makes the floorboards squeak as I make my way down the steps.

I just know I have to check one more time.

And there, as bold as can be, is a new email from Lauren.

Rachel,

Hey, sorry again that I didn't write back right away, but I tend to get on my computer pretty late at night. And I'll be honest. It's been kind of messing with my mind to read your emails. Please don't think that means I don't want you to write to me. Only that reading what you're going through brings a lot of stuff back.

Yes, I have been swimming. And yes, in a two piece. It was the most glorious feeling in the world. Don't tell Pastor Garrett! Ha ha. Go ahead. Tell him. I don't care what he thinks.

I wish we could meet in person, but I know that probably isn't possible. I remember the extraordinary precautionary measures I would take when I still lived with my parents just to do the smallest things. Like how I hid books I wanted to read inside the box spring of my mattress. And how I wrote down poetry I knew they wouldn't like and tucked it behind gaps in the wallpaper of my bedroom. It seems like it happened to a different person now, but I did those things, and I know that the fact that you are emailing me at all means you could be putting yourself in danger.

At this, I stop reading and listen to the house around me. Lauren is right. Even when I lose myself in the computer, even as my risk-taking grows ever riskier, a part of me is always waiting to be caught. As if that's the only thing that could happen next.

I take a breath and start reading again.

Anyway, I know there's a really strong possibility that I'll never hear from you again because it's too dangerous, so just in case I wanted to leave you with a quote I really like. It comes from a poem written by a woman named Mary Oliver, and I wish I'd heard it when I was still part of your world. And the "me" in the quote isn't me, Lauren Sullivan. Maybe some poetry expert would tell me I'm wrong, but I think the "me" is *you*.

Tell me, what is it you plan to do with your one wild and precious life?

xoxo Lauren

The question expands, filling every ounce of space in my mind.

It only takes a second to search the words Lauren's quoted and the poet's name. And suddenly the full poem is staring back at me.

The Summer Day

By Mary Oliver

Who made the world?
Who made the swan, and the black bear?
Who made the grasshopper?
This grasshopper, I mean—
the one who has flung herself out of the grass,
the one who is eating sugar out of my hand,
who is moving her jaws back and forth instead of up and down—
who is gazing around with her enormous and complicated eyes.
Now she lifts her pale forearms and thoroughly washes her face.
Now she snaps her wings open, and floats away.
I don't know exactly what a prayer is.
I do know how to pay attention, how to fall down
into the grass, how to kneel down in the grass,
how to be idle and blessed, how to stroll through the fields,
which is what I have been doing all day.

Tell me, what else should I have done?
Doesn't everything die at last, and too soon?
Tell me, what is it you plan to do
with your one wild and precious life?

Tears are running down my face, and I try to stop them but I can't. I can't make sense of the words—not all of them—but something about them makes me catch my breath. Makes me read them again and again. Especially the final two lines.

Tell me, what is it you plan to do with your one wild and precious life?

The fact that this question now exists in my brain makes me feel like a million bubbles are exploding under my skin all at once.

How long has this question existed? How many other people have asked themselves these very words?

What is it I plan to do with my one wild and precious life?

My wild life?

My precious life?

To be a godly wife to my future husband and raise my children in the service of the Lord.

It's been my answer all my life. It's always come so easily.

Maybe because I've never asked the question first.

10

"*So as we leave this evening*, brothers and sisters, let us remember that wonderful verse from John," shouts Pastor Garrett, his chest puffing up as he preaches, one hand clutching his Bible, the other palm up, toward Heaven. "'Love not the world, neither the things that are in the world. If any man love the world, the love of the Father is not in him. For all that is in the world, the lust of the flesh, and the lust of the eyes, and the pride of life, is not of the Father but is of the world. And the world passeth away, and the lust thereof, but he that doeth the will of God abideth forever.'"

"Amen," the congregation responds with enthusiasm.

"Amen," I add, under my breath.

Tonight is Wednesday night fellowship. Sometimes on Wednesday nights there are meetings like the one about modesty, but other times Pastor Garrett speaks to the entire congregation. Dad always says it's like refueling in the middle of the week.

As we sing the closing hymn, I see Mr. Sullivan, Lauren's father, several rows over on the far side of the church, singing but barely moving his mouth as he does. His hands hang at his sides, and I imagine them curled into fists, beating his own daughter. My heart hardens just looking at him. Mrs. Sullivan nods her head as she sings, as if each nod brings the words more meaning.

As we trail out of the church, my father moves close to me and touches my shoulder.

"I'd like you to visit with Pastor Garrett for a moment," he says, his steady voice revealing nothing. I open my mouth to ask why but shut it just as fast.

"Hello, Rachel," Pastor Garrett begins as we approach him just outside the door of Calvary Christian. He's not a large man, but his presence takes up so much space. His voice and the way he carries himself command attention, and his bright blue eyes focus on you in a way that almost makes you want to look away.

"Hello, Pastor Garrett," I say, my pulse quickening. I see Mom standing a few feet away, holding a sleeping Isaac in her arms, her eyes on us. The service has gone on even longer than normal—Pastor Garrett's sermon was almost a full hour—and dusk is falling around us. A mosquito lands on my arm, but I don't dare to swat it away. I just stand before Pastor Garrett, trying to breathe.

"Rachel, your father has asked that I give you a special

blessing this evening," he says. "And I'm happy to do so. Please bow your head and pray for God's blessing."

I tip my head forward and shut my eyes immediately. We often see Pastor Garrett praying over a courting couple, soon to be married, or a member of the congregation who isn't feeling well. But why has my father asked him to pray over me tonight? Mom and Dad must think I need this extra blessing because of something, but what, exactly, might they suspect? My heart, already hammering, picks up speed.

I feel Pastor Garrett's hand on my forehead. A moment later, I feel Dad's grip on my shoulder.

"Father God," Pastor Garrett begins, his voice rising and falling, his hand pushing harder and harder into my skull, "Scripture tells us that you are faithful and that you will not let your followers be tempted beyond their abilities, and that with temptation you will always provide a way of escape, that we may be able to endure such temptation. Father God, we ask you to watch over your servant Rachel and guide her through trials and storm as she grows in your grace and wisdom. Stay with her, Lord, and show her the way. In the name of Jesus Christ our Savior, amen."

"Amen," my father shouts, and he squeezes my shoulder tight.

"Amen," I say, my chest tightening. When I open my eyes Pastor Garrett is smiling at me. I try to catch a glimpse of those around us, wondering who's witnessed what's just occurred.

Whispers. Bits of whispers. Gossip in the form of prayer requests. Juicy information in the form of concerned words.

I slide into the van, and Ruth shoots me a sympathetic look, but we don't talk. Isaac and Sarah are asleep, and as we drive home in silence, I peer out into the inky blackness. A heaviness surrounds me as I think back to the words I typed last night after everyone had gone to sleep.

FROM: rachelwalker123@freemail.com
TO: butterflygirl@mailservice.com

Dear Lauren,

I really love that Mary Oliver quote. I don't know why, but it's all I can think about since I read your email. The words keep running through my mind. I read a little about Mary Oliver and I was surprised she's still alive. For some reason, poetry seems like something people did a long time ago.

Actually, I found the poem you quoted and read the whole thing over and over. I don't completely get it, but part of it felt like it was speaking right to me. Let me tell you, if God took paying attention and being idle as prayer, I would be the world's greatest at praying. I would be better at it than anyone I know.

I haven't hidden anything in my box spring or behind the wallpaper, but I did have to get rid of a book I loved called *A Wrinkle in Time*. I still miss it.

I keep wondering what your life must be like. Working. Living alone. Do you like working with animals? I keep thinking of questions I want to ask. I keep thinking so much in general. I keep paying attention.

I'm terrified about what will happen to me if I get caught writing to you. But I'm also terrified about what will happen to me if I stop. I want to keep writing to you, even if I can't explain why in words.

I just can't stop thinking about that poem. I want to keep it in my mind and repeat it over and over. Like I'm praying the poem.

Rachel

If Pastor Garrett knew what I'd written back to Lauren late last night, he would have recommended right then that my parents send me away to Journey of Faith.

When we get home, Ruth and I tuck the younger ones in. Wednesday night fellowship means a break from Bible time with Dad, and I take a deep breath of relief at the thought. There's no chance to check my email, but maybe I can go back downstairs after everyone is asleep again. Although the lack of sleep from late night visits to the computer is starting to take a toll. I yawn loudly as I slip into bed.

"Rachel," Ruth asks from her bed across the room. Her voice is quiet and tight. "Why did Pastor Garrett want to pray over you?"

I flush and am grateful it's too dark for Ruth to notice. "I'm not sure," I tell her.

"Is everything all right?"

"Yes, Ruth," I answer. "Everything is."

Everything's not, but I don't think a thousand late night cuddles with my little sister would give me time to explain the turmoil inside of my heart. Still, one might at least help me feel better.

"Do you want to snuggle up?" I ask.

Ruth takes a deep breath and lies back on her bed. Speaking toward the ceiling, she answers, "I want to stretch out tonight, I think."

"Oh," I answer. "Okay."

I slip under my covers and stare at my bedroom wall. I can feel the prick of hot tears and I try not to let them get the best of me, but a few spill over. Squeezing my eyes shut, I try to wish myself to sleep.

I hear little Sarah's steady breathing and the tick of the clock and the rush of water through the pipes—one of my older brothers is taking a shower. Soon, I hear the creak of footsteps behind me. Rolling over, I see Ruth making her way to my bed.

"Scoot over," she says, and I do.

"I'm so tired," Ruth says, like it's nothing that she's changed her mind and decided to cuddle up with me.

"We're always so tired," I whisper. "If we had a nickel for every time one of us told the other we were tired, we would be rich."

"The first thing I would do with the money is buy a bigger bed, so we could snuggle up without you kicking me," Ruth says, but I can see she's grinning.

"Very funny."

"Good night, Rachel."

"Good night, Ruth."

She drifts off, her warm little body curling in on itself as sleep overtakes her. I gaze at her sweet face.

Oh, little sister, what is it we'll do with our wild and precious lives?

I sleep hard through the night, and by the time I wake up it's too late to check my email before anyone else gets up. But by the time we're settled in for morning lessons, I can't fight the compulsion. I give the old excuse about checking the business website, but I open an extra window and find a new message from Lauren.

FROM: butterflygirl@mailservice.com
TO: rachelwalker123@freemail.com

Rachel,

I never read *A Wrinkle in Time*, but I'm sorry you lost it. People love that book. The writer wrote a whole bunch more about the same family, did you know?

I totally appreciate the risk you're taking writing me. I really, really do. And I'm really glad you want to keep writing to me.

Maybe paying attention is prayer. Maybe being idle is prayer. Who said it can't be?

It's too bad we can't meet, probably. Even if you could get away, it's Clayton. Someone might see us. It's so weird to be back here sometimes. It's so different in the city. Anonymous, you know? And exciting. Sometimes I miss it. And sometimes I don't.

But things are good here, too. I love working at the animal hospital. I used to visit it all the time when I was younger and still at home. I would find these stray animals (or they seemed to find me) and then I'd try to nurse them back to health. It drove my father nuts. Then I'd bring them to Dr. Treats when I could. Isn't that the best name ever for a vet? Dr. Treats. It's his real last name, too, and it's like the dogs know that he has Milk-Bone biscuits in his pockets all the time. When I called him asking for a job, he was nice enough to give me one, and I'm so grateful. Do you have any pets? I have two cats again, Mitzi and Frankie. Right now as I type this they're attacking my shoelaces like the shoelaces are alive.

Okay, I need to eat and relax in front of the television. Rachel, there is this WHOLE AMAZING PLANET called television. I could tell you about it sometime. There's this show called *Law & Order* and apparently it's been on for over 20 years, so I think I have enough episodes to last me the rest of my life.

xoxo Lauren

"What are you reading, Rachel?"

I spin around in my seat and find my mother standing behind me, staring into the screen, her face full of concern. Lauren's email is still up on the screen. My heart drumming away, I quickly minimize it. What has she seen?

"Nothing, Mom, just work stuff for Dad," I say. Turning around so fast has only made me seem more guilty.

My mother tucks some stray strands into her otherwise neatly styled hair.

"Could you please turn off the computer and come join us at the kitchen table for lessons? I'm sure what you're working on can wait."

"Yes, of course," I say, and I exit out of email.

Numbly, I sit down next to the twins so I can correct their latest assignment. My mother strokes Sarah's head and smiles, so totally at peace. And I'm so angry. For weeks she locked herself up in her room while I tried to keep the house running, and just when I find Lauren she decides it's time to come out.

No, Rachel, you're selfish. She's your mother and she loves you. You shouldn't be angry at your own mother. No. I ball up my fists and squeeze.

"Rachel, are you all right?" my mother asks. I look up. My mother's eyes search mine.

My throat locks up, and I want to cry. Because I've been

caught. Because something is wrong with me and it's not getting better. Because of everything.

"I'm fine," I say, and I force myself to smile. The same tight, forced smile mom used all those weeks she wasn't well. If my mother notices the smile isn't real, she doesn't say anything.

That night toward the end of supper, my father looks at me and says, "Rachel, I appreciate everything you're doing on the computer for the family business, but I've prayed on it, and I think you need to stop for a little while. I think it's taking far too much time away from your duties around the house."

The chicken sandwich in my mouth turns tasteless. I keep chewing so no one will think I mind. I tell myself I can still sneak downstairs at night to get on the computer and email Lauren.

"Also," my father continues, "I've changed the password so you won't be tempted."

Stay calm. Don't give yourself away.

But I can't. I swallow and open my mouth. "Dad, no, please. Let me explain. I really think that—"

"Rachel Walker, are you questioning my authority?" my father snaps.

Everything stops. My mother stares at me, her eyes wider than I've ever seen them. My older brothers put down their forks. Even baby Isaac looks around, wondering what the exchange means.

My father has never raised his voice like that before. Maybe because neither my siblings nor I have ever talked back to him before.

"Remember Colossians," he says, his voice quieter now but his face still stern. " 'Children, obey your parents in all things, for this is well pleasing to the Lord.' " He briefly looks down at his meal and then back at me. He's not used to reprimanding us like this, I know.

"Yes, Father," I answer.

"We take computer time and usage very seriously, Rachel. Time on the computer should not be spent lightly."

My mind pictures James Fulton again, forced to show repentance in front of all of us. A reminder of what happens to children who disobey.

I try to take another bite of my supper, but I can't bring myself to do it. I want to cry—hard—but I can't in front of everyone. Maybe this is God's way of telling me I'm wrong, a sinner. Maybe this is God's way of stopping me from losing control.

But what about what Lauren said in one of her emails? Why would God give me my mind if he didn't want me to think these things, notice what I notice, question what I question?

And now I'll never be able to write Lauren back. I'll never

be able to find out why she left the city and came back to Clayton, and I'll never be able to find out what happens to her, and I'll never have the space or time to share my mixed-up feelings with someone who won't think I'm sinful or sick for having them.

I force myself to keep moving and keep breathing. Somehow, I make it through supper and through Bible study. After the little ones are in bed and my father sits with his Bible in the family room, I approach him for my routine blessing, but his words float over me like the directionless moths that hover outside the light on our front porch. They go nowhere, least of all my mind or my heart.

11

It's been over a week since Dad changed the password on the computer, but I keep thinking about Lauren Sullivan. I'm alone in the upstairs bathroom trying to get ready for another day, but instead I'm thinking of things I want to ask Lauren or the things I want to tell her.

Like . . . what other poetry does she know that's like Mary Oliver's?

And . . . what does she eat if she doesn't eat meat or eggs or cheese?

Or . . . didn't it hurt when she got those tattoos?

All these little comments and wonderings are piling up in my head until they feel like they might tip over and crash. But I have to accept that Lauren Sullivan isn't part of my life anymore. I should probably be glad it's all over, and I don't have to worry about getting caught or hurting my family or maybe even risking God's love . . . if I ever really risked it at all.

On that I'm not sure.

I frown at my own reflection in the mirror. "What's wrong with you?" I whisper as I brush my long, dark hair. My reflection stares back at me, looking as confused as I feel.

And it's not just Lauren. I still have my outdated encyclopedias and textbooks, but since Dad took away the computer, I miss the ease of being able to quickly look things up that aren't even related to her at all. Like why do lunar eclipses happen and how do airplanes actually work and where is Mount Everest located?

I even miss how I got the chance to stretch my brain when I worked on the Walker Family Landscaping and Tree Trimming website.

Everything feels foggy and dull edged and gray since I stopped using the computer, even though I'm getting more sleep than ever before since I'm not sneaking out of my room at night anymore.

"Rachel, could you please come back down to the kitchen?" my mother's voice calls.

I clomp down the stairs, forcing myself to smile.

"It sounds like a team of horses making its way down here," my mother says, but her eyes are kind.

"I didn't mean to be so loud," I tell her.

"It's all right, dear," she says.

Mom's recovery seems like it's lasting, but she also can't stop talking about Faith's new baby. Of course she must understand this new baby is Faith and Paul's and not hers. Still, she keeps talking about this child almost as a replacement for Joshua. Piles of baby clothes are stacked up in the family room, and the other morning I found a list titled Baby Names on a notepad on the kitchen counter. The carefully printed words—Luke, Martha, Josiah—made me pity her.

The phone rings, and Mom answers it. I make my way over to the breakfast table where Ruth is working on her math lesson. Her cheeks are ripe red apples.

"Are you feeling all right?" I ask her, pressing my hand to her forehead.

"I feel like everything inside of me hurts," Ruth says softly, and she lays her head on the table.

"You're hot," I say. "Burning up."

Mom walks in from the kitchen. "Rachel and Ruth, you have to run by Faith's house," she says. "Little Caleb has a terrible cold, and she wants to borrow the humidifier for his nap."

"Caleb isn't the only one who's sick," I say. "Ruth has a fever."

Mom walks over and feels Ruth's forehead. "To your room, Ruth."

I watch them head toward the stairs as I make my way to the family room floor where Isaac and Sarah are playing with a worn deck of alphabet flash cards. If I distract myself, the idea just born in my mind will go away. I take a sticky card and show it to Sarah.

"This is *B* for *banana*," I say. "*Banana.*"

Oh, idea, leave me alone.

"*B-B-B banana,*" Sarah says, blowing me a raspberry.

The idea is burrowing into my brain like a worm. It isn't listening to me. At all.

"This is *D* for *dog*," I tell Sarah, holding up another card. "*Dog.*"

Dogs that go to animal hospitals like Clayton Animal Hospital on the corner of Pickett and Claremont.

Oh, stop it, brain.

When my mother comes back downstairs from getting Ruth into bed, I hand Sarah the *H* is for *hat* card and stand up like something just occurred to me. Like what I'm about to say just flew into my mind as I sat here playing with my little sister.

"Mom, I could take the humidifier to Faith's if you want me to," I say.

Mom glances at the twins working at the table.

"Well, you could take one of the boys with you," she says.

We never go anywhere alone. That's not allowed unless it's an emergency. Proverbs says that iron sharpens iron, and one man sharpens another. When we travel in pairs, we keep each other accountable to the Lord. At least that's what Dad has always told us.

Jeremiah looks up from where he and Gabriel have been practicing long division.

"Well," he asks, "can I take a snack with me in the van at least if I have to go? I'm starving."

"You just ate breakfast," my mother says.

"Mom," I say, "don't make the boys go. It's just a half hour to Faith's house. I'll call you when I get there."

Mom looks out the window at our beat-up family van with the cardboard taped into the space where one of the back windows broke. She runs a finger along her bottom lip.

"I can always send one of your older brothers tonight," she says.

"But doesn't she need it for Caleb's nap?"

Mom takes a breath. She looks out the window.

"I want you to call the second you get to Faith's," she tells me. "It shouldn't take you more than thirty minutes. And then call right before you leave. All right?"

I nod and go find the humidifier. I'm tingling all over with excitement and fear and the sense that I've reached some point of no return.

The inside of the van smells like everything I know. The earthy smell of my dad's work boots and the faint, queer odor of the Fels-Naptha soap we buy in bulk to save money and the strange, unnamable scent that belongs to me, to us, to the Walker family.

I turn the key and start driving, and soon the spaces between houses get smaller, and eventually I'm driving through the streets of downtown, far, far away from Faith's house.

When I pull up to Clayton Animal Hospital, my heart is hammering away. What are the odds she'll even be here? I didn't stop to think about that when I was coming up with this grand, secret, crazy idea.

But I know it's Lauren the second I dart inside. Even as the door is closing behind me, I know I've spotted her standing at the counter, her hair the color of the sky. She's wearing matching cotton pants and a tunic like doctors and nurses wear. Hers are covered with cartoon cats.

"Can I help you?" she says, looking up at me, and the minute she smiles at me I want to cry, but I don't.

"Lauren, I'm . . ." I stop myself. My eyes dart around the waiting room. People from Calvary Christian own pets, of course. They could be here. But there's only an old man I don't recognize sitting in one of the waiting room chairs, scratching the ears of an ancient mutt.

"Are you all right?" she asks. Her eyes scan me up and down, and her smile collapses a bit. Do I look odd, yet familiar? Does she remember wearing long skirts in the middle of May? Loose-fitting blouses when worldly girls and women cooled off in strapless shirts and swimsuits? Does seeing me make her sad? Or angry?

But then she smiles again, a smile so contagious her eyes catch it, and they smile too, crinkling at the edges.

"Are you . . ." she asks, her voice dropping to a whisper, "Rachel Walker?"

I nod. She knows me. "Yes," I answer. "I'm sorry I came by your work. I can't really stay. I just needed to explain something."

Lauren nods, her eyes wide. "I can't believe you're here," she says. "When I last saw you, you were a kid. But I recognize your face." She peers behind me.

"I came alone," I say, suddenly aware of how fast my heart is still pumping. "But I have to get back before they notice I'm missing."

Lauren nods, understanding.

"Mark," she calls behind her, "can you come up here for a second and just watch the front desk?"

From a back hallway appears a boy about my age wearing a red T-shirt dotted with holes. It reads CLAYTON TRACK AND FIELD in faded black letters.

"Hey," he says, "who are you?"

I blush and glance at my feet.

"Mark, we need a minute," Lauren says, rolling her eyes slightly. She darts around the counter and takes my hand, pulling me into an empty exam room. The lights are off, and it smells like cleanser and wet dog.

"Are you all right?" she asks.

My want-to-cry feeling becomes a must-cry feeling, and suddenly I'm wiping tears away and I can't speak.

"Rachel, it's okay," Lauren says, lightly touching my shoulder. "Are you okay?" she asks, uncertain.

I nod, still not able to talk and only crying harder. Lauren keeps her hand on my shoulder and her face looks into mine. Her eyes are knowing and sad.

"It's just that I wanted to tell you why I stopped emailing you back," I say. "I didn't want you to think I didn't want to be your friend anymore." I blush at the word *friend*. Did Lauren even think I was her friend? Or just some strange little kid from her former life? But Lauren smiles at the mention.

"What happened?" she asks.

"My dad thought I was spending too much time on the computer. He didn't know I was talking to you, of course." I think about Pastor Garrett's special blessing. I think about what my mother might have seen that last day I was allowed online. "But I think he might have been . . . suspicious. So he changed the password and now I can't ever get on it again. At least, not for a really long time."

Lauren nods like she expected as much. "I'm so sorry, Rachel."

"I am, too," I say. "I really liked talking to you. I mean, writing to you. It was just . . . really nice."

Lauren nods. "Yeah," she says. "It was."

I hear the sound of the front door opening and voices in the waiting area. How much time have I spent here? Five minutes? Ten? Faith will be calling Mom any second, asking where I am.

"I have to go," I say, panicked. "Now."

"I know," Lauren says, nodding. "But wait. Here." She grabs a note pad and pen from the counter and scribbles something down, then hands me a slip of paper.

"This is the number for my cell phone. I always have it with me. Memorize it, okay? And call if you need anything at all."

I glance at the note pad, which has the name of some sort of flea and tick medicine at the top. Scrawled underneath is a phone number. Lauren left her name off, for which I'm glad. It's safer that way until I can memorize it.

"Thank you," I say, tucking the paper into my pocket. When we walk out that boy Mark is sitting at a chair, his long legs propped up on the counter.

"Mark," Lauren says, "feet."

Mark sighs and lowers his beat-up shoes down to the ground.

"So who are you, anyway?" he asks me.

"A friend," Lauren answers for me, walking me to the front door. "Call me," she says. "Anytime. Okay?"

"Okay," I say.

"And Rachel, remember. You can make your own choices in this life. I promise you. You really can."

I nod, but Lauren's wrong. I can't make any choices. I can't even choose what to wear or what to read. I don't have a choice in the world, and I'm not like Lauren. I can't just leave home like she did.

I walk out to the van and climb in. I start up the engine, and the classical music station comes on. I grab the dial and spin it, listening to static mixed in with words and snippets of songs I don't know—and will never know—and more and more static. I turn the volume up and scream as loud as I can.

12

When I get to Faith's, I call and tell Mom a truck stalled out and blocked the road and that's why I'm a few minutes late. She seems to believe my lie. Faith thanks me for the humidifier, and I give her a minute to rest while I rock a stuffed-up baby Caleb. He curls up against me, and I whisper in his ear that he's a little sack of sugar. But he's so congested that he snores like a little old man.

Faith and Paul only have one car, so Faith spends most days alone in their two-bedroom house. I count the creaks of the rocking chair and picture myself in a home like this one with my future husband, whoever he is, and a sick baby. It takes me five minutes to memorize every inch of the walls of Faith's house, and I imagine the crushing tediousness of every day exactly the same as before, full of backbreaking housework and a future husband who sets the rules for me just like Dad.

I want to scream again, just like I did in the van.

That night back at home, I make supper, bathe the little

ones, and put them to bed. I've already memorized Lauren's number to the tune of "Amazing Grace," my favorite hymn. In the days that follow, I sing her phone number in my mind over and over. Even though I can't email her anymore, having her phone number reminds me she's a real person out there in the world.

Maybe I can find a way to be like Lauren but different. Still part of my family but something new. Maybe I could ask my parents about living at home while attending community college.

But Mom and Dad would never approve of that. Not ever. And Scripture says that God commands us to honor our father and mother. *He that curseth father or mother, let him die the death.* It's what the Bible says.

But what about what my mind asks? What about what my heart wants?

What about my one wild and precious life?

I'm a stick of dynamite with a lit fuse. I can feel it in every bit of my body, and I find myself walking around the house ready to explode.

These are the thoughts that are racing through my mind on the Saturday after I meet Lauren, when my mother finds me in the kitchen scrubbing out the breakfast pots and pans.

"Rachel, we're out of a few things, and I need you to run to the grocery store," she says. She hands me a slip of paper with a few items listed on it and a folded-up twenty dollar bill. Normally we go to the discount warehouse closer to the city to buy in bulk, and when I see toilet paper and bread on the list I glance at my mother, uncertain.

"Don't we have enough of these things in the garage? In storage?"

"I'd like them just in case," my mother says. Her eyes avoid mine, and for a moment, I worry she's getting sick again. I go to the coat rack to get my purse.

"Ruth is coming with me, right?" I ask. I can't imagine my mother will let me go out alone again, especially since I was late getting to Faith's the last time.

"You can go alone," my mother says, straightening the chairs under the kitchen table, still not looking at me. "I trust you."

I mull over those three words in the van on the way to the store. I trust you. She's never said them before. She never needed to.

I walk through the aisles of the grocery store finding everything on the list. Music seeps through the air, and something about the song that's playing catches my ear. I strain to hear the lyrics.

I never hear popular music except for in stores, and usually there are so many of us talking I can't make out any of it. When I reach the register, I load up the groceries on the conveyer belt. I don't talk to worldly people very often, but this cashier is an older woman with a kind smile.

"Excuse me, but what is this that's playing?" I ask. I point up at the air, sheepish.

She grins. "It's the Beatles," she says. "But you're too young to remember them, right?" She winks.

I'm too something to remember anything. But I don't tell this to the cashier.

When I make it home, I get to the kitchen door and open it, struggling with my bags.

"Jeremiah, Gabriel, can you come help?" I say, trying to haul everything inside. The handles of the plastic bags cut into my palms.

But there's no response.

Suddenly, my father appears in the doorway between the kitchen and the family room. He fills up the entire space, he's so large.

"I'll get these, Rachel," he says, coming toward me. "I need you to go into the family room."

They've caught me. I know it as well as I know the Lord's Prayer. As well as I know the digits in Lauren's phone number.

I know it as surely as I know my own name.

"Where is everyone?" I ask. The house is weirdly quiet.

"Your younger brothers and sisters are at Faith's house," my father tells me. "Your older brothers are at a job site."

The trip to the grocery store is clear to me now. They had to get everyone out of the house while I was gone.

Oh, Ruth, what did they tell you I did?

When I walk into the living room, I see Pastor Garrett sitting with Mom in the family room. Pastor Garrett's been to our home before. Once when Faith still lived with us and was recovering from an emergency appendectomy and another time when one of the twins had a serious case of the flu. But no one is sick in our house now. Not physically, anyway.

My father follows me in and sits down, and three sets of eyes are on me. Everything in me is racing. My heart, my mind, the blood in my veins.

"Hello, Rachel," Pastor Garrett says. "It's good to see you." His voice is as loud and booming and full of self-importance in my family room as it is at church.

"Hello," I say, so softly I can barely hear my own voice.

"Rachel," he continues, "please sit down with us while we pray."

I swallow and sit down on the hard-backed chair someone has pulled out from the kitchen table. Mom and Dad are perched on the sofa across from me, and Pastor Garrett walks over and stands next to me, placing his hand on my shoulder.

Take your hand off of me.

I squeeze my eyes shut. I can't think that way about Pastor Garrett. He's a man of God.

But haven't I just thought of him that way?

And don't I want him to take his hands off me and leave?

"Father God, we all fall short of your glory," Pastor Garrett begins, "and we ask you to cleanse us of all unrighteousness.

Redeem our souls and restore us. We ask you in Jesus's name for your love and the atoning blood of Christ Jesus. Amen."

I'm the only one in the room who has fallen short of God's glory. Cherry-red hives are breaking out all over me, crawling up my neck like hungry spiders.

"Rachel," my father is saying, and his mouth is moving but my brain is so muddled I have to strain to even understand his basic English. "Your mother and I received a phone call the other day from Donna Lufkin's mother. She was in downtown Clayton picking up a prescription, and she saw you leaving the Clayton Animal Hospital across the street. She thought we would want to know that you were somewhere strange unchaperoned."

It's over. I'm finished.

"You know we've been concerned about your computer usage, and we called Pastor Garrett for guidance."

Pastor Garrett has taken a seat on the edge of my father's recliner, and he's nodding along with everything my father is saying. Concern fills in every wrinkle of his matchstick-thin face.

I want to run so fast. I want to run so fast I disappear.

"Pastor Garrett recommended Ken Mason come over to examine our computer," Dad continues, almost as if he's practiced this speech before. He takes a pause in between each sentence.

Ken Mason is one of the church elders. I don't know his

family well, but I know he runs some sort of computer business out of his home.

"Mr. Mason came over the other evening after all of you were in bed, and he found this on the computer," my father continues, handing me a stack of printouts. I'm not sure if I'm supposed to take them, but my father holds them out long enough that I do. My mother is crying now, but she's not making any noise. Tear after tear is sliding down her face, each one in a race against the next.

I look at the papers in my father's hands. It's all of my emails with Lauren. Every single one.

I know everyone expects me to be next—to get married and have babies just like Faith. And I really love kids. I love my little sister Ruth, especially. Even though she's not that little anymore. But the thought of having babies of my own in just a few years—I know it's what I should want. But it just isn't.

Let me tell you, if God took paying attention and being idle as prayer, I would be the world's greatest at praying!

I'm terrified about what will happen to me if I get caught writing to you. But I'm also terrified about what will happen to me if I stop. I want to keep writing to you, even if I can't explain why in words.

"But these were private," I say, my voice barely audible. But I don't have any privacy. Not really.

"Have you been communicating with Lauren Sullivan?"

Pastor Garrett asks, his voice serious and clipped. "Is that who you went to see when you went downtown?"

"Yes," I whisper. They want to make me say it. Even though they already know the answer.

My mother's cries turn into sobs when I admit out loud what she must already know.

"It's my fault," she says. "I was sick. I wasn't able to keep my closest eye on her heart. Oh Father God, forgive me."

"It's not your fault, Mom," I say, reaching out for her. But Dad places his hands between us. I shrink back into my chair.

"Your mother and I have discussed this at length with Pastor Garrett," Dad continues. "You need to reconnect with Christ. God wants to heal your heart, Rachel, and He needs you to be in a place without distractions. We feel it's best for you to spend some time at Journey of Faith camp."

I remember James Fulton's shame-filled face when he returned from Journey of Faith. I remember Lauren using the word *brainwash* to describe what happens there. And suddenly, even though I feel as if the floor underneath me is giving way, I feel something so deep inside of me I know it must be true.

I can't let them take me to that place.

"What if I don't go?" I ask.

My mother's eyes pop open, and she stares at my father and Pastor Garrett.

My father glances at Pastor Garrett, who nods just slightly.

"If you don't go," Dad says, "you can't continue to live

under our roof. You're not a godly influence on your younger siblings."

"Yes," I say. "I understand."

There's silence, and Pastor Garrett clears his throat. I squeeze my hands together. They're so slick with sweat they slide up against each other and slip apart.

"Rachel, we want you to get ready to go now," Pastor Garrett says. "Mrs. Garrett and I are prepared to drive you to Journey of Faith this afternoon."

"All right," I say. "Of course."

I try to breathe. My own parents don't want me unless they can send me off to a place that terrifies me because of what it might do to me. Psalms says *when my mother and my father forsake me, then the Lord will take me up.* But where is the Lord now? *God, where are you?*

"May I go upstairs to pack and to have time to myself to pray?" I ask. My throat is coated in sandpaper. I don't know how I'm speaking. I can't look at anyone so I look at the floor instead.

"Yes, of course," says Pastor Garrett. I glance at him and he's smiling like butter wouldn't melt in his mouth.

I want to slap him.

I get up and as I turn the corner and walk down the hallway to the staircase leading up to my room, I grab the cordless phone hanging on the wall, quickly. I hear Pastor Garrett's voice, still as loud as ever, leading my parents in prayer.

I hold the phone and race up the stairs.

Amazing Grace, how sweet the sound . . .

"Hello?"

I slip inside my room and shut the door.

"Hello?"

"Lauren?"

"Yes, who's this? Wait. Rachel?"

"Yes," I say, my voice a whisper. My body numb. "They want to send me to Journey of Faith," I tell her. "Do you remember that place?"

"Journey of Faith? Oh, fuck no!"

I wince, and Lauren seems to sense it.

"I'm sorry," she says, "but no, Rachel. No. You cannot do that. You don't know what they do to people there. You can't go. I swear to you. Do not go. You'll come back lobotomized."

"I don't know what that means," I say. I'm standing in the middle of my bedroom now. The only bedroom I've ever known. The corners and quirks and cobwebs are all familiar to me. I know them like I know my own heartbeat.

"You'll come back not you," Lauren says. I can hear a dog barking in the background. She must be at work.

"I don't know who me is," I say, my voice barely audible. And I burst into tears. Finally.

"Rachel, Rachel, take a breath," Lauren commands.

I try but I can't. I've never cried like this before, like I've lost control of my body entirely. "My parents say I have to leave if I don't go," I manage. "They're asking me to leave if I don't go, but I don't want to go there, Lauren."

"Listen to me," Lauren tells me, her voice insistent. "Listen. Listen to me, Rachel. Pack a bag. Can you pack a bag? What's your address?"

I tell her through my sobs.

"I know where that is. By the Nielsen farm, right?"

"Yes," I tell her. I'm gulping for air.

"I'll be there in less than half an hour. I'll honk my horn twice, Rachel, and you will come out of that house. You'll see me, and you'll come out of the house and you'll get in the car. It's an old red Honda. You have to run out, do you understand? I can't come in for you. Tell me you understand. Say, 'Yes, I understand.'"

"Yes, I understand," I say through my tears even though I do not understand at all. I understand none of what's happening to me except for some tiny little core piece of my heart that knows I can't go to Journey of Faith. I can't and I won't and I won't.

"Pack a bag, Rachel. And bring your driver's license. Do you have it?"

"Yes, but it's downstairs with my purse."

"Grab it if you can. I'm leaving now. Two honks."

She hangs up, and I stand there, finally able to swallow my cries. Don't think, Rachel. Just do. On the floor of the closet, I find an old, navy blue tote bag I used to use as a diaper bag for Isaac when he was smaller. I grab what I can and roll each piece of clothing into a tight ball, trying to make as much room as possible. Underwear, my resale shop bras, old denim skirts, a nightgown, and loose-fitting blouses. I take my hairbrush off the dresser. I open my nightstand and snatch a notebook where I like to keep a list of my favorite words (*persnickety, mortified, magnanimous, freewheeling*) and a postcard Aunt Marjorie sent us from Hawaii some Christmas long ago. Dad threw it out, but I took it from the trash and kept it. I liked to stare at the glorious beach scene on the front as much as I liked to reread the chicken-scratch handwriting on the back from the aunt I'd never had the chance to know.

Merry Xmas from The Big Island!!
It's bee-yoo-ti-full here! Lots of Love to All
xoxo Marjorie

How many bee-yoo-ti-full places exist on this planet? How many has God made? How many will I never see if I stay here?

I slip the card in my bag and check the clock radio on my nightstand. It's been fifteen minutes. How long will Pastor

Garrett and my parents let me hide away upstairs before they come and get me?

I look at Ruth's tidy bed and the throw pillow she's arranged to cover the ink stain on the bedspread we got cheap at the Goodwill. Sweet Ruth. Good Ruth. My eyes sting, and I start to cry again.

What if I forced myself to go to Journey of Faith? What if I forced myself for Ruth?

But what if I can't survive it? The physical labor, the isolation, the constant barrage of Scripture and correction, Lauren's promise that I'll be forever changed and not for the better. Even if I survive all of that, then what? Could I go to community college? Read whatever I want? Tell my father I don't want to get married until I'm older?

I find a notebook in Ruth's stack of schoolbooks on her nightstand and tear out a fresh page, then search frantically for a pen until I find one.

Ruth, I love you so much. I'm so sorry. I will get in touch with you soon, I promise. Please forgive me, Ruth. Please know I wouldn't be doing this if I had another choice. I love you so, so, so much, Ruth.

Love,
Rachel

I slip the note under Ruth's pillow where she'll be sure to find it. Then my eyes stop on the framed Bible verse she keeps on the wall next to her bed. Her favorite. From Hebrews.

Now faith is the substance of things hoped for, the evidence of things not seen.

I hear two honks in quick succession. I imagine Mom and Dad and Pastor Garrett downstairs in the family room, glancing at each other with *what-was-that?* looks on their faces.

When I peek out the bedroom window, I see a dusty red Honda parked in the yard, its engine still running. Two more honks.

Come Out. Come Out.

I grab my bag. I head for the door. I open it.

Without looking back, I race down the stairs.

13

It's been over a week since I moved in with Lauren, but I still haven't gotten used to the smells I've encountered in her one-bedroom apartment. Sriracha sauce. Cats. Peppermint-scented body lotion. And something Lauren calls Nag Champa incense.

"I promise, it gives off good vibes, good energy," Lauren says as she lights a second stick of the strange, sweet-smelling stuff and gray smoke starts to make cursive letters in the air. "That sounds corny, but I'm trying to make you laugh." She watches me from the broken-in pink arm chair in the corner. It's like she's counting how long it will take for me to start crying again.

One.

Two.

"Rachel," Lauren says, her face falling as I burst into tears, her voice dropping into a whisper, "I wish I could make this all easier."

I sniffle and let the tears flow for a minute. I'm curled into the corner on the couch, which is in no better shape than Lauren's pink armchair. But the couch is comfortable, which is good because it's where I've been sleeping at night.

"I just needed to cry," I say out loud. "Again."

"I know," Lauren says, nodding. "It's normal. I think I cried every day for weeks after I left, I was such a wreck. But I have an idea. Diet Coke. That always cheers me up. You want one?"

"Sure."

I've had soda before on a few rare occasions. Wedding receptions at church. The one time my parents took me to Red Lobster for my birthday. But mostly it's an indulgence we can't afford. Lauren says Diet Coke is her "one vice" since she left the city. When she told me that, I had to ask her what a vice was. Something not so good for you, she says. But of all the vices, she tells me, soda is probably the least bad one.

We sip our drinks, and I let the fuzzy, cool bubbles pop against my tongue. The cold can feels good in my hand. Finally, I'm calm enough to really talk.

"I keep picturing what happened when I left," I say. I can't forget the way I grabbed my purse from the hook near the door and turned to tell my parents and Pastor Garrett in between sobs that I couldn't—wouldn't—go to Journey of Faith. I can't forget the strange, contorted expression on my mother's face that I tried to unsee the moment I saw it.

"Where are you going?" my father bellowed, raising his voice for the first time in my memory. "How can you abandon Christ's path for you?" And Pastor Garrett prayed in a loud voice, " 'To open their eyes, and to turn them from darkness to light and from the power of Satan unto God!' Open your servant Rachel's eyes, Father God! Open her eyes, we pray!"

I couldn't find the words to answer or explain, and I was afraid if I tried I would lose my nerve, so I ran outside and found myself inside Lauren's red Honda, crying so many tears I thought I'd never have enough to cry again. The first night at Lauren's apartment I'd only been able to calm down after I'd called home from a phone we borrowed from her next-door neighbor. Lauren didn't want anyone from Calvary to be able to reach her.

My father answered when I called, and when I told him where I was and that I was safe but I just needed some time away and that he could reach me at this neighbor's number, he used a voice he'd never used with me before. But I recognized it anyway. It was the detached, measured voice he uses with worldly clients who hire him to trim their crepe myrtles. The careful, better-than-you voice he pulls out with the cigarette-smoking mechanic—the only one in town who can keep our van running.

"Rachel Elizabeth," he said, "when you are ready to return to the Lord, to His service, to walk with righteousness and be healed by attending Journey of Faith, you will contact us. Until then, you are not permitted to communicate with this family. We're praying for you, Rachel Elizabeth."

And he hung up the phone, just like that. I held the receiver for minutes after, sure I was mistaken. Certainly that wasn't all he could have to say to me, his own daughter.

"That's what I keep running over in my mind the most," I say to Lauren. "What my dad said when I called. That my own dad said that." I wait for tears to start again, but my body won't have it anymore.

"It's like how I couldn't picture that my own dad could beat me up like he did, but he did," says Lauren, her black fingernails tapping against the edge of her soda can. "Just because our dads are our dads doesn't mean they're perfect or even right. I know that's weird to hear, but I think it's the truth."

I curl my knees up under my chin. I want to tell Lauren that at least my dad never hit me. That maybe my dad just needs more time to understand me. But I keep quiet and nod.

Lauren picks up the little black cat that's clawing at her chair. He's the one she calls Frankie. She rubs one of his ears, and he purrs contentedly.

"Tell me again what makes Journey of Faith so bad?" I ask Lauren. Maybe there's some small part of me that's still considering toughing it out—just to be able to see Ruth again or hug my mother, however briefly.

"You know the stories," Lauren says. "But I can show you a website where kids from all over the country talk about having gone to camps like Journey of Faith. Waking up at four in the morning, forced hikes and these weird survival exercises, constant memorization of Scripture. They wear you down so they can force you to think the way they want you to think. It's brainwashing, basically. Plus, they serve runny eggs. I'm talking seriously disgusting food."

Lauren likes to make jokes when she's been serious for too long, and I'm not sure if I appreciate this or if it bothers me. But I remember James Fulton confessing to all of us after looking at pornographic images on the computer, and I remember seeing him hiding out alone after services, the shame on him as thick as Pastor Garrett's personal copy of the King James Bible. Even after his return James was still looked on as an outsider, as someone who deserved our sympathy but who earned our sidelong glances and gossip masked as prayer requests instead. Lauren is right about Journey of Faith. I can't go there.

Lauren gives Frankie one last cuddle and stretches her arms. "My lunch break is almost over. I've got to get back to work," she says. Clayton Animal Hospital is a few blocks down the street, not far from this little eight-unit apartment complex Lauren's been renting her place in since early spring.

"I'll do the lunch dishes," I say. I can't be a bother to Lauren as long as I'm staying here.

"I already did them," Lauren answers. "There were only two dishes and two glasses."

I grin in spite of everything. "That's a lot less than I'm used to," I say.

"I figured," Lauren says, and as she walks past me toward the front door, she gives my hair a gentle ruffle like I'm one of the cats she loves so much.

After she's gone, I stare around the empty apartment for a moment. The second day I was here, Lauren showed me how the television worked, but the few times it's been on, I can't think straight because watching it feels like being with someone who won't stop talking to me. I've been around televisions a few times, like in the waiting room at a doctor's office. But I don't see how anyone can handle having one on all the time. Fortunately, Lauren only turns it on once in a while. Last night she and I watched one episode of *Law & Order*. Lauren explained it's set in New York City and is about criminals and the attorneys who try to put them in prison. The women on the show had such short skirts and immodest clothing I couldn't believe anyone with a television could just turn it on and see something like that whenever they wanted. Out of habit, I kept averting my eyes whenever the female district attorney walked into the room, then I'd glance back to see what happened next.

Now, alone in the apartment, I stare at my reflection in the big, black TV screen.

"Get up, Rachel," I tell myself. "You have to get up off the couch. You can't just lie here all day long." I think back to my mother in the bedroom after the miscarriage. Maybe this is what great sorrow does to you. It makes you unable to move. To do anything.

Everything around me is so unfamiliar I decide to try and find some peace in something familiar. By the time it's almost the end of Lauren's shift, I've dusted, straightened, and cleaned every last bit of her tiny apartment, and I've only thought about my parents and Ruth and everyone else back home every other second instead of every second. Lauren's apartment is full of distractions. As I tidy her bedroom, I find a photo of Lauren kissing a boy with jet black hair tucked into the frame of her bedroom mirror. I first notice it while making Lauren's bed, and I quickly look away, just as I did while watching television. But then I glance back, more than once, and with each glance back I stare for a few more moments until I'm inches away from the photograph, studying it carefully. Lauren and this boy kissed with their mouths wide open and their eyes closed. Their whole faces just full of wanting. Staring at it too long makes my heart race, and I finally force myself not to look at it anymore. I don't know what to make of a kiss like that, but the truth is I don't know what to make of most kissing. When Faith and Paul kissed for the first time on their wedding day, I looked down at my maid of honor bouquet, embarrassed at their awkwardness on display for everyone to witness. My stomach turned at the hoots coming from the congregation.

In the kitchen there are no photographs, just a refrigerator full of strange magnets that say things like "Meat Is Murder" and "Well-Behaved Women Rarely Make History." Lauren's bookshelf is full of mystery novels and all these thick books with titles like *Sisterhood Is Powerful* and *Quivering Daughters: Hope and Healing for Daughters of the Patriarchy*. Part of me wants to read them, but I don't know if I should touch them yet. I don't think Lauren would mind me reading them, but something about the titles frightens me, like they might be more than I want to think about right now. As I sweep the closet-sized kitchen, I wonder what Ruth is doing. Getting supper ready? Finishing her schoolwork? Maybe attending an emergency prayer meeting for me? *Rachel, stop it. You can't keep asking yourself these questions if you have any hope of not crying for at least a few hours a day.*

As I finish making peanut butter and jelly sandwiches for supper—because I can't find much else in the kitchen—I hear Lauren's keys in the front door.

"Such a dutiful daughter," Lauren says, when she finds me in the kitchen, hands on her hips, one eyebrow raised.

"I'm not trying to be dutiful," I say, blushing. "I'm just trying to help." I take the dish towel I was straightening and toss it on the counter instead. I want to show Lauren I don't think I have to be perfect all the time, but I don't think it's very kind of her to call me dutiful. Even if she was just trying to be funny in her own strange Lauren way.

Lauren raises both eyebrows. "Wow. Very good, Rachel. I pissed you off and you called me out on it. Keep doing that."

I take my plate and follow Lauren out to the living room where we've been eating our meals. I take a bite of my sandwich but I'm thinking about Lauren's words. She was right. I guess Lauren did irritate me, but I don't understand why she thinks I should tell her about everything she does that irritates me. Speaking about your emotions so often seems like it would only cause arguments or hurt feelings.

"Thanks for making these," Lauren says, taking a bite. Lauren doesn't pray before we eat, but I still offer a rushed blessing over my meals privately inside my mind. Praying before meals hasn't ever been something I've minded; I actually like the idea of it. Except for when Dad asked Paul to offer the blessing and the food was practically cold by the time we started eating.

"You really don't eat any meat or cheese or anything?" I ask.

"Yeah, well," Lauren says with a shrug. "I try not to. Because I feel really strongly about animal rights. But I don't think it's going to be very easy to keep that up living here where there's only one grocery store. Tom Thumb doesn't exactly stock soy milk and fake chicken nuggets." She rolls her eyes.

"When'd you start? Not eating meat, I mean."

"When I moved to Houston. Some of the kids I'd gotten to know had friends there. I ended up renting a room in this big house and a lot of them were vegetarians and everything. Then I started working and putting myself through vet tech school and the more I started to work with animals, the more I just couldn't eat that stuff anymore."

I nod, not even able to visualize moving to the city and living with almost total strangers. I've rarely even been into the city, and whenever I have it always seems so big and swarming and overwhelming to me. At least I'm only a thirty-minute drive from home. And Lauren isn't really a stranger. Not like that.

"Why'd you come back?" I ask. Now that I'm staying here—I can't say living here—maybe Lauren will tell me why she moved back to Clayton.

Lauren pushes her sandwich around on her plate. "Honestly, I never thought I would come back here. Too close to everything that happened. But money was one reason. It's so much cheaper here. The vet office I was working at in Houston closed, and I hadn't found a new job yet. Some of the other kids I was hanging out with could, like, go and ask their parents for help or move back home for a few months with their families if they had to. And I couldn't. Obviously."

I nod and wonder how close Lauren came to having nowhere to go. The idea makes me shiver a bit.

"Anyway, remember how I told you about Dr. Treats, the vet I work for?" Lauren continues. "He'd always been so nice to me when I was younger, when I would bring him all these stray animals I'd tried to take care of. He knew I was part of Calvary and he never made a big deal of it or anything. I think he was worried about me even. A few months after I ran away I got him to write my letter of reference for vet tech school, and he told me if I ever needed a job, I was welcome back here. So here I am."

She gets up to take her plate to the kitchen and keeps talking. "Plus, I needed to leave the city because there was all this stuff with this guy I was dating . . . but that's a long story . . ." Her voice trails off.

I think about the boy with the black hair, his lips on Lauren's, the picture still tucked in a spot where she can see it every day. If she keeps his picture up then was the stuff that happened between them good? Or bad? It had to have been bad if it made Lauren move away, but then why keep the picture up? Suddenly, Pastor Garrett's threatening voice is in my head. *The Bible reminds us that dating is just practice for divorce. How can we fully commit to our future partner if we have the attitude that it is all right to spend time with someone only until we tire of them?*

If Lauren hadn't dated that boy, would she be happier? Was Faith happier for having courted Paul under the watchful eyes of our parents?

"So, remember the other afternoon how we kind of talked about how you have to get out of this apartment?" Lauren says, walking back into the living room. "I think it would be good for you. And I think I've found you the perfect opportunity."

"Oh," I say, putting my sandwich down, suddenly too anxious to take another bite.

"What about a job?" she continues, giving me a hopeful smile. "I think I found you one."

Now I really can't eat. Of course I've seen how Lauren keeps careful track of her money, adding and subtracting numbers on a piece of paper she keeps along with her bills in a file folder by the television. I can't expect to simply live here, stay here, and have her pay for everything. I can't be a burden to her. Perhaps I've already become one.

"What kind of job?" I ask. I can't possibly be qualified to do anything.

"Dr. Treats's wife is a real estate agent," Lauren says, tucking her feet underneath her as she sits down again. "I was telling him about everything that's going on, and he said he had an idea, so he called his wife. It turns out she needs help rearranging her entire filing system and updating stuff on her computer and some other random stuff in her home office. It was supposed to be her big summer project, but it's not going well. She needs serious help. I've met her a couple of times and she's super nice, plus it's perfect because

I can walk to work and you can use my car to get to her house."

"Does she know I'm only seventeen?" I ask.

"You'll be eighteen at the end of the summer, Rachel," Lauren reminds me. "That's not so far away. The job would only be a few days a week, but she doesn't have any problem paying you in cash. Ten dollars an hour."

In a few weeks I'll be eighteen. It means I'll be a legal adult, and my parents can't do anything to me if I keep staying here. Even though I can't imagine them coming after me since they made me leave in the first place, it still hurts that my own parents don't want to at least come and check on me. Do they truly not care? My throat starts up with that old familiar ache. It's been a few hours since I cried last, and I'd like it to stay that way. I swallow hard and ask Lauren, "Do you think I can do it? The job, I mean."

"Yes, Miss I-Learned-to-Navigate-the-Internet-All-By-Myself," Lauren says, taking her laptop from where she keeps it by the side of her chair. "You can totally do it. You're a smart cookie, and not just about housekeeping and babies, all right?"

"Okay," I say. "Then I'll do it. Thank you, Lauren."

"Sure," Lauren says. "Diane—that's Mrs. Treats—says you can come by tomorrow around ten in the morning. I'll give you the directions later."

"Wait, tomorrow?" I say.

"Yes, tomorrow," Lauren says, shaking her head at me and smiling. "You know the saying. Tomorrow is the first day of the rest of your life."

"I don't know that saying," I say.

"That's because it's not in the Bible. But seriously, there's some truth to it. Don't stress, Rachel. Mrs. Treats is crazy nice. She even baked me a vegan cake as a housewarming gift when I moved back to Clayton. Hey, wouldn't it be so hilarious if her first name was Candy? Then she'd be Candy Treats."

I snort. Lauren's humor confuses me sometimes, but sometimes it helps. Even though I'm still trying to comprehend the idea of going to a job tomorrow. My job.

"I'm gonna dick around—mess around—on my computer, okay?" Lauren says. She's been trying to watch her swearing since I showed up, I can tell.

"Okay," I say. Lauren knows I'm not used to bad words, and watching her language is a way of trying to make me feel more comfortable. I'm grateful for this small kindness. But Lauren's word choice doesn't bother me so much as this strange time after dinner. I've been here over a week, and this is always the time of day that I feel most unsure. Lauren likes to get on her laptop, and I sit on the couch, flipping through some of Lauren's less threatening books, unsure what to do with myself. Sometimes Lauren watches television, and that's interesting but sometimes exhausting.

It's not very late at night, and I have no babies to wash or supper table to clean up. No Ruth to snuggle up with. Just an immense stretch of time in front of me until Lauren decides she's sleepy and goes into her bedroom and I make up my bed on the couch. This must be what people refer to as free time. Time to be free. What a strange idea. I've always wanted this kind of time to read or study, but now that I have it I can't even focus.

I glance at the front door to the apartment. I've barely been outside since I arrived. "I think I'll go outside and get some fresh air," I say.

Lauren looks up, surprised. "Okay, but be careful on the wild streets of Clayton, Texas, at dusk," Lauren says. I know she's joking, and I offer back a small smile.

The steps from Lauren's second-floor apartment lead down to a small garden in the complex's courtyard that no one seems to be maintaining. There are a few plastic lawn chairs that don't match and a small metal bucket filled with sand and cigarette butts. I push my sleeves up past my elbows and untuck my pale peach button-down blouse, letting it fall over my long, denim skirt, and I sit down in one of the chairs.

I try to imagine the house I'm going to tomorrow for this job. I rehearse in my mind how I'll knock at the door and smile brightly and say hello. I'm not used to interacting with people who aren't part of Calvary, and my heart starts racing a bit at the idea of being in such a strange place, charged with something I'm sure I'm not really experienced enough to handle.

The scent of hot tar on the streets and the whispers of fresh bread from the industrial Sunbeam bakery on the edge of town waft through the air. Live oaks and juniper trees dot Lauren's street. The sun has gone down just enough that it's almost pleasant out. I take a deep breath to try and slow down my heart, imagining the air entering my body from the soles of Faith's black boots, the only shoes I brought with me when I left. I exhale. Faith must be so ashamed of my behavior. She tried her hardest to help raise me into a godly young woman, and now I've done everything wrong. It's been a week since I've heard Dad's voice read the Bible or since I tried to pray. Lauren doesn't keep anything about Jesus or God in the apartment, not even one Bible or a single wooden cross.

I take another breath. *Breathe, Rachel. Breathe.*

I remember the poem Lauren sent me, and I remember how I tried to pray the poem. I think about the final words over and over again. What will I do with my one wild and precious life?

God, guide me.

The words come to me suddenly. I haven't been missing services at Calvary Christian or Pastor Garrett's booming voice, even if not missing them makes me feel guilty somehow.

But I think I miss God. The idea of God.

I breathe and repeat.

God, guide me.

Breathe.

Repeat.

I keep breathing until I feel better. Until the anxiety relaxes its grip.

14

Lauren's little red Honda is easier to handle than my family's ancient van. I follow the handmade map Lauren drew for me with blue ballpoint on the back of a receipt, and ten minutes before ten on Tuesday morning I find myself parked on Atwell Street, sitting outside a cute two-story home with green shutters and red azaleas planted out front.

I squeeze the steering wheel to prove it's real. To prove I'm real. A week ago I was living at home, not even able to use a computer. And here I am about to walk into a job. A job that will pay me money. My own money. I squeeze the steering wheel one more time, then spread my sweaty palms out over my skirt, straightening out the wrinkles. What would Ruth say if she was with me now? What would she possibly think?

Oh, how I wish I could talk to her. Cuddle with her. Does

she hate me now? Does she miss me? I miss her. So much. Did she ever find my note, or did Dad find it first and throw it out?

I can't cry. Not when I'm about to have to go inside and introduce myself to Mrs. Treats. Lauren got me this job, and I can't mess it up or it might upset her. I take a deep breath and count to one hundred, then check the car radio. It's 9:58.

God, give me the strength to do this.

I get out and walk slowly toward the house.

"You must be Rachel," Mrs. Treats says when she opens the door. She smells like vanilla and her smile is big and open. "I'm so glad Lauren set this up. She's such a doll, isn't she?" Mrs. Treats says, leading me into a sunny entry area with an umbrella stand and a painting of bluebonnets. "Can I take your purse?"

"Thank you, Mrs. Treats," I say, trying to smile.

"Oh, you have to call me Diane," she says. "Otherwise I feel about five hundred years old."

She's wearing a cream-colored skirt and jacket that would last five seconds in our house before Isaac or Sarah dumped something on it or accidentally stained it with grubby hands. But Mrs. Treats—Diane—is impeccable. And beautiful. She's a little older than Mom—maybe in her early fifties—but her honey-brown hair is carefully styled and she wears high heels that match her suit. My mother is beautiful, too, I think, but she doesn't look as young as Diane. A thin, gold chain rests around her neck. She hangs my purse on a hook by the umbrella stand and click-clacks into a room to the right, off the front entryway. A small black cat bounds up to her and winds itself around her legs for a moment before bounding away.

"That's Boots, the dumbest cat in creation," Diane says. "But we love him anyway. Over there's the kitchen, and you can help yourself to anything," she says in a Texas twang that's stronger than most as she motions toward the back of the house. "Don't be shy for even a second, okay? Just help yourself. Now this . . ." She motions at the room. "This was supposed to be my summer project, but it's gotten away from me. I'm so grateful that you're so sweet and kind to help me out with it. For ten dollars an hour, of course."

A large desk of dark wood holding a phone and a computer many years newer than the one back home sits in the center of the room, surrounded by plastic crates of papers and pamphlets with headlines that read, "Sweet Treats! Latest Listings! Find Your Dream Home!" and "Experience Has Its Rewards—Diane Treats, Realtor!" A few FOR SALE signs with pictures of Diane smiling eagerly lean against the back wall under several plaques that look like some sort of awards. Mountains of paper spill out of desk drawers and three black filing cabinets along one side of the room look like they're about to tip over from the weight of the papers barely stuffed all the way inside.

It's as though a bomb blew up and no one has bothered to call the police.

"It's a mess," Diane admits. "You can say it. But I have faith you can help me. Please say I'm right?"

I stand there, not sure of what to say or do. I guess Diane isn't really looking for an answer because she just keeps talking. For the next twenty minutes she explains how she thinks I can make sense of the chaos, pointing to various piles of paper with fingers that end in shell-pink nail polish. I try to keep track of her instructions even though there are so many, and I'm grateful when Diane decides to hand me a pad and paper so I can take notes. She also shows me how to use the computer to input information into a database, including uploading pictures of houses for sale. Diane tells me she helps people buy and sell homes in towns all over the area—Clayton, Healy, Dove Lake—and business has been good, which means the paperwork is awful and her office work has gotten ahead of her. She also has several stacks of bright blue flyers that need to be stuffed into envelopes and a mailing list that needs to be updated.

"I'll be out with clients for a few hours, but you can call my cell whenever," she says, scrawling a number on a notepad. "Oh, Rachel, I feel like I'm leaving you with a ridiculous task! It's ridiculous, isn't it?" She pouts a little.

"It's not so ridiculous," I say. What I want to tell her is

that it feels ridiculous that I have a job, but of course I don't say that.

A smile spreads on her face, and she reaches out to hug me. I freeze up a moment and then carefully put my arms around her and pat her back gently, scared I'll ruin her suit. The vanilla scent she wears is even stronger up close. Like cookies. It's a little unnerving to be hugged by a stranger, but Diane seems so nice it's comforting at the same time.

She lets me go and clicks around until she finds a large leather bag that she hauls over her shoulder.

"Oh, I almost forgot. My son went out for a run. He should be back soon, but then he'll probably disappear upstairs to the cavern he calls his bedroom, and you'll not see hide nor hair of him again."

"All right," I say.

After Diane leaves I sit down in the large, soft office chair. It tilts back unexpectedly, and I gasp and catch myself. This chair feels like it's made for giants.

I sort through the papers on the desk. While Diane's instructions made my head swim, as I look over everything, I realize that what she wants me to do is not that different from the type of work I did for my father's business. I might even be able to figure out a way to make sense of all of this. At least I hope I will because I know Diane is expecting it of me.

Boots the cat decides to join me, curling up in a small,

purring ball by my feet as I start tackling the pile of paper closest to me, aware of every sound in the house. The whir of the refrigerator in the nearby kitchen, the ticktock of the clock on the wall to my right, the hot exhale of the computer on the desk. How peculiar that a house could sit alone all day long, with only a little black cat to keep it company. I think of my house, where there are always voices talking, bodies moving. Right now Ruth is probably helping the little ones with their lessons and my mother is busy preparing lunch.

No, Rachel, you can't think about home or it will take over your mind. You can focus. You need to do this. Soon I've worked through an entire stack of papers and entered quite a bit of information into the computer. There's a small pleasure that comes with completing this task quickly and correctly—until I look around and realize how much more there is to do.

Just then I hear the sound of keys in the front door, the door opening, and then a slam that makes the windows rattle. Suddenly, a boy is standing there. A boy my age, covered in sweat and catching his breath.

"Hey," he says matter-of-factly, standing there in the middle of Diane's office. "Don't I know you?" He has a towel around his neck which he uses to mop his face before tossing it toward the stairs without looking to see if it lands on the railing or the floor. It hits the railing, but only barely, then swings precariously for a moment or two.

"Um, I'm working for your mom? So . . ." I say. I can

barely hear my own voice. He stares at me like he expects me to say something more, but when I don't, he nods slowly like something has just occurred to him.

His hair is hanging in his face. How does he even manage to see two steps in front of him? When he drags his hand through it and looks straight at me, I can finally see how dark his eyes are. Like two cups of black coffee.

"Oh, yeah, riiight," he continues, still nodding. "She said something about someone coming over and something. I kind of stop listening after a while when she's delivering copious amounts of information in one sitting."

He plops down on the love seat by the stairs and leans back, draping his entire body over the piece of furniture like a throw blanket. "So, what's your name?" It comes out, "Sowhatsyername?"

"Rachel," I tell him. Guilt twists my stomach in two. It's the first time in my entire life that I've been alone with a boy my age. But this boy is acting as if it's nothing. As if we're not strangers.

"Wait," he says, "I remember how I know you. You came by to talk to Lauren that one time. At my dad's office? I'm Mark Treats. The vet is my dad. Your boss is my mom. Small town coincidence number three hundred and twenty-nine. You know the deal."

"Yes," I say, not knowing at all. If I keep working, I'm afraid I'll look rude. But I'm so nervous I don't think I can do much else but sit and wonder if I should look at him or at the desk.

"I'm gonna go make a ham sandwich," he announces as if there are more people than just me in the room and it's an urgent declaration. "Running makes me hungry, you know?" I nod. It's all I can think to do. "You run?" he asks. I shake my head no. He starts unlacing his shoes.

"You want one?" he asks. "A ham sandwich?"

He doesn't wait for me to answer. He just pulls off his running shoes and cracks his toes against the floor. "God, my feet are totally sweaty," he continues. "I gotta start running earlier in the morning. But what's the point of summer vacation if you can't sleep in, right?" He gazes off, staring at some point in the distance like he sees something interesting on the wall behind me or somewhere beyond. I sit, still holding the same piece of paper I was holding when he first walked in. Suddenly he pops up and grabs his shoes, flinging them up the stairs to the second floor where they land with two quick thumps.

"So, ham sandwich?" he asks. "I make a mean one. I'm serious."

The easiest response is to accept his offer.

"All right. I mean, if you don't mind. Thank you."

"You got it," he says, loping off to the kitchen. I look down and try to get back to filing papers, but he keeps hollering from the back of the house, asking if I want mayonnaise or mustard or lettuce or tomato.

"Just make me whatever you're making for yourself," I respond.

"What? I can't hear you."

"Whatever you're making for yourself is fine!" I repeat, louder this time. It's strange to raise my voice over a ham sandwich when I'm not used to raising it even in anger.

I realize I'm so anxious I've misfiled the last few papers when Mark walks back in with two plates, each carrying a ham sandwich as big as my head, bordered by heaps of thin, golden potato chips. He puts my plate down on the desk and carefully balances his own on the couch.

"Drink?" he asks, pointing at me.

"Water's okay."

"We have soda if you want it."

"Oh," I answer. Is it more polite to accept the offer? "Um, do you have Diet Coke?"

"Uh, I think my mom has some in the fridge in the garage. I can go look."

"No, that's okay. Water is fine."

"No, I'll go, no big deal," he says, and then as he walks out he adds, "You ladies and your Diet Cokes."

The ham sandwich is one of the best I've ever tasted. If I asked one of my older brothers or my father to make me a ham sandwich, they wouldn't even know where we keep the ham in the refrigerator.

We eat in silence, my growling stomach suddenly letting me know how hungry it's been since subsisting on Lauren's peanut butter and jelly and pasta and marinara sauce.

"So, how much work does my mother have you doing?" he asks in between chews. "Does it involve filing every piece of paper since the Egyptians invented paper?"

I look down at my sandwich. "I'm happy to help your mother," I manage.

"It's nice that you are, otherwise I would be stuck helping her with this, and the less I'm around her the less she can tell me how much I'm always screwing everything up. And anyway, I would probably make matters worse, given my total and complete lack of organizational skills." He says the word *skills* like it ends with a long string of Zs.

"Oh," I say.

"I'm lifeguarding at the Clayton pool most afternoons," he says, even though I didn't ask. "I'm probably gonna get skin cancer out there in this damn heat. I must have been nuts to take that job but the pickings are pretty slim around here. And, you know, it's basically essential to my mother that I not spend all summer farting around or developing a secret plan to overthrow the government or, like, playing video games every day. She schedules her life to the second, and she thinks everyone else should, too." He takes an enormous gulp of water and wipes the bit that spills down his chin with the stretched-out neck of his T-shirt.

"Did you know," I ask, "that the Egyptians didn't actually invent paper? It was the Chinese. During the Han Dynasty." What on Earth am I saying? I must sound impossibly rude. And he probably doesn't even remember that he *mentioned* that the Egyptians invented paper. That was at least ten sentences back.

But Mark just furrows his brow and stares at me, like he's figuring out a math problem in his mind. "The Egyptians didn't invent paper? Are you sure? Huh."

"Yes. I'm pretty sure it was the Chinese," I say. "I can look it up on the computer. If you want."

"Okay, yeah," Mark says. "Yeah, now I'm curious. But wait, what did the Egyptians invent then? I thought they invented everything."

"I know they invented embalming dead bodies," I offer, wrinkling my nose at the thought before turning in my seat to type *where did paper come from?* into the search engine. The familiar act of finding something out on the computer puts me slightly more at ease.

"Embalming. Gross," Mark says, standing up and wiping his hands on the back of his shorts. "Okay, what did you get?"

I pull up a Wikipedia article that explains how the Chinese invented paper. Mark comes over behind me, leans over my shoulder, and peers at the screen. The distance between us could only be measured in centimeters. I do a quick modesty check, peering down to make sure Mark can't be tempted by the cut of my loose-fitting, three-quarter-sleeved blouse. But Mark only seems interested in reading about nineteenth century advances in papermaking. He's not even looking at me.

"Oh," he says. "Okay. Fact for the day learned. The Chinese invented paper. Way to go, China." He stands up and stretches, his spine cracking with a couple of pops. "I'm going upstairs, but let me know if you need anything. Like, more incorrect facts about history or another incredible ham sandwich or whatever."

It's impossible not to smile. "Okay," I tell him. "I'll let you know."

He heads up the stairs two at a time.

"Thank you for the sandwich!" I yell.

"Welcome!" he yells back, and soon I hear what sounds like a shower running.

I get back to work, listening carefully to the noises coming from the second floor. It sounds like Mark is talking to himself, but maybe he's just on the phone. He stomps around like a herd of wild animals. Later, I hear music, something definitely not classical, with strains of guitars and a chorus of voices yelling.

I worry I haven't finished enough. I haven't even started stuffing the flyers yet. I want Diane to be pleased with my work, but my mind keeps reminding me that there's a boy upstairs. A boy my age. And he could come back downstairs at any moment.

The thought makes my skin flush.

I squeeze my eyes shut, overwhelmed, and open them again. I set my mouth in a firm line and work as quickly as I can, careful not to make a mistake. Mark doesn't come back downstairs, and when Diane gets home, she sees I've stuffed at least fifty envelopes and made headway on uploading an entire stack of listings on to the computer.

"Sweetheart, you are a gift from God, I tell you what," she says, sweeping in for another embrace. After hugging me, her cell phone rings and she fishes it out of her purse before scowling at it and tapping her finger.

"Yes? Yes, the house on Morningside. Yes, they're very motivated sellers."

Diane is just like Mark. Neither one seems able to sit still.

By the time she gets off the phone she's found her wallet and she counts out forty dollars for me.

"Can you come back Thursday?" she asks.

"Sure," I say, slipping the bills into my pocket. I've never had so much money before that was all mine. Once, Aunt Marjorie sent me five dollars for Christmas, but Dad made me put it into the collection plate at church.

"Oh, your son came home," I say as casually as I can as I walk toward the door. "He's upstairs."

"Well, maybe he'll stay up there until he can learn to make his bed," Diane says. I'm not sure how to respond, so I just nod and offer Diane a small wave before heading back to the car, where I start up the engine and head down the street. At the end of the block I take a peek at my reflection in the rear-view mirror, trying to see if going to a job and talking to a strange boy has made me look any different. I don't think my appearance has changed, but my reflection stares back at me warily, as if to ask what comes next.

15

With the money Diane pays me, I buy a few simple things at the grocery store on my way home. I scout each aisle before heading down with my cart, wondering if I'll run into someone from my family or from Calvary Christian, even though it's unlikely. Mom likes to do her grocery shopping early in the morning when the store isn't so crowded, and since we do most of our shopping at the discount warehouse, it would be odd to find them here on a Tuesday afternoon.

It's so weird to buy food for just two people. Everything I've picked up barely covers the bottom of the cart—and that includes the treats I buy for Mitzi and Frankie. But it feels good to hand the money over to the cashier. My money. The cashier is the same older woman who told me the song I was listening to was by the Beatles. The same day Pastor Garrett turned my life inside out by saying I had to go to Journey of Faith.

No, that's not right. Pastor Garrett told my parents I

should go to Journey of Faith. But my parents agreed with him. And they set the consequences for me if I didn't go. They made me leave, not Pastor Garrett.

The truth makes me wince, but it's the truth as sure as anything.

I get home and put away the groceries, then put the eight dollars I have left in change on Lauren's bed. It doesn't feel like enough given everything she's shared with me, but at least it's a start. I wish Diane would have me back tomorrow. There was something enjoyable about figuring out how to make her business run smoothly, plus I want to prove to Lauren that I'm worth the trouble of keeping me here.

In an effort to show her as much, I do a load of laundry in the tiny room downstairs. It has two washers and two dryers that everyone in the complex is supposed to share, and I realize—not for the first time—how much easier laundry would be at home if we could afford two of each machine. How many hours did Ruth and I spend willing the machines to spin and dry faster so we could get another basket of clothes in before suppertime? But there's so little clothing between Lauren and me it only takes a short time to do one load. As I'm sorting the pieces, I pull out several black bras and underpants with a leopard print on them, and I stare at them for a full minute. I can't fathom that any woman would ever wear something so revealing, and then I try to fathom that I'm living with a woman who actually does. I stare at them, wondering where anyone would even buy such things in Clayton. Then again, Lauren probably bought them when she lived in the city. I wonder if the black-haired boy from the kissing picture ever got to see them. The thought makes my cheeks flush again, and a delicious shiver runs up my back.

For to be carnally minded is death, but to be spiritually minded is life and peace.

Quickly and with urgency, I shove Lauren's underwear into the laundry basket under some blouses.

It's not right to think of such things. I don't want to go to Journey of Faith, but I also don't think God would approve of me forgetting to guard my heart against lustful thoughts. That doesn't seem all right.

Suddenly, I'm filled with panic. Was I lusting after Mark this afternoon? Is that why I thought about him so much that it was hard to get work done? And is God angry with me for it?

I take the deepest breath I can and exhale.

"God," I whisper, "guide me. Help me to honor you in my words and actions." At home, the words didn't come to me so easily. Not like Ruth with her secret messages from God. But just now, here, in the middle of the laundry room, the words appeared to me. I didn't even think them, really. They were just there. I repeat the words over in my mind. *God, guide me. Help me to honor you in my words and actions.* I take one more deep breath for good measure. I feel better. Less anxious at least.

When Lauren gets home around six, she drops her purse on the floor and smiles at the pasta salad I've set out on the table for supper.

"Oh, Rachel, this is so nice, and I want to hear all about your first day at work, but I have to figure out an outfit for tonight because I have"—she pauses dramatically—"a hot date." She leans back against the door and sighs.

A hot date. I think about the underwear and the kissing boy picture and am suddenly gripped with the fear that I've taken on too much by living with Lauren. She's been nothing but good to me, but what if she wants me to be as worldly as she is to stay here? What if I can't be? I don't know if I even want to be.

"Who are you going on a date with?" I ask, trying to manage conversation. I look at the dinner I've made. At least the salad will keep until tomorrow. At least I hope it will. It took a while to make, too.

"Don't be mad," she says. "You don't have to eat alone. Just bring your plate into my room and I'll tell you all about it."

I pick up my plate and join Lauren in her tiny bedroom. The only place to sit is her unmade bed, so I curl up in the corner and balance my pasta salad in my lap.

"How could you tell I was upset?" I ask. "About you not joining me for supper?"

Lauren opens her closet door—on it is a poster of a serious-looking woman with dark lipstick and blue eye shadow, and it says BLONDIE in black and white letters over her bright yellow hair. Her gaze is so intense it's like she's staring right into my brain and reading my thoughts.

"I could tell you were upset because you, like, did a little frowny face when I told you I couldn't eat," Lauren answers from inside the closet as she throws pieces of clothing on the floor, searching for something to try on before taking a shower. "I know you're not used to, you know, sharing negative emotions." She exits the closet and wags a finger at me, speaking in a singsong voice that reminds me of Faith's. "'Every man according as he purposeth in his heart, so let him give, not grudgingly or of necessity, for God loveth a cheerful giver.'" Then she rolls her eyes—very *un*-Faith-like.

"That's 2 Corinthians," I say.

"Trust me, I remember," Lauren answers. "I'll probably never forget even though I try."

"It's strange to hear you quote the Bible," I say.

"Remember, Rachel, that I was also part of a repressive religious cult that hates women and thinking for yourself and gay people." Lauren takes off her vet tech scrub top and slips on a tight black T-shirt before stepping back to examine herself in her full-length mirror.

I take a bite of pasta salad so I won't be able to agree or disagree. I'm not sure what to say.

"I mean, you were afraid to tell me how you *really* felt just a few seconds ago, right? Over something like supper?" She turns and stares at me, hands on hips. She looks at me as intently as the girl on the BLONDIE poster.

"Yeah," I say quietly. "Yes."

"But why? Because a bunch of men who chose to interpret the Bible in a super specific, super ridiculous way decide that to love God and Jesus you can never be sad or mad or angry? I mean, give me a fucking break. Human beings get sad. We get mad. We get angry! If God didn't want us to feel this way, why did he create these emotions in the first place?"

I take another bite of pasta, but it tastes like cold rubber in my mouth. Lauren's face is reddening. She frowns at her reflection in the mirror.

"Sometimes I wish I could go right back and look at my dad's face and say, 'Fuck you, Dad, I hate you so much,'" she spits. "And you know what? That would be my right."

My eyes widen. I know Lauren's curse is maybe the worst curse a person can use short of taking the Lord's name in vain. She is clearly not trying to protect my ears right now.

Lauren slips off her bottoms and slides into dark denim jeans that hug every curve of her body, each one of her movements filled with a rage that sits just below the surface, about to pop. "Sometimes I wish I could go back to my parents' house dressed like this just to piss them off. They would be so *royally* pissed." She takes a brush off her dresser and flips her head upside down and whips her brush through her blue hair so hard I'm sure it must hurt. When she swings herself back up she flings the brush across the room until it hits the baseboard with a thud. The redness of her cheeks has spread south, filling her neck with strawberry hives. There's a scowl on her face, but she's not looking at me. She's just staring off at her bedroom wall.

I sit for a moment in silence, my heart thumping. I'm frightened. Maybe I remind Lauren of everything she hated about Calvary. Maybe she won't want me around anymore because of that, but I'm not sure I know how to act around someone who gets so angry so easily. Actually, I'm not sure I know how to act around someone who gets angry at all. I'm just not used to it.

I carefully put my plate of pasta down on the bed. I stare at my sad little supper. And then I remember Lauren's words about telling people what you feel when you feel something. I take a breath. "I . . ." I start.

Lauren looks at me as if she's suddenly remembering I'm there.

"Yeah?" she says, not unkindly, only curious.

"I just . . ."

"Rachel, you can say it. It's okay." Her voice is soft all of a sudden.

"I'm a little bit scared right now," I hear myself saying, my voice like it's about to crack. "Because I'm not sure what I'm supposed to do when you get so angry."

There. I said it.

I hear a long exhale, and when I meet Lauren's eyes, they're a little wet, like she might cry, too, but she isn't crying. She's just wearing a tiny, forlorn smile.

"Oh, Rachel," she says, her shoulders slumping. "I'm sorry. I don't mean to scare you. I'm—I just . . . I get . . ."

"You get mad," I say, my voice almost a whisper. "About what happened to you."

"Yeah," she says, nodding, her voice calm again. "I get really mad about everything. A lot. But you know what? My anger saved me. I really do believe that. If I hadn't gotten angry I would be married with three kids right now, and I would be out of my damn mind. For sure."

I nod, but I'm not sure I feel the same way. I don't feel like I left my house in anger. In sadness, yes. In confusion and frustration and fear, definitely. But in anger? I don't know.

"Hey," Lauren says, crawling onto the bed next to me, carefully, so she doesn't spill the pasta salad. She looks me right in the eyes. "Look, sometimes I blow off steam. And if it gets to be too much, you can tell me to shut the hell up. Or just tell me to shut up, you know." She's trying to make me laugh again, and it's working. "Promise you'll tell me? If I get to be too much?"

"Promise," I say, appreciating Lauren's directness even though it still feels so foreign.

"Okay," she says. She reaches out and touches me on the forehead, like she's checking to see if I have a temperature, but the gesture comes out feeling nicer than that, somehow.

"What's this?" she asks, looking down to find the eight dollars I left for her.

"The money left over from my work today, after I did the groceries. It's for you."

"No, it's for you," Lauren says, firmly putting it in my hand. "You pay for your groceries and gas with that, okay? It's your money."

"Are you sure?"

"Yes, absolutely," Lauren tells me.

Grateful, I slip the money into my skirt pocket, and Lauren slides back off the bed.

"How'd it go today, anyway?" she asks.

"Okay," I answer. "The work isn't too hard, but Diane's office is kind of a mess." I pause. "I met her son. Mark. I'd seen him before, though. That one time I saw you at your work."

"Oh my God, Mark Treats," Lauren says, examining her face in the mirror carefully. "He's such a goofball."

"What do you mean?" I ask.

"Just, you know, goofy. He never stops moving around, and he's kind of loud," Lauren explains. "When he hangs out at the office he's always asking everyone questions and just trying to crack everyone up or whatever. And Greg—that's Dr. Treats—is always after him to do better in school, like he's not working up to his full potential or something. You know, if I had parents like Greg and Diane, I would be so thrilled I would earn straight *A*s every day just to make them happy. I mean, I know Diane is a little bit of a control freak perfectionist, but still, they're really sweet people." She finds her bathrobe and heads to the bathroom to take a shower.

Later, as she dresses, she tells me her date's name is Bryce and that she met him just that afternoon, when he brought his dog in all the way from Dove Lake because he'd heard good things about Dr. Treats.

"What are you going to do?" I ask as she checks her makeup for the tenth time.

"Who knows. I guess get a bite to eat. Maybe a drink. You don't have to wait up, okay?"

"Okay," I say, although I'm sure I will because I want to make sure Lauren gets home all right.

"This is a little weird," she continues. "My first date since moving back from the city. I don't know if these country boys are ready for me." She puts her hands on her hips and shoots me a saucy look, then rolls her eyes and smiles. I can only smile back uncertainly, unsure about what it means to be ready for a boy.

When Bryce shows up he looks more normal than I expected. I guess he is a country boy. His hair is short and brown, and he's wearing a dark-blue collared shirt and jeans that even my older brothers would find acceptable. Part of me thought he would have green hair and a T-shirt with strange words on it.

"This is my roommate, Rachel," Lauren says as she grabs her purse. Her voice sounds lighter, dreamier somehow, when Bryce arrives. "Rachel, this is Bryce."

"Hey," says Bryce, nodding his chin at me.

"Hi," I say back from my spot curled up on the couch.

"Okay, I'm ready," Lauren announces, and as she waves goodbye to me, I watch as Bryce puts his arm around the small of her back and they shut the door behind them.

Dating is practice for divorce. That's what Pastor Garrett and Dad always say. You have to guard your heart because if you give pieces of your heart away to every boy who comes along, when your future husband arrives, you won't have a whole heart to give him. That's why Faith courted Paul only after she had Dad's approval. That's why she never spent any time alone with him until they were married. So she didn't give her heart away by accident.

Mitzi the cat jumps up on the couch and starts kneading my stomach with her snow-white paws.

"But if a mother is supposed to have enough love for more than one child, how can a heart have to save up love for a future husband?" I ask Mitzi. "Isn't there an unending supply of love? How much love does one person contain, anyway?" Mitzi yawns and starts carefully licking her paws.

"Fine, ignore my questions," I say. But I'm still thinking

about them. It does seem odd to me that Faith and Paul went from never being alone together to becoming husband and wife, but going on dates with boys you met that day like Lauren is doing doesn't make any more sense to me. I wonder where Lauren and Bryce are, and I hope she's all right.

It's so quiet and I'm so eager for a distraction from my racing brain that I turn on the television. It's set to the channel that shows *Law & Order* episodes over and over again, but I click through until I find a program about the Sahara Desert. It's on one of the channels that Lauren never watches because she says it's boring, but the program isn't boring to me. The narrator's voice has a soft, foreign accent, and the glorious pictures are as soothing as her voice. After watching for a while, my eyelids start to feel heavy, but I'm alert as soon as I hear the sound of keys in the door.

"Rachel?" Lauren's voice is a loud whisper.

"I'm here," I whisper back in the dark, sitting up and popping my head over the back of the couch. "How are you?"

"Fine," she answers, tiptoeing over to me. "Sorry I smell. The bar we went to was smoky, but I don't smoke or anything. But I'm going to have to take a shower again."

"Okay," I say. "Did you have a nice time?"

"Yeah, it was all right," Lauren says, sounding less excited than she did a few hours ago. "He was a super nice guy and a real gentleman, so of course I found him too boring. I swear to God, if I could afford it I would get some therapy or something." I don't exactly understand what Lauren means, and I can't tell if she's joking or not. I would think a nice guy would be something good.

"I don't want to keep you up. We'll talk about it more in the morning."

"Okay," I say.

"Rachel," she says, pausing, "you're not mad at me, are you? For earlier?"

"I was never really that mad," I answer.

"Really?"

"Yeah," I say. "I was mostly just scared, like I said."

"Okay," she says. "Thanks. For not being mad." She suddenly reaches down to give me a hug.

She does smell, but I don't mind. It's the first time she's hugged me and it's nice. It's a strong hug like my mom's, but she doesn't let go right away.

"Thanks for waiting up," she says into my ear.

"I wanted to," I respond, relieved she doesn't think I'm being too much of a snoop for staying awake until she got home. Finally, Lauren lets go and walks back to the bathroom, and soon I hear the shower running. Snuggling deep under my blanket, I feel cozy. Not exactly like how it feels to cuddle with Ruth, but close anyway.

16

Diane answers the door smelling likes cookies again, this time dressed in a plum-colored suit and matching plum heels, her makeup carefully applied. She must spend a lot of time looking in the mirror, but I doubt it makes her worry about being vain. Her skirts are shorter than any mother at Calvary Christian would ever think of wearing, but her shoulders-back, head-up, big-steps approach to walking suggests a confidence I know I've never felt.

I think Diane likes being pretty.

After giving me a few instructions on my tasks for the day, she gathers her briefcase and a few files full of papers. "Please make sure you get yourself something to eat!" she adds as she runs out the door.

I stuff two hundred envelopes and get three paper cuts. I think it's good progress, but how should I know for sure if it is or it isn't? I just want Diane to be happy with my efforts. As I stuff another envelope, I hear a sound and jump out of my seat, half expecting Mark Treats to walk in the front door. But it's just Boots the cat, who saunters in and promptly falls asleep at my feet. I shake my head, grateful no one but a cat witnessed my reaction. After another hour or so of steady work, I realize how hungry I am and wander down to the kitchen.

Either side of the hallway is lined with built-in bookshelves. So far I'm only sure of three people who live in this house, and they have more books here than all of the books in my house combined. I stop and study some of the titles.

Siddhartha by Herman Hesse

How to Stop Worrying and Start Living by Dale Carnegie

The Stranger by Albert Camus

Ariel by Sylvia Plath

The Seven Spiritual Laws of Success by Deepak Chopra

I see one Bible, but of course there are none of the homeschooling books and Bible study guides that make up the stacks of books back home.

And then I spot them. I gasp out loud when I do—*A Wrinkle in Time, A Wind in the Door, Many Waters, A Swiftly Tilting Planet, An Acceptable Time.*

My eyes wide, I run my finger down the spines. I remember Lauren mentioning there were more books about Meg Murry and her family, and here are all five of them. Five. Five!

I can't help it. I slip *A Wrinkle in Time* off the shelf and thumb through it, smiling at the names of familiar characters as they pop off the page like they're saying hello. I put it back and flip through *A Wind in the Door*, but I'm scared to open it to the first page. I can't. If I start reading it, I'll never stop.

All right. Maybe the first few lines. Just to see.

I stand there in the middle of the hallway reading, flipping through the pages. I walk toward the kitchen still reading, letting my eyes float outside the perimeters of the book just enough to make sure I don't bump into anything. I spot a bowl of fresh fruit on the fancy granite countertop, and I sit on one of the kitchen stools and eat an apple and keep reading.

I'll give myself twenty minutes.

I eat two apples and some saltines that I find in a cupboard and keep reading. Twenty minutes pass.

All right, just five more minutes, I bargain with myself.

"Rachel! Are you here?" I hear Diane's heels as she makes her way down the hallway and I jump. Two apple cores and saltine crumbs are spread out before me on the counter, and I'm reading a book instead of working.

I'm scarlet when she walks in, even though I manage a quick "Hi!" and quickly start sweeping the crumbs into my hand and taking the apple cores to the garbage can in the corner. "I'm really sorry. I was eating, and . . . I just . . ."

"Rachel," Diane says, plopping a stack of manila file

folders on the kitchen table, "didn't I tell you that you could get something to eat? Please don't apologize."

"I know, but I was reading and I . . ."

Diane raises an eyebrow slightly. "Sweetheart. Listen. It's all right."

"Thank you. But I'll just put this back," I say, holding the book up. I scoot down the hall and slide it next to its friends on the bookshelf. Page thirty-two is where I stopped, but I probably shouldn't try reading on my break again. Diane is just being nice.

Should I go back to the kitchen where she's waiting or go back to her office? I press a hand to my right cheek. Still warm from blushing. How stupid I am.

"Come in here! Let me pay you for your work today," Diane calls from the kitchen, so I go back to find Diane counting out several bills from her wallet. "Here's thirty for today," she says.

"But I spent the last thirty minutes reading," I tell her. Maybe it was even forty minutes.

Diane tosses her head back and laughs. It's more of a hoot, actually.

"Can I hire you to teach my son how to be even half as conscientious as you are?" she says. "Honey, I meant what I said about you taking a break to eat. I'm not running a sweatshop here. I offer paid lunches, all right?" She takes a carefully manicured hand—even her fingernails are plum—and pushes her long, thick hair back behind her shoulder.

I nod. I haven't been caught. To Diane, I was just eating lunch and flipping through a novel. That's all. Nothing more.

I slip my money inside my skirt pocket, relaxing a little. Grateful. "I just want to say," I start, trying to speak up, "that I truly appreciate you giving me this job, Mrs. Treats . . . Diane."

"Of course," Diane says. "What about setting up a regular deal? Mondays through Thursdays from nine until noon? Maybe Fridays if I decide to be a real taskmaster? Does that sound good to you?"

"Sure," I say, thinking about page thirty-two and all the money I could earn. I'd be so independent, Lauren really wouldn't mind keeping me around.

"I'll walk you out," she says, and we head toward the front door.

I grab my purse to leave, and Diane puts her hand on the doorknob as if she's about to open it. But she doesn't. Instead, she pauses and looks at me.

"Rachel," she starts, "I'm sure Lauren's told you that we've sort of, well, looked out for her a bit. Made sure she had a job and could get started on her own here when she needed to. She's such a sweet girl, and a hard worker, too. And I'm sure you know that Lauren has shared with us some of what's going on with you. And with your family. I want you to know that I'm sorry for what you're going through." Her voice drops down to almost a whisper, no longer big and theatrical. As soft and lilting as she sounds, I bet she could put Isaac to sleep with just one reading of *Goodnight, Moon*. The thought of Isaac's sweet baby face makes my throat tighten, and I try to focus on Diane's words.

"I admit there's a little part of me that worries that you're still technically a minor," she continues.

"I turn eighteen in a few weeks," I say, my voice soft. I wonder if this means she wants to call my parents. I tense up at the idea.

"You know, when I was eighteen I was putting myself through community college," Diane says. "My father thought I was a little bit touched in the head for that," she says, tapping at her temple.

I must look confused because Diane smiles. "Did you know I was Miss Teen Lake O' the Pines 1988? Of course you wouldn't know, but that's a beauty pageant, and I won it. And I was first runner up for Miss Texas Teen the very same year."

"Oh," I say. "Congratulations." I think that's the right thing to say.

Diane grins and shakes her head a little at the memory. "Congratulations for what? Standing around in a one-piece bathing suit with spray glue on my tush while I talked about how children are the future? Please." She pauses and peeks over her right shoulder, then looks back at me with a frown. "Although I must confess, my tush certainly looked a lot better back then than it does now. But what can you do?"

"Oh," I say again because it's all I can think to say.

Diane and I stand in silence for a moment and then she starts up again, her words coming out in a rush, her voice still quiet. "My father once said to me, 'Diane, sweetheart, with that face you won't have to work a day in your life.' My father was a bit of a peckerwood, to tell you the truth. But you know what, Rachel? My life was for me just like your life is for you, and you've got to live it like you want to, and that's why God gave it to you. Now you may look like you wouldn't bite a biscuit, but I know a girl who goes after what she wants. And you're that kind of girl, I think. Remember that. All right, I've talked your ear off, so go on and I'll see you next time."

And with that, she turns the doorknob and opens the door, a wave of summer heat hitting us both.

"Thank you," I say.

"Bye, sweetie," she answers, her voice back to its usual charged self.

I slide into Lauren's red Honda. A girl who goes after what she wants. I admit I like the sound of it, but the problem is, I'm still not sure what on Earth I should be wanting.

The next day is Friday, and Diane doesn't need me to come in. I sleep in—it's odd how I have so much less work and yet the week feels so long and exhausting somehow.

Still, I almost wish I could go to work at Diane's. Not just for the money but so I could have something to do to distract myself. There are only so many times I can tidy up Lauren's apartment before my mind is tugged back to life at my parents' house. I'm sure my mother and father expected me to come home by now, my lesson learned. But if I'm gone long enough, maybe they'll take me more seriously. Maybe they'll let me come back without making me go to Journey of Faith.

I drag a paper towel slowly across Lauren's bathroom mirror and stare intently at my reflection.

"Don't be ridiculous, Rachel," I reprimand myself. "You know you would still have to go." I frown and scrub extra hard at some nonexistent stain on the mirror. Diane said I was a girl who could go after what she wants. But I look just as I did when I left home. Same long dark curls, same unremarkable face. Same girl.

After work, Lauren comes home with a small paper bag. In it is a bottle. She serves herself some of whatever's inside it in a little juice glass covered with flowers.

"I need to take the edge off this day," she says, collapsing into her pink chair.

I tuck my knees under my chin and set aside the book I'm

reading—Lauren doesn't have the same selection the Treats have, but she has a nice set of Agatha Christie mysteries that I'm working through at a pretty quick pace. So far, I've been able to figure out the ending to each one before actually finishing the book—something that fills me with some small pride, one that I'm allowing myself to enjoy.

"Red wine, I've missed you," Lauren announces, taking a sip from her glass.

Romans says it's better not to drink wine in case it makes your brother stumble. No one at Calvary drinks. But the same verse says it's better not to eat meat—something almost everyone at Calvary does anyway. Lauren doesn't eat meat, but she does drink wine, apparently. So is she just as good— or just as wrong—as the people at church? Since moving out of my house, I've noticed how many contradictions there are to question, but I'm still not sure how a person goes about deciding which side of the contradiction is right.

"Did you have a bad day?" I ask. Sometimes she has to help put an animal down. I know she hates those days the most.

"Work was fine," she says. "It's just that . . . sometimes I have these days when I just. I don't know."

"I think I know what you mean," I say.

Lauren smiles, nods, and takes another gulp of wine.

"Do you want me to get you some supper? I made spaghetti. I already ate, though."

"Maybe later," she answers. "Thanks, anyway." She picks at a loose thread on the chair and scowls. "That guy Bryce texted me today and asked me if I want to go out again, but I said no. I don't know why."

"You didn't like him?" I ask. "You said he was nice."

"Too nice, I guess. I don't know. I keep thinking about Jeremy."

"Is he the one you have in the picture in your bedroom?" The kissing picture. The boy with the black hair.

"Yeah," says Lauren, sighing. "He's the one."

"What happened?" I ask. The way Lauren is bringing him up, I think it's safe to ask.

"He started off super nice, you know?" Lauren says. "Gentle. Funny. He loved animals like I did. He had this big pit bull named Johnny who would sleep in bed with us."

This is the closest Lauren's ever come to telling me she's had intercourse, and I'm shocked by it. I suppose I knew she had, but hearing her say it out loud makes her suddenly seem so worldly, sitting there with her glass of wine. So apart. So different. And she's my friend, too. I mean, I think she is. My brain works that contradiction over a few times before I can manage to speak again.

"What happened?" I ask.

"He smoked a lot of pot," she says. "Pot's a drug. An illegal drug. I mean, not like a crazy bad drug like cocaine or whatever, but it kind of made him broke all the time and sort of, like, not that motivated to do stuff. Which honestly didn't bother me that much because he was sweet and fun to hang out with. But one night at a party I caught him messing around with another girl." Lauren's voice is matter-of-fact. Detached. "He was kissing this girl named Mary Beth who hung out in our group. She thought she was so punk rock or whatever because she was in a band that sometimes played in Austin. Whatever. Anyway, they were kissing, like, in the bathroom. Isn't that gross? Who kisses someone in the bathroom?" Maybe she's trying to joke again, but her voice is empty. She doesn't smirk at her own humor like she normally does. She just stares out into space and takes another sip of wine.

I'm sad for Lauren, and I try to make sure my face registers that instead of stunned surprise. The entire time I'm listening to her speak, I'm also trying to keep a list in my head of things to look up or mull over later. Like punk rock. And kissing in bathrooms. But I also wonder how any boy would be so cruel. Sometimes Paul is as irritating as a leaky faucet in the middle of the night, but he would never do something like that to Faith, that's for sure.

"I'm sorry that happened to you, Lauren," I tell her when she's finished with her story.

"Yeah, well," Lauren answers with a shrug, like it's nothing. "It turns out it wasn't the first time. I don't know. Maybe he and Mary Beth are together now. She smoked pot, too."

Lauren and I only ever hugged that one time, the night she got back from her date. Part of me wants to hug her now, but Ruth's the only person I've ever really felt like I could hug without worrying if it was all right first.

"You're looking at me like I have cancer," Lauren says. "Or leprosy." This time she smirks for real.

"No, I'm not," I say, cracking a smile. "I'm just sorry that happened to you is all." And I am sorry. But I'm also still marveling at Lauren's story. She could have been telling me about hiking through the Amazon rain forest she sounded so exotic and strange.

"Yeah, well, in the grand scheme of things that have happened to me, it's just one more shitty thing," she says.

For the first time since I've come here, I feel like Lauren needs me. If only to listen. Somehow, even though Lauren's story was strange to hear, I now feel sort of more relaxed around her.

Lauren is relaxed, too, but I think it might be from the wine. She gulps down what she has and pours herself another glass, then peels off her uniform top and flings it in a corner. Her bra is blue, like her hair.

Lauren never minds getting changed in front of me. At home, Ruth and I would get changed in the closet or the bathroom because we were so concerned with modesty. But Lauren stretches her arms over her head and pulls an oversized T-shirt with a cat on it that says PURRFECT IN

EVERY WAY out of the laundry basket in the corner. She slides it on, unhooks her bra and pulls it out through one of the sleeves, and turns on the television. Then she starts sipping her wine again.

When it gets late and I start yawning, Lauren sends me to her bed to sleep and tells me she'll take the couch tonight—she wants to stay up late and watch more TV. By now she's on her third glass of wine and she's laughing at the strangest things, like commercials for fabric softener and the way Mitzi the cat cleans herself.

"You're sure you're okay?" I ask.

"Yeah, just go to sleep. I don't want to keep you up."

Lauren's bed smells like Nag Champa incense and cat, but I'm so tired I don't care. I drift off, thinking of how much I wish I could cuddle with Ruth in this bed and whisper about what's on my mind. But maybe what's on my mind now would be too much for Ruth.

When I wake up the next morning, Lauren is sitting on the couch, her hair in tangles around her face and her skin the color of chalk.

"Never. Drinking. Again." The bottle of wine, almost empty, sits on the floor.

"Are you all right?" I ask.

"Yes, but I'm sorry you had to see me go full Janis Joplin last night," she says.

"Who's Janis Joplin?"

Lauren sighs and rubs at her eyes. "I keep forgetting you don't get any of my references. Sometimes when you drink too much, the next day you're . . . It's called being hungover. And you feel sick. And Janis Joplin was this bad girl from like a million years ago and she was, like, Queen of the Hangovers. Because she was a bad girl. A rule breaker. Let me put it this way. You saw me go full Delilah last night. Full Jezebel."

"Full Salome," I add, understanding.

"Full Lot's wife," says Lauren.

"Full Eve," I say.

Lauren grins. "Bad women of the Bible trivia. Poor Eve. She gets blamed for everything."

"And Lot's wife doesn't even get a name," I say, the realization coming to me for the first time.

"Too true," Lauren answers. "I'm going to go dump the rest," she says, and gets up to take the leftover wine to the kitchen. When she comes back she collapses on the couch again with a wince. "This is my Saturday on, but I cannot go to work. I'll call Dr. Treats in a second."

Lauren is the older one. She's the one whose name is on the apartment lease and who pays the bills and knows how to manage life in the outside world. But right now, I feel like the grown-up. Only a grown-up who doesn't know what to do or say next.

"Can I get you anything?" I ask, simultaneously

promising myself that I'll never drink alcohol and also wondering what you do for someone who is hungover. "Do you want something to eat?"

"God, no," Lauren says. "I'm really sorry, Rachel. I haven't had so much to drink in a really long time. It's just stupid."

"It's all right," I say. I'm not sure it is, but I know I want to help Lauren even if it isn't.

"Hey," Lauren says, stretching onto her stomach on the couch, her voice muffled, "will you swing by my work later this afternoon to pick up my check?"

"Sure," I say, and I spend the rest of the morning trying to make as little noise as possible as I make myself breakfast and get dressed and tidy up a bit. It's a bit of a relief when it's time to go because I'm not sure how long being hungover lasts and for how long I should be quiet, and I don't want to bother Lauren by asking her.

I could walk, but it's so hot I drive the few blocks to Clayton Animal Hospital in Lauren's Honda, and when I walk in I see a man in a white coat with a thick salt-and-pepper moustache scratching the head of a calico cat who's sleeping on top of the front desk.

"Hello," he says, smiling easily.

"Hello," I say. "Excuse me, but are you Dr. Treats?"

"Last I checked," he answers. The cat suddenly decides it has an important place to go and leaps off the counter and trots off down the hall.

"That's our clinic cat, Hermione," Dr. Treats says. "She was a stray my son found hanging around outside our house one morning, but she didn't get along with our cat, Boots. So Hermione came to live here."

Suddenly there's a male voice from the back office. "Dad, who are you talking to?"

Mark appears, all dark eyes and soft hair and broad shoulders. My heart accelerates, and I redden a little and look down at the counter. If I'm not supposed to notice his looks, I'm not sure why God made him so noticeable. Unless he wanted me to have one more contradiction to puzzle over.

"Hey," he says. I manage to make eye contact, and Mark's smiling just enough to make me feel like it's okay to smile back. He's wearing jeans with holes in them and a white T-shirt that says THE JAM.

"Hi," I answer. At least I think I do. My mouth moves and my brain tries to make the word come out, but maybe I'm just imagining my entire response.

"You know each other?" Dr. Treats asks.

"This is Rachel. Lauren's friend. The one doing work for Mom?"

He remembers I'm Rachel. He remembers my name.

Dr. Treats nods, then looks at me more carefully. Maybe searching for a sign that I'm from that same strange world as Lauren. But he just smiles again and says, "Of course. Pleased to meet you."

"It's nice to meet you," I say, trying to pick out each word carefully. "I know Lauren called you to tell you she isn't feeling well, but I just came to pick up her paycheck."

"Of course," answers Dr. Treats, and he sorts through some papers on the counter before handing me a white envelope. "Tell her I hope she feels better."

"Thank you, I will," I say, tucking it into my purse. Not sure what else there is to say, I offer a little wave and start to head toward the door.

"Hey," Mark asks, "could you give me a lift to the pool? I'm supposed to be there for an afternoon shift and I've got my bike, but it's so freaking hot." He scratches at the back of his neck and looks at me, waiting for my reply.

"God forbid you have to exert yourself," Dr. Treats says dryly, gently patting Mark on the back.

"Hey, man, isn't it enough I have Mom on my back every minute? And I ran five miles this morning," Mark says good-naturedly to his father. Then he turns to me.

"So?" he asks, cracking a grin. "Would you? Mind giving me a ride?"

Alone in a car with a worldly boy whose voice and smile and irises the color of chocolate make me temporarily mute. I can't. It's not appropriate.

"Oh," I say, my heart thumping in my ears, my stomach, my two baby toes. "I . . . well . . ."

Impossibly, Mark's grin spreads even wider. "Hey, it's no big deal if you can't."

When I say yes, I'm not sure if it's the smile or my fear of appearing rude that makes me do it.

"Thanks," he says, grabbing a beat-up green backpack from behind the counter. "I'll put my bike in your trunk. Ready?"

The walk to the car is quiet. I'm worried I should be saying something. That it's rude to keep quiet. Only, what is there to say? I open the trunk and wait by the front door as Mark works to squeeze his bike into the Honda.

"Thanks for the lift," Mark says, folding himself into Lauren's car. "Just head straight a few blocks and make a right on Front Street."

I fumble with the keys and finally manage to get the car started.

"Mind if I turn on the AC? Hot as Hades in here," he says.

"Sure," I answer. I'm so nervous I didn't even turn the air conditioning on. But Mark fiddles with the knobs, gets the cool air blowing, then does a little drum flourish on the dashboard to finish off the task.

"So," he says, "my mom says you like Madeleine L'Engle. That you were reading her the other day when she got home."

I expect him to tell me he's heard I've run away or left a bizarre world where I don't go to normal school and never cut my hair. But he wants to ask me about Madeleine L'Engle? Something in me eases up a little. Uncoils.

"Well, I've only ever finished *A Wrinkle in Time*," I answer, "but I loved it so much. Have you read it?"

"Oh, yeah. That and the ones that came after. Actually, they were so great I read them all twice. But how come you only read the first one?"

"It's the only one I had," I say.

"Why not get the others? Oh, make a left on Donaldson."

I turn the steering wheel and ignore his last question.

"Why not?" he persists.

"It's hard to explain." I see the sign for CITY OF CLAYTON MUNICIPAL POOL and pull up in front. Mark doesn't get out.

"My parents felt those books weren't godly," I finally offer. The car is still in drive. My foot is pressed into the brake and it's shaking just slightly. I can feel Mark looking at me intently, not breaking his gaze, but I keep glancing back and forth between his face and the view out the windshield, not making eye contact.

"Godly like God wouldn't approve?" he asks. "But Madeleine L'Engle was Christian. The whole series has, like, what do you call them . . . allusions. Allusions to Christianity."

"Exactly!" I say, excited. The fact that he knows this about Madeleine L'Engle makes my heart race even faster than noticing his broad shoulders. Suddenly I have so many questions I want to ask him about the second book, like is Charles Wallace sick with some awful disease and are there actually dragons in the Murry garden. But all I can do is sit there with my foot on the brake, smiling stupidly.

"You're not living with your parents right now, right?" he asks.

"No, I'm staying with Lauren." I go ahead and slide the car into park.

"Yeah, that's what my mom and dad told me," he says. "I guess that must be . . . pretty cool? Lauren's pretty chill. And no parents telling you what to do, right? Nothing stopping you from reading whatever you want now."

"Like I said before . . . it's difficult to explain. I miss my family. Even if they wouldn't let me read Madeleine L'Engle. But yes, Lauren is . . . chill."

Mark cracks both his thumbs and nods.

"Yeah, my mom is a bear when it comes to rules and doing my best and not screwing up my potential and being the best-looking family for the Christmas cards and all that, but the truth is I guess if I didn't live with her I would miss her, you know?"

"I think I do," I say. But I don't, and suddenly I feel a little prickly even though I know Mark didn't mean to make me feel that way. I understand wanting to love your parents no matter what and missing them no matter what, but Mark has no idea what it means to live with rules. No idea what it means to question what love actually looks like and feels like.

"Oh, hell," he says suddenly, leaning back in his seat and closing his eyes. "Speaking of moms, I just remembered I told mine I would go to this SAT prep thing at school this morning and I sort of, like, bailed on that. I mean, I think subconsciously I knew I was going to bail on it, but now I am consciously aware that I actually did bail on it. Damn."

He opens his eyes again and stares ahead glumly.

"What's SAT prep?" I ask.

"This thing," Mark says with a dramatic sigh. "This thing that claws open your chest and takes your will to live and just crushes it with one intense death grip." He clenches his fist for added emphasis.

I can't help but laugh just a little, and he glances at me sideways, clearly pleased with his ability to make me smile.

"Actually, the SAT is, like, a test people take and then colleges look at the score and the better your score is, you know, the better school you get into," he says. "So SAT prep is this class where they help you prepare for the test. To do well on it."

"Oh, I get it."

I wonder how well I would do at SAT prep. I've always thought I was the smartest of all my brothers and sisters—even if it was prideful to think it—but I bet in a room full of people my own age like Mark, I'd actually realize I'm not that bright at all.

Suddenly, I really want to know how I would do on this SAT test.

"Well, there's another class next Saturday," Mark says, his voice resigned. "I'll go then."

"So you're going to college?" I ask.

"That's the plan," Mark answers through a yawn, like the topic of college is one he's discussed too many times. Just then, two girls about my age stroll down the sidewalk past us. They're wearing pink bathing suits the color of strawberry ice cream, and Mark's eyes shift for a sliver of a moment, glancing at their backsides as they make their way toward the pool.

I flush as pink as the swimsuits.

"My shift started two minutes ago," Mark says, turning toward me, as if he's not even aware he looked at the girls. "So I guess I should be going. I really appreciate the ride."

"Sure," I say. "Don't forget your bike."

"Thanks," he says.

Then he stops for a minute and looks at me, right in the eyes. It takes me by such surprise that I don't have a choice but to look right back, and my breathing quickens. There's a crease of confusion between Mark's dark brown eyes.

"I seriously cannot believe they wouldn't let you read *A Wrinkle in Time*," he says at last.

"Well," I say with a small shrug, looking back at the steering wheel. "I think if I told you all the things I wasn't allowed to do, that actually wouldn't seem like a very big deal."

I glance back at Mark, just to check his reaction, and he shakes his head softly, like he's lining up guesses in his mind about all the things that were forbidden. "I'll see you later, Rachel." I watch in the rearview mirror as he hauls out his bike, slams the trunk, and starts heading toward the pool. I hear him calling out to the girls in the strawberry ice-cream suits, and I watch as they slow down to let him catch up. I keep watching until they all head beyond the pool gates and away from my line of vision, but I sit there long after they've disappeared, wondering what people my age talk about on a Saturday afternoon at the pool. Wondering what it must feel like to dive headfirst into that cool, blue water.

By that night, Lauren is feeling better. She's still in her PURRFECT IN EVERY WAY T-shirt from the night before, but she's munching on saltines and sipping Diet Coke while she fiddles around on her laptop. I'm dressed in my nightgown, flat on my stomach on the couch, flipping through one of Lauren's mystery novels. But my mind can't focus. It keeps replaying my conversation with Mark from that afternoon about SAT prep and *A Wrinkle in Time.*

And it keeps replaying those two girls in strawberry swimsuits strolling past the car and the way Mark's eyes rested on them for just a moment.

"What's it like to wear a bathing suit?" I ask.

Lauren's eyes pop up from behind the screen.

"What?"

I look down, rubbing a finger up and down one of the beat-up paperback pages. "I'm just wondering," I say, like I'm having a conversation with the book instead of Lauren. "I'm wondering what it's like to wear a bathing suit."

"Wearing a swimsuit is fine, but what's incredible is swimming," Lauren answers. I look at her for a moment, and she's eyeing me carefully as she closes her laptop. "When you're swimming, you're just . . . weightless. It's transcendent."

I nod, remembering how I watched my brothers swim that day in Galveston Bay. "How'd you even learn how to swim?"

"Jeremy taught me," Lauren admits with a quick eye roll. "His mom's apartment complex had a pool. We weren't technically supposed to use it without her, but at least I learned."

"You never felt . . ." I reach for the right word. "Exposed?"

"You mean immodest?" Lauren says, raising an eyebrow. "At first it was weird. But it was all weird. Getting to be comfortable with my body as, like, my body. My body that belonged to me and wasn't just something to cover up so I didn't tempt men."

All of Pastor Garrett's favorite verses and sayings about how a woman should help a man resist lust flood my mind. But without his actual booming voice ringing in my ears or my father's stern expression to give them extra weight, they don't roar as loudly as they once did.

"But don't you tempt men when you wear a bathing suit?" I ask. I can barely manage to look Lauren in the eye when I say it, but I hear her take a sharp breath, like the night she threw the hairbrush and yelled. I glance back at her, and she closes her eyes for a moment before opening them to speak.

"I mean, yes, honestly," Lauren says carefully. "But sometimes Jeremy tempted me. I guess I wouldn't use the word *tempt*. I mean, he attracted me. Like when he would take his shirt off and swim in his shorts. He was cute. We attracted each other. That was the whole point."

I think about Mark Treats and his broad shoulders and his eyes on those girls and how my first impulse was to think it was wrong. Immodest. It was even a little scary for a moment to realize I'd just been in a car with a boy who could look at a girl like that.

But then I think about Mark Treats looking at *me* like that. And about what it would feel like to know his eyes were on me, unable to look away.

Suddenly, there's a fuzzy tingle running through every fine hair on my arms, down to my skin, like a million fuzzy tingles at one. And there's a gentle thud between my legs that makes me catch my breath. I stare at the words on the page in front of me.

What I'm feeling is pleasant, but it's something I've never allowed myself to feel.

I sit up and blink hard.

"The thing is, Rachel, that humans get attracted to each other," Lauren's voice continues as I try to pay attention to her words. "Our bodies attract each other. And girls can get attracted to guys, too." I can hear the energy and urgency picking up in her voice. "That's how it works, you know. That's why all of us are here. Because we get hot for each other. And the way you and I were raised, we were just handed these totally warped ideas about sex and our bodies, you know? Like girls can't feel attracted to guys and guys are just animals who can't control themselves, so we have to rein them in by wearing pillowcases on our heads, practically. It's body shame and guilt and all of that, and it pisses me off just thinking about it."

Lauren's gotten started and now she might never stop. She can only choose her words for a moment before she starts sounding just like her blog posts. And her blog posts mean something to me. They're what got me to think there might be something else out there for me, something besides just living a life like Faith's. But sometimes Lauren sounds just as strident as Pastor Garrett.

Lauren's still talking but I stop listening. I want the space for just my thoughts. Even if they frighten me sometimes. Even if I don't know how to answer myself most of the time.

When there's a knock at the door, Lauren stops mid-sentence. The two of us glance at each other, confused.

"Who's that?" she asks, walking over toward the door and looking through the peephole.

In the millisecond it takes me to turn my head toward the doorway, one thought enters my mind: It could be my father. It wouldn't be that hard for him to find out where Lauren is living.

It could be him. And any swimmy, fuzzy, tingly feelings I felt a moment ago have disappeared. My hand grips the back of the couch, and I'm not breathing.

I don't want my father here.

But I also want him to want to be here. To be looking for me. To make sure that I'm all right.

My lungs are burning, about to explode.

Lauren turns back from the peephole with a bemused expression and turns the knob.

Mark Treats is standing there, holding a paper bag from the grocery store, wearing his THE JAM T-shirt, holey jeans, and a freshly sunburned nose.

"Hey," Mark says. The word comes out like a shout. He walks in like he lives here. "Uh, I tried calling, but Lauren didn't answer her cell."

"I put it on silent," Lauren says, shutting the door behind him.

I'm still clenching the back of the couch, but my shoulders drop as I finally allow myself to exhale. Not that I relax. Just seeing Mark in the living room is enough for my heart to keep a quick pace. At his own house or even in the car this afternoon it felt less strange, somehow, to talk to him. But here in the apartment with me dressed in my nightgown it's something much different. My cheeks warm.

"If you need a place to stay, the couch is taken, Mark," Lauren asks, rolling her eyes. But there's a smile on her face.

"No couch needed. I was just wanting to bring these over tonight. For Rachel." He lifts his chin in my direction. "Hey." Then he sets the paper bag on the table where Lauren and I sometimes eat our meals together.

"What's in there?" Lauren says, peering into the bag. I still haven't said anything. Not even hello.

"Those Madeleine L'Engle books from my house," he says to me, not Lauren. "All of them."

Lauren is digging through the bag, pulling out the worn paperbacks with faded covers and piling them on the table, and Mark is standing there staring at me, smiling a crooked smile and maybe, probably, I am trying not to cry.

"I mean, my dad read them to me when I was a kid and then I read them again when I was older and my mom's not into them, so they're just sitting there being, like, not read. So I thought, you know, if you haven't had the chance to check them out or whatever. No rush in getting them back or anything."

"Oh," says Lauren. "Wow. That's really nice of you, Mark. Isn't that nice, Rachel?" She looks at me, and her voice reminds me of when I prompted my younger siblings to talk by spoon-feeding them the right words one at a time.

"I . . ." I swallow. "Thank you. Mark."

"You want to sit down for a sec?" Lauren says.

"Yeah, sure," Mark answers, scooping the books up from the table. He flops down on the other end of the couch. A bare kneecap sticks out of a hole in his jeans. In blue ink someone has written DINOSAUR BREATH.

"Anyway, see, I numbered them on the spines with a Sharpie so you know what order to read them in, just in case you get confused," he says. His DINOSAUR BREATH knee is bouncing. Is he ever still enough to sleep? The small pile of books sits between us, and I reach out for one and flip through it, just to have something to do with my hands.

"Mark, this is so nice of you," I say. Something about holding the book steadies me a little. My heart is slowing down and so is my breathing.

"Hey, I have to make a call," Lauren says, searching around her chair for her cell phone. "I'm in my room if you need me." She raises an eyebrow at me as she heads to the back of the apartment.

"So," Mark says, "I gotta tell you I got into trouble today." He sticks his finger in his right ear and wiggles it around. "Damn. Water in the ear. One of the downsides of my profession. That and the sunburn."

"What happened?" I ask.

"My parents found out I didn't go to SAT prep," he says.

"How?"

"Well, my parents speak to each other. They've been married for, like, a hundred years, but they still enjoy spending time together and talking, so it didn't take long before my dad mentioned that I'd been over at the office this morning and then my mom was like 'did he mention SAT prep' and my dad was all 'he had SAT prep he never said anything' and she was all 'you need to stay on top of that boy' and then it was, you know, 'Mark we need to talk to you come to the kitchen immediately' and blah, blah."

"So then what happened?" I have my knees tucked under my chin. Maybe this way he won't be able to tell I don't have a bra on under my nightgown. Since moving in with Lauren, it's been one of the habits I've given up. At home I wore one all the time, even when I was sleeping, just in case we had to wake up in the middle of the night for an emergency and my dad or brother saw me.

"The usual is what happened," Mark says with a shrug. "Sad head-shaking from Dad. A lecture from Mom about how SAT prep class is going to help me get into a good college and how I shouldn't miss out on such an amazing opportunity and all that. Then they told me I was grounded and when I started complaining, my dad said not to push it because they can ground me all summer long if they want to."

"That's it?" I ask. If he expects commiseration, I'm not quite sure how to start.

"I know. It could be worse. They didn't even mind me coming here to drop off these books. I think my mom thinks you could be a good influence on me," he says.

"It's really nice of you," I say.

"Sure."

"How'd you know where Lauren lives?"

"My parents gave her some of our old furniture and stuff when she came back here. I hauled that table over there up that flight of stairs, actually."

"Oh," I say. "It's nice how they've helped Lauren. And me. I mean, since I . . . left my house."

"You mean since you ran away?" Mark asks.

The words make me sound more dangerous and exciting than I think I am.

"I guess I ran away, yeah," I say. Or was I kicked out? Or both?

"My parents know things were rough for you at home, and rough for Lauren, too," Mark continues. "Because of, like, your church, right? And that's why you're not living with your families anymore."

"I guess that's one way of putting it," I answer.

I expect Mark to ask me a million questions. Is it true I can't cut my hair? Is it true I've never watched television? Is it true I haven't ever been to a public school? But he just sighs and looks around Lauren's apartment, decorated in resale shop finds and tattered posters of nothing I recognize or know—pictures of bands, pieces of artwork.

"What's DINOSAUR BREATH?" I ask, pointing to his knee.

"Man, I forgot that was there," Mark says with a laugh. "It's the name of this band I might be in. With some other lifeguards from the pool. But we may not be Dinosaur Breath. We might be Blueberries for Sal. Or the Betty Whites."

"Oh. What instrument do you play?"

"I don't actually play anything yet," he says. "But if Dinosaur Breath is formed, I think I'll play bass. But I have to get a bass first. And, you know, learn to play it."

I laugh. A band that doesn't exist based on instruments that don't exist.

"What? That's funny to you?" But his big smile tells me he knows it is. I love how his smile eats up almost all of his face.

"A little," I say, grinning. "No, a lot."

"Yeah, it is," he says, standing up and stretching. Should I get up, too? Is he leaving? I don't have a road map or directions for How to Be with a Boy. Especially one who brings me books and glances at girls' rear ends and wants to be in a band that plays secular music. Especially one with broad shoulders and suntanned calves and dark eyes that first strike me mute and then make me feel like a head without a body, all warm and floaty.

"I'm gonna get a glass of water from your kitchen if that's cool. You want one? I mean, if it's cool that I get a glass of water."

He doesn't want to leave. Not yet.

"I can get it for you," I answer, daring to lower my arms from my chest. I have little goose bumps up and down my arms, from the ends of my short-sleeved nightgown to my wrists.

"I can walk," Mark says. "You want one?"

I won't be able to hold it I'm still so trembly.

"No, that's okay."

When he comes back he downs the water in three gulps.

"Excellent water. Five stars. High quality water."

I laugh again, but I don't know what to say. Do I seem stupid just sitting here laughing? Or do boys like girls who laugh at everything they say?

"So . . ." he says, putting the empty glass on the coffee table, "are you going to go to school in the fall?"

"You mean . . . Clayton High School?"

"Yeah."

I bet Clayton High has a library, full of even more books than the Treats have in their house.

"I don't know. I don't know if I'm staying here long term," I answer. "I'm not . . . I don't. Like I said. It's complicated."

"Your parents don't want you here, right?" Mark asks, picking at a mosquito bite on his ankle. His fingernails are short and clean, and I'm struck by this tiny attention to detail hidden in the middle of his jittery, jumpy self.

"No, they don't want me here," I tell him. "They want me to come home and go to, um . . . a church camp. Because I wasn't . . . behaving appropriately."

"What did you do?" Mark says, an eyebrow raised.

"I went on the computer without their permission." And I thought for myself and had questions and wondered if maybe things might be different for me. But I don't say that part.

Mark whistles. "That's it? You went on the computer and you have to go to a church camp?"

I nod, reddening. Did Mark think I did drugs like Lauren's old boyfriend? Drank alcohol like Lauren? Snuck out without permission? If Mark thinks I'm a dangerous runaway, I guess I've just proven him wrong.

"Is the church camp that bad?" he asks. "It's not just sitting around, like, singing and rapping about Jesus?" He pantomimes playing a guitar, nodding his head from side to side.

"I think the church camp would be bad," I say. Maybe it's the tone of my voice, but Mark lowers his hands and looks at me right in the eyes, and he stops all the silliness. "I think if I went to that church camp it would, like, kill my spirit," I say, my voice a whisper. "It would make me not be me anymore." Whoever that is.

Mark nods. He has lashes like a girl's and a tiny scar

in one of his eyebrows where the hair doesn't grow anymore.

"What do you mean not be you?" He keeps his gaze on me.

"Oh," I say, the question catching me off guard. "I'm . . . well . . . I like to read," I manage. "I like to know things. I guess I'm curious. Maybe too curious. That's probably what my parents would say. And my pastor. But I don't think . . . I mean, I know . . . you're not allowed to be curious at church camp."

Mark's face softens, and he smiles. "I think liking to know stuff is good. I'm glad you didn't go."

"Me, too," I say. "I'm really glad I didn't. Even if I don't know what's going to happen to me next."

Mark picks at a cuticle. "This is making my SAT prep class problem seem pretty trivial. You're, like, trying to answer philosophical questions about your existence on the planet, and I'm, like, basically trying to get away with not having to memorize a million vocabulary words, like what *mendacious* means."

"It's funny you should say *mendacious*," I tell him, "because it means prone to lying."

"There is no way that's what it means," Mark says, taking *A Wind in the Door* from the pile of books between us and tossing it at me gently.

"Yes, it does, honest!"

"All right, all right. I believe you. Man, you probably have a bigger vocabulary than my older brother, and he got into Georgetown."

"What's Georgetown?"

"This fancy schmancy school for people who are going to become fancy schmancy doctors," he says, leaning back on the couch and staring at the ceiling. "My parents are thrilled, to say the least. And I know my mother loves to imagine how amazing it would be to tell everyone both her sons are doctors. Whatever."

"Well," I say, "there are a lot of doctors, but there's only one bass player for Dinosaur Breath."

Mark laughs hard. As hard as he's made me laugh. I can't believe I did it. After he recovers, he asks if I have a brother.

"I have six," I answer. "And three sisters."

"No way," he says, his eyebrows popping. "Seriously?"

"Seriously."

"Whoa."

"There's a family at my church with twelve kids," I say, enjoying myself. "And the mom is pregnant again."

"Really?"

"Really!"

"Where does everybody sleep?" he asks, stunned.

"Bunk beds, I think. It's what my brothers do." The mention of sleeping makes me think about my little twin bed, and my mind hits on the image of Ruth snuggling up with me. The lightness of my mood darkens a bit, but then Mark jumps and glances at the phone he pulls out of his pocket, grimacing and shoving it away again just as quickly. "Parental units beckon me," he says, frowning. "And after the SAT prep situation, I can't screw up again."

"Yeah, you wouldn't want to botch things up even more," I answer. "Is *botch* an SAT word?"

"Probably," Mark says, standing up. "*Botch*. It sounds like a skin disease. She's got a serious case of botch."

I follow him to the door, smiling at the joke. "He's got a terrible case of the bumbles," I try.

Mark nods in mock seriousness. "She's suffering from bungle disorder," he adds.

"I can't think of another one," I say, laughing. "Wait, I can. Flub."

Mark bows his head, shaking it sadly. "He ate right, exercised, didn't smoke, yet when the doctors performed the autopsy, his heart was full of flub. Such a shame." When he lifts his head back up, his wide grin meets mine. Then he opens the door to head downstairs. "Hope you like the books," he says to me.

The books. I was so focused on our last bit of conversation I managed to forget that was the entire reason he came over. In fact, I was so focused I managed to forget that I stood up in front of him without a bra on underneath my nightgown.

"Oh," I say, quickly crossing my arms in front of me. "Mark, thank you so much. Thank you for the books."

"No problem," he says, giving me a little wave as he heads out. "I'll see you around, Rachel."

I shut the door after him and rest my cheek against it, closing my eyes as I listen to the sound of his feet making their way down the steps.

18

I'm not sure where Diane gets all these addresses or how much she spends on postage, but there's another stack of bright pink flyers to stuff when I get to the Treatses' house on Monday morning.

"I asked the print shop for shell pink and I get this," Diane says, tapping the flyers with her finger. "Don't you think the shade is too Pepto-Bismol?"

"No," I say, even though they are a little bright for my taste. "I think people will notice them."

"They say Sweet Treats and are the color of a box of Good & Plenty," she continues, picking up a flyer with a grimace. "I'm going demand my money back. People are going to think I run a candy store. They're going to be calling me up asking me how much I charge for Mars bars and Kit Kats."

I can't help but grin. It's easy to see where Mark gets his quick humor.

"Should I still stuff them?" I ask.

"Yes," Diane says, sighing. "But I've got to make a note to myself somewhere about calling that print shop to complain."

She strides over to the mirror and checks her reflection one more time, using a carefully manicured pinkie finger to tug a stray eyebrow hair into place. Her carefully tailored peach suit skims her knees and hugs her curves, and matching sets of slim, gold bracelets shimmy along her tanned, freckled forearms. The scoop neck of her top shows off the tiniest sliver of cleavage. Diane really likes looking at herself in the mirror, and I'm amazed she can stare at herself so much and not feel her behavior is vain.

Finally, she smiles appreciatively at her reflection and then turns to me.

"Not bad for a former beauty queen, right?" she asks like she doesn't need my answer because she already knows it herself. But something in her voice tells me she'd like hearing the answer from me anyway.

"You always look pretty, Diane."

"Oh, you're too sweet, but I miss the days when my skin was in its prime. Treasure your pores, honey." Then she tilts her head at me and says, "Hey, have you ever thought about wearing your hair up? I mean, your hair is lovely. All those dark chocolate curls and everything. But your face is so gorgeous, and it's like I can hardly see it."

I flush at the word *gorgeous*. I've been called dutiful, patient, hardworking, and virtuous, but never gorgeous. Not even pretty. I squirm a bit in my seat.

"I've never thought about it, I guess," I respond, glancing down at the stack of flyers.

"Oh, I didn't mean to make you uncomfortable," Diane starts.

"You haven't," I say in a soft voice.

"I have," she says.

I manage eye contact with Diane, whose face is clouded with concern.

"Am I really . . . gorgeous?" I ask, the words sounding silly as soon as I say them.

But Diane grins, her worry vanishing, and her eyes crinkle up at the sides. "Yes, dear. You are. You're lovely."

I flush again, and because I'm not sure what else to do, I start stuffing envelopes. "Thank you," I answer, almost under my breath.

"You know," Diane says, getting her purse and phone and heading toward the door, "I've always loved that part in Song of Solomon. The part when the man tells his love that her lips are like a scarlet thread and her cheeks are like pieces of a pomegranate behind her veil. I just think it shows us how much God wants us to appreciate beauty. Human beauty, too."

I stop midstuff, and I know I'm staring. I'm not sure if the Treats go to church, but Diane just quoted Scripture with the ease of a preacher.

Diane notices my surprise and winks. "In addition to being Miss Teen Lake O' the Pines 1988," she says, "I also won Covenant Baptist's Bible Bee six years in a row. All right, I'm heading out now, Rachel. Help yourself to lunch."

After Diane leaves, I walk over to the mirror and pull back my curls, twisting them up and away from my face, exposing my neck. We didn't study the Song of Solomon much—Pastor Garrett always said it was a metaphor about Christ and his church, not about people—but I remember what comes after the Scripture Diane quoted.

" 'Your neck is like the tower of David, built for an armoury, whereon there hang a thousand bucklers, all shields of mighty men,' " I recite to my reflection. I smile at myself before I let my hair tumble down around my shoulders. I can't tell if it looked pretty or not. It definitely looked different.

I stuff every flyer and upload five new houses to the database. My ears are on alert, wondering if I'll hear the jangle of keys in the front door and Mark's shout of hello. If he shows up, I could tell him how much I loved *The Wind in the Door.*

But Mark doesn't show up, and soon I go make myself a sandwich and eat it at the kitchen counter. I picture Mark in this kitchen every morning, joking around with his parents and making up excuses for why he can't go to his SAT prep class. I imagine a lot of laughter and words and silly sayings that only make sense to them. My own house wasn't usually filled with much joking, but still, we had our own little routines and our Walker way of doing things. Now that exists without me. And I don't have a family to be part of. I wait for tears but there aren't any. Just that same weight of sadness I'm always carrying that grows heavier when I least expect it. I allow myself a sigh and then start tidying the kitchen so I can get back to work.

After lunch I upload a few more houses, alphabetize several files, and do some general tidying up. Finally, I write a small reminder note that reads Call the Print Shop to Complain About Flyers. I know Diane will be back soon, and she'll be pleased with what I've done. I sit in silence for a moment and survey the neat and orderly desk and smile. It's good to feel capable.

As I consider what else I can finish, I run my fingers along the computer keyboard, still in wonder that I'm able to look up absolutely anything I want whenever I'm here. Of course, I've been so serious about working hard for Diane that the only time I let myself search for something that wasn't related to work was when I wanted to show Mark who invented paper.

Diane wouldn't mind if I looked up something. Something I've been thinking about. I do a quick search and click on the link.

Welcome to Clayton High! Home of the Cavaliers!

Right in the middle of the home page are a group of girls in red and black uniforms of small skirts and sleeveless tops. They surround a young man dressed in a funny suit, red cape, and a big black hat with a red feather sprouting out of the top. He's brandishing a sword, and I figure he must be a cavalier. I can't help but grin, but my smile is no competition for the bright smiles of the girls on the home page. My eyes scan the menu to the left.

Summer Reading

Summer School Meal Plan

Fall Registration Info

Fall Athletics

Booster Club

Campus Directory

Campus Map

Student Information

I remember catching brief glimpses through the window of our family van of students while they waited at bus stops. Sometimes I'd see them hanging out by the Stop N' Go when I went in to pay for gas. My dad always referred to public schools as government-run schools, places where little children were stripped of values instilled at home. As a little girl, I felt superior to them as I drove by—my father cared enough about my soul to protect me from God haters and sinners. As I got older, I saw them clustered together, laughing, talking, sometimes even holding hands. They spoke their own private language.

They looked like they were having fun.

At the bottom of the page, I find a link to the Clayton Independent School District. I click on it and am bombarded with words and tabs and links to other links about policies and procedures and curriculum. I minimize the page and stare for a few moments at the picture of Boots the cat that Diane uses as a screensaver, then take a deep breath and go back to the district website. I slowly read every word until finally, under a heading titled Admissions and Withdrawls, I discover the following sentence: *The adult student (over age eighteen years and under age twenty-one years) or the student, who has had the disabilities of minority removed through marriage or as otherwise permitted by law, may enroll without parental involvement.*

Over eighteen but under twenty-one.

In a few weeks that will be me.

I print out the page, fold it in half, and tuck it inside my purse. I decide to try and make sense of one of Diane's file cabinets bulging with unfiled things, but a few minutes later, I take the paper out and unfold it, smoothing the crease with my finger. I read the sentence over and over again until I'm sure I could recite it with my eyes closed.

❧❧❧

A week later the information about school enrollment is still in my purse like some sort of talisman. I haven't done anything with the information, but just knowing the paper exists at the bottom of my bag makes me feel like good things could happen to me.

But unfortunately, its charms aren't working at this moment. It's Friday night and I'm curled up on the couch, trying to focus on a different piece of paper—a blank one. Gripping a pen in my hand, I write the word *Ruth* in my careful script.

The name stares back at me expectantly from the lined paper. I chew the end of my blue ballpoint pen in response, frustrated.

I've tried to write Ruth every few days since I came to Lauren's, but I can't find the words to explain everything that's happening in a way that I know won't scare her. All I have is a handful of letters that don't say anything about what I really long to share with her. In my last letter I spent a full paragraph explaining what I made for supper one evening, but I haven't told her about my job or the Treats or watching television because I know how much it would frighten and confuse her to know I'm doing all of those things. After all, those things still frighten and confuse me a little, and I'm actually here, living them and trying to make sense of them.

In the note I left under her pillow, I promised Ruth I would get in touch, but I can't figure out a way to get the letters to her. Even if I leave my return address blank, my parents are sure to open any mail addressed just to Ruth. And even letters about mundane things like making supper are forbidden if they're written by someone like me.

Since I can't call her, a letter is the only way. Maybe the day my letter arrives might be the day Ruth gets the mail. But I think she'd probably show it to my parents.

I bite down harder on the pen and frown. Finally, I think about the one thing I wish I could tell Ruth right now. And it's not mundane and it wouldn't scare her. It's just the truth.

Ruth, here in the place where I am staying, I sleep on a friend's couch. And sometimes at night I hug my pillow and pretend it's you, and I whisper all the things I want to tell you.

My throat tightens up. Now that I've found something I want to say, I can't even get the letter to her.

"How do I look?"

Lauren interrupts me by walking out of her bedroom. She's wearing tight black jeans and a skin-hugging red T-shirt. Her red lipstick is the color of fresh apples. Her eyes are framed with dark liner, and her hair—still blue—is artfully arranged in soft curls around her face.

"You look pretty," I say, grateful for the distraction. I swallow a few times until the lump in my throat is gone and examine Lauren's outfit again. I still can't imagine myself in anything like what she's wearing, but Lauren does look pretty. Light-up-a-room, notice-me pretty. Confident pretty. Pretty pretty.

"Thanks. Jeremy's picking me up in a few secs, so . . ."

"Jeremy? Your old boyfriend?" The one she caught kissing someone else?

"Yes, and I don't want to talk about it. Just tell me to have fun, okay? Please?" She smiles brightly and slips off to the kitchen. When she comes back she's sipping from a glass. She finishes it pretty quickly as she messes around on her phone.

"Okay, he's downstairs," says Lauren, setting her glass down on the table. "Don't wait up."

"All right," I say, wondering why Bryce came to the front door to meet Lauren and Jeremy just sends her a message from his car outside. "Have a nice time."

After Lauren leaves, I watch *Law & Order*, figuring out the plot twist long before the assistant district attorney does. I usually choose nature shows when I'm in the apartment alone, but when Lauren and I watch *Law & Order* together she has me guess the ending at the halfway point because she knows I'm almost always right. I have to admit I enjoy solving the puzzles. I've even gotten used to the short skirts. When the show's over, I turn off the television so I can go read some more of the Madeleine L'Engle books Mark brought. I haven't seen him at Diane's this week, and I'm starting to wonder if I'll ever see him again. And I want to. I want to see his kind smile and hear his silly jokes. I'm not sure what to do about the fact that he makes my heart beat double time, but I do know the last time I went to Diane's I thought about pinning my hair up to show off my face even though I didn't do it.

I change into my nightgown and lie down to read on the couch until a little past eleven. Reading whatever I want for as long as I want to read it makes me sigh out loud with happiness even if there's no one around to hear me sighing. I'll never get sick of it.

Suddenly the door to the apartment swings open with a wild force. I jump at the sound, my eyes wide.

"That guy," Lauren spits. "I seriously hate that guy." She slams the door so hard the framed *Don't Mess with Texas Women* poster she has hanging by the door skitters off the wall and lands with a crash on the hardwood floor.

"I hate that fucker like I hate my dad," she yells, her voice cracking. Two black half moons of melting eye makeup stain her face, and her carefully applied lipstick is now smeared, careening off her mouth and down her chin like a child's scribble.

"What happened?" I whisper, but Lauren takes the glass she left on the table and hurls it at the door. Then she crumples into a ball right there on the floor, and in that moment she looks impossibly tiny. Younger than me.

"Lauren!" I shout, and I scramble to her, careful not to step on the glass. She's sobbing now, hard. The choking, can't breathe sobs I know from my first days away from home. Mucus runs freely down her nose, but she doesn't seem to notice or care.

I help her up and walk with her to her bedroom, grabbing

a bunch of toilet paper from the bathroom on the way so she can clean her face. In the dim light shining in on us from the hall, I can see she's finally stopped crying. Her breathing is shaky, coming in fits and starts. She falls into her bed, not even changing her clothes.

"I'm sorry about the glass," she finally says, her voice soft. Not at all like the bombastic Lauren I'm used to. "I'll clean it up tomorrow."

"No, I'll do it later," I say. "Don't worry."

"Oh, you don't have to, Rachel."

"I don't mind."

"Thanks," she says, scooting closer to the wall, making room for me. I sit next to her and bring my knees up to my chin.

"Can I ask what happened?"

Lauren shrugs and doesn't make eye contact when she answers. "Stupid stuff. Drinking stuff. We messed around." She glances up at me. "I mean, we kissed and everything."

And everything. I wonder what the *everything* part means.

"Anyway, we spent all night hanging out, and I thought it was going really great, like all the crap that had gone on between us was in the past, but then when I brought up maybe, like, starting to hang out again, he said he thought I had too many issues and he wasn't the right guy for me because he wouldn't be able to help me in the way I needed help. God, it sounds so awful and gross just saying it out loud." She rolls onto her back and stares at the ceiling. "I mean, that is so him. He makes it sound like he's doing me a favor while he breaks my heart."

Tears start sliding down her face, but she wipes them away with the back of her hand.

"The truth is, he's right. I do have too many issues. I'm seriously fucked up. I'm just this fucked-up girl, and I'll never *not* be fucked up. And no one will want to be with me."

"Lauren, that's not true," I say. My hand sits uncertainly for a moment and then I reach out, pushing her hair away from her face. I pet her gently for a while, and I sense Lauren's shoulders start to sink just a bit and hear her breathing even out.

"How is that not true?" she whispers, still avoiding my eyes.

"You left your house when you were my age, but you didn't have anyone to go to. And you did it. You made it. I couldn't have done that. I couldn't have left without you to go to."

"Yes, you could have."

"But you did it, Lauren," I insist. "You did it all by yourself. And you got your GED and a job and an apartment. You're a hard worker, and you care about people. You spend all day helping animals. And you're helping me now. You're a good person, Lauren."

Lauren sniffs a little and manages a tiny, wry smile. "Remember how Pastor Garrett always used to say it didn't matter if we were good? How good people went to hell every day? How the only thing that mattered was whether or not we were born again in Christ Jesus?"

"Yeah, I remember," I say. And suddenly I know—suddenly I accept, in every space in my heart—that Pastor Garrett is wrong.

"What's going to happen to us, Rachel?" Lauren asks. "What's going to happen to our lives?"

To our wild lives. Our precious lives.

"I'm not sure," I answer. "I wish I knew."

"Me, too," Lauren whispers, and she stifles a yawn.

"You need to go to sleep."

"Sit with me till I do?"

"Sure."

I wait until she's drifted off. I take a deep breath.

God, help me. Guide me. Give me the compassion to be there for Lauren as I know you would want me to be. Help me to show her love, God.

I pray and breathe and watch Lauren sleep, and when I'm sure she's resting deeply, I tiptoe out of her bedroom and set to picking up the shards of broken glass.

19

Diane asks me to come in next Friday even though it's usually my day off, and when I knock on the door, I expect to be met by trails of Diane's sweet perfume and the tap of her high heels. But when the Treatses' front door opens, I'm face-to-face with Mark.

"Oh, hey," he says, grinning. "Long time no see."

"Hey," I answer. "I mean, hi." My face feels warm.

"Hey, hi, *hola*, it's all the same thing," Mark says, heading into Diane's office. He takes a big bite of an apple he's holding and bellows out, "Mom! Rachel's here!" in between bites. Then he stretches out onto the love seat and keeps eating. I put my purse down on the desk just as Diane walks in, dressed in a mint-green suit and matching pumps.

"It's so lovely for you to let me know in a calm and measured tone that my responsible employee is once again on time for her job," Diane says to Mark, rolling her eyes. "And take your shoes off the love seat." She's carrying a large paper bag full of clothing which she places alongside some others by the front door.

"Mom, come on," Mark replies. He finishes the apple and tosses the core into the garbage can where it lands with a thud. But he drops his feet down to the floor.

Diane sighs. "Mark told me you've got six brothers," she says to me. "How do you handle all that male energy?" She drags out the last two words, like saying the phrase "male energy" alone is exhausting.

"Well, I have sisters, too, so I guess it all balances out," I say.

Diane smiles, then glances at the bags by the door.

"Mark, we have to get all of these things out to the car. The church is having that big yard sale to raise money for the women's shelter, and I said I'd donate what we could."

Mark groans again and doesn't move.

"Rachel, that gets me thinking," Diane says, ignoring Mark. "I know you used to go to church with your family, and I was wondering if maybe this Sunday you'd like to come to church with us?"

"Oh, man," Mark says, sitting up straight. "Mom, don't be weird."

"What's weird about church?" Diane shoots back. "Don't be so negative, Mark. It's a lovely church. Peace Lutheran of Clayton." She looks at me and adds, "Mark and his brother were both baptized there."

Mark gives me an "I'm sorry" look. "My mom is so good at selling houses she doesn't stop there," he says. "Although I guess as churches go, it could be worse."

"Oh," I say. "I guess . . . well." I can't be rude. Not after everything Diane has done for me. And anyway, it's the church Diane goes to. It's not Calvary Christian. "I'll go. Sure."

"You will?" Mark answers.

"Wonderful!" Diane adds. "This Sunday at nine a.m. Do you want us to pick you up or just meet us there?"

"I can meet you there," I say.

"Terrific. It's a really warm and welcoming place, Rachel. I think you'll enjoy it."

"Thanks," I say, my mind catching up with my mouth. I just agreed to go to church with Mark and his parents.

Diane explains my tasks for the day as Mark makes several trips to the car with the sacks of old clothing. When he's finished, Diane swats him gently on the head with a stack of folders before heading out the door. "If you want a ride to work," she calls, "this is your chance. See you Sunday, Rachel!"

As I take my seat at the desk, Mark stands in the open doorway. "I guess I'll see you Sunday, too," he says. "Hey, how are the *Wrinkle in Time* books?"

"Oh, they were all so good," I say, smiling.

"All?" His eyebrows pop a bit.

"I finished them last night," I answer. "I should have brought them back, but . . ." I hesitate. "I thought maybe I could reread one or two, if that's okay. If you don't mind me keeping them for a little while longer?"

"You finished all those books in less than two weeks?" He tilts his head and looks at me carefully.

"Yes, is that fast?"

"Uh, yes, that is fast," Mark says. Then he grins. "It's expeditious."

I smile, remembering our vocab game from the other day. "It's hasty."

"It's accelerated."

"It's rapid."

"It's brisk."

"It's swift," I answer, not sure what I like more—coming up with the words and challenging Mark, or the fact that Mark doesn't seem to mind that I challenge him.

"Mark, let's go!" rings Diane's voice from the front yard.

"Saved by my mother," Mark says. "But you won anyway. And no rush on getting the books back."

I'm still smiling after he's shut the door.

But as I set to work, my smile fades. I've agreed to go to church. I've missed certain parts of my family life—Ruth's hugs, Isaac's sticky kisses. But I haven't missed church. I haven't missed Pastor Garrett's blustery sermons that leave me full of contradictions and questions. I'm guessing the Treatses' church won't be like that, but I'm not sure. I've never been to any church but Calvary Christian, so I have no idea what to expect. Part of me is curious, of course. And part of me just doesn't want to hurt Diane's feelings.

I'm still muddling over what Sunday will be like when Lauren gets home from work that evening, just in time for dinner. We sit down at the table and share tomato soup and saltines and something Lauren found called tofu pups that taste like rubber unless you douse them with ketchup.

"So how was Diane's today?" Lauren asks me.

"Well," I say in between bites, a little nervous and not entirely sure how Lauren might react to my news, "I'm going to church with Mark Treats and his parents this Sunday."

Lauren swallows and looks at me. "What?" she says. From the steady tone of her voice, I can't tell if she's concerned or angry. Or both.

"I said I was going to church," I say, my voice small. "With Mark Treats and his parents."

"Oh," she says. She takes a big bite of her supper and chews slowly, like she's keeping track of the number of bites in her head. After she swallows she takes a sip of her Diet Coke. "You actually want to do this?" She makes me going to church sound like I'm about to go camping in the wilderness by myself for a week.

"I don't know." I shrug. "Diane asked, and I didn't want to be rude. Plus, it might be sort of interesting to see a church that's not like Calvary."

"Interesting?" Lauren answers. "Well, that's laughable." She looks me dead in the eyes. "Rachel, you cannot go back there."

"Go back where?" I ask, and irritation starts to build inside. "I'm not going anywhere I've been before. Like I said, it's not like I'm going back to Calvary." I didn't think Lauren would be thrilled at my news, but I mostly thought she would just roll her eyes in her Lauren way and forget about it. Instead, she's furious.

"Calvary, the Treatses' church, St. Patrick's down the street," Lauren continues, dragging her hands through her hair in frustration, "it doesn't matter. Church is church. It's all just a bunch of guys trying to sell us the same exact crap. You don't get it."

"But you're the one who said Dr. Treats and his wife are such nice people, and they've helped you out so much," I manage. "You even said Mark was so lucky to have them as parents. So now they're horrible people because they go to church?"

Lauren crosses her arms and shakes her head. "They're not horrible people. They're just . . . They don't get it."

I stare at my food, uncomfortable with what's happening

between us. I hate the idea of fighting with Lauren. Because I hate the idea of fighting with anyone, period.

But at the same time, I can't help but feel annoyed at the idea that Lauren thinks she can tell me what to do.

"What do you mean they don't get it?" I say, my voice just above a whisper.

"Religion brainwashes you, Rachel!" Lauren taps her temple twice, hard. "Haven't you figured that out by now? You're doing so well here. You're not just buying their Jesus God crap all the time like some Christian robot."

I squeeze my eyes tight for a moment, trying to figure out the words I need. Trying to decide if it's even worth it to fight back. "I'm pretty sure I can . . . make my own decisions about what to think about this," I tell her, still avoiding eye contact.

"I'm not telling you what to think, I'm just trying to protect you!" Lauren replies, her voice growing louder.

"Protect me from what? From God?" My voice rises suddenly, and it takes me by surprise as much as Lauren. I finally manage to look at her. "You know I still believe in Him, right? And I still pray?"

Lauren just huffs and rolls her eyes. "Whatever," she mutters.

We both sit there, silent. We're two messed-up girls who will never have enough words to explain ourselves. Not ever.

"Okay, fine," says Lauren, her voice still frosty. "I'm going to bed."

"It's seven at night," I answer, fighting the lump in my throat.

"I know," Lauren answers. "Good night."

Even the cats go with her, leaving me by myself on the couch.

In the moment, telling Lauren how I felt seemed like a good idea. Like a release. But now I just feel terrible. Maybe I should have kept my mouth shut. But that didn't feel right either. I burst into tears, loud enough that I think Lauren might come back. But she never does. I cry myself to sleep on the couch.

⚜

The next morning is Saturday, and Lauren goes to work. I'm not sure if she's scheduled to or if she just wants to get out of the apartment, but from my spot on the couch, hidden under blankets, I see her slipping out the front door dressed in her work scrubs well over an hour before Dr. Treats's office opens. She doesn't even eat breakfast. Or glance in my direction.

When I finally get up, I pour myself some cereal and eat it on the couch.

Maybe Lauren is right. Maybe all churches are the same. And I don't have to go to church to keep talking to God in the way I have been.

But I can't possibly know if all churches are the same if I've only ever been to one in my whole life.

Eventually, I have to get out of the apartment or I'm afraid I'll go stir-crazy, so I go for a walk with one of the only mystery novels in the apartment that I haven't read, making sure to head in the opposite direction from Clayton Animal Hospital. I have nowhere to go, really, so I spend most of the time in a park with my book. It's so hot there aren't any other people there. It's so hot I can't even concentrate on my reading.

But it's probably not just the heat that's making it difficult to focus.

First my father wanted to protect me and now Lauren does. When I didn't want to live as my parents wanted me to, I had to leave their home. If I don't want to live my life like Lauren thinks I should, maybe I'll have to leave her home, too. And then I'll have nowhere to go. I take a shaky breath or two and feel sorry for myself.

Mosquitoes are feasting on my ankles and forearms, so I head back to Lauren's apartment. When I get there, I pull out some paper from my pile of unsent letters to Ruth and consider what I want to say to Lauren.

At least I'll be able to get this letter to where I want it to go.

Lauren,

I don't want to be in a fight with you. You mean too much to me.

I remember in your very first email to me you asked me why God gave us brains if He didn't want us to use them to learn about anything we wanted to learn about. And later you sent me a poem that said it was all about me asking myself what did I want to do with my one wild and precious life? I don't think you know how often I've thought about that question since you sent me that poem.

I'm not totally sure why I'm going to church with the Treatses, but I do want to feel like I can decide whether or not I can go. I feel like that has to be up to me. Like I can make that kind of decision about my life.

You've done so much for me, and I don't want to make you angry at me. But I also think it's important that I try to figure this out for myself. I don't know if this is making any sense, but I hope you read this and know I care about you so much, and I *hope you understand what I'm trying to say.*

Love,
Rachel

I've never told Lauren I love her, but signing the letter this way seems right. I do love Lauren for her spirit and energy and kind heart.

I hope she loves me back. Even after yesterday.

I leave the letter on the table where she'll be sure to see it, and then I curl up on the couch. All of a sudden I'm exhausted, even if I haven't done much but take a walk and write a letter.

The next thing I know, I feel a gentle shake on my shoulder, waking me up. When I open my eyes I see Lauren, dressed in her work scrubs with her blue hair piled up on top of her head in a ponytail.

"Hey," she says in a quiet voice. I can see she has the note I've written to her in her hand.

"Hi," I say, trying to read her face.

"I just wanted to say . . ." she starts, holding up the piece of paper. "Oh, hell." She falls down next to me on the couch, and I can see her eyes are wet with tears, but she's holding on to them and not letting them fall. "Rachel, I'm sorry. I'm really sorry." I know from Lauren's rants that she loves to be right. So I know the words "I'm sorry" are a big deal for her. They don't come easily.

"You read my note?" I ask.

Lauren nods. "Me freaking out about you going to church," she says, "that's my own issue. You should go with the Treatses if you want to. I mean, I can't say I get it. I don't ever want to go to church again. But you're not me. You're you."

My chest lightens, grateful for this truce we seem to be forging.

"Thanks, Lauren," I say softly.

She nods toward the kitchen.

"I think I need a Diet Coke," she tells me. "And a huge piece of cake."

"You mean that weird vegan cake you made the other day?" I ask her, anxious to feel back to normal as soon as possible.

"Yes, that weird vegan cake," she says, getting up. "You know you love it."

We sit together on the couch, and when we're finished eating, there's comfortable silence for a little while. Lauren picks at a loose thread on one of the couch cushions.

"Rachel," she asks gently. "Do you really still pray?"

"Sort of," I answer. "I never felt very good at it before. At home, I mean. But now I do this thing where I focus on a few words instead of trying to remember Scripture. It sort of helps me, I guess."

"I couldn't pray without hearing my father's voice in my ears," Lauren says. "So I just stopped doing it."

"Yeah," I say. "Sometimes I hear my dad's voice, but lately not so much."

"That's good."

"If you saw your dad now, do you still think you'd tell him that you hate him?" I ask.

"I used to think so," Lauren answers, tugging at the loose thread now, wrapping it around her finger until the tip is beet red. "But now I think I would just walk away. He's not worth it."

Lauren's answer makes me so sad. I picture kids all over the planet—kids in Mongolia or France or Peru—sitting at home with their families. Talking. Arguing. Growing up.

And we don't get to be those kids.

"I don't love my parents anymore . . ." Lauren continues, "I mean, I don't think it's wrong if you still love your parents. I think it's so hard to put into words, Rachel. I've been gone a lot longer than you. My dad beat me up. My dad was . . . he was awful. For a really long time. And your parents . . ."

I close my eyes for a moment. They haven't always been awful. I can't even say they're awful now. They're only doing what they think in their hearts is right.

I exhale and look at Lauren again. "I don't want to talk about it anymore. It's just overwhelming."

Lauren smiles. "I get it. You want to numb out on TV and watch, like, three episodes of *Law & Order* with me?"

"Definitely," I say. "But let me put on my nightgown first. Hey—where's my bag that I brought with me?" I usually keep it in the living room.

"Oh," Lauren says, her eyes on the television. "While you were napping, I cleared out a drawer in my dresser and some space in my closet. And I put your clothes in there. I hope that was okay."

"Sure," I say, and there's a familiar lump in my throat again. But if I let myself cry this time, I think the tears would be happy ones instead of sad ones. "Thanks. A lot."

"No problem," Lauren says.

As I head back to change, Lauren stops me.

"Rachel, I'm really sorry."

"Thanks," I answer. "And I'm sorry if anything I said hurt your feelings, and just because I'm going to church tomorrow doesn't mean . . ."

"Rachel?"

"Yes?"

"Go get your nightgown on. I want to watch *Law & Order.*"

"Okay."

I go back to the bedroom to change. *God*, I whisper when I get there, *thank you for Lauren.*

20

Mark is wearing knee-length khaki shorts and a pale-blue collared shirt and he smells like soap and something minty.

And I'm sitting two inches from him. If either of us shifted just a bit we might touch.

"Want a Tic Tac?" he says to me, sliding a small plastic case out of his pocket.

"Sure," I say.

"Hey, I'm not saying your breath smells or whatever," he tells me, knocking a few tiny mints into my open palm. "I'm just offering. I always think people are going to think I'm telling them their breath smells when I offer them a Tic Tac."

"Well, thanks for reassuring me that my breath doesn't smell," I answer, popping one of the mints into my mouth. Mark smiles at me—his warm, takes-up-half-his-face smile—and I bite down quick on the Tic Tac, my heart picking up speed just a bit.

"We're so glad you're with us, Rachel," Diane says in a loud whisper. She's sitting on the other side of Mark, and she leans over him and squeezes my forearm. "I think you'll really enjoy the service." She smiles at me and so does Dr. Treats from the end of the pew, his big bushy moustache curling up along with his grin.

Mark slides the Tic Tacs back into his pocket. "What I really think you'll enjoy about this service is the pastor has it down to fifty minutes flat," he says, loud enough for his mother to hear him. She glares at him, but he just shrugs.

Peace Lutheran is certainly physically different from the wooden, airless structure that houses Calvary Christian. Peace is a big, modern building with large windows that let in lots of sun. An enormous felt banner with a picture of corn stalks and pumpkins hangs to my left. It reads *Give Thanks to the Lord for He Is Good!* Another on the right reads *Let Everything That Has Breath Praise the Lord!* A big flat-screen projects the word *WELCOME!* along with an animated white dove flapping its wings. At Calvary, sometimes the women bring fresh flowers from their gardens and put them at the front of the church, but Calvary is too poor to even afford pews, so we use folding chairs. The pews at Peace Lutheran are padded and covered in dark green fabric.

In big, bold letters on the inside of the Sunday program are printed the words *All People Are Welcome Here! No one is excluded! No matter who you are, or what you have done, God loves you and is glad you are here!*

No matter what you have done. The first time I read those words I get goose bumps on my arms. I read them over again. I'm a girl who's left her family behind, and even if I know I have good reasons for that, in my heart I've felt guilty for it. For leaving Ruth and my mother and all my responsibilities behind.

I imagine God looking down on me. If God loves me and is glad I'm here, is it the same gaze of the God who looked down on me at Calvary Christian? Did that God welcome everyone? Sometimes Pastor Garrett didn't make me think so. But if God is God, it has to be the same God, doesn't it?

Soon it's time for the service to begin. A full band in the corner with a piano player, a drummer, and several men playing guitars starts up with "Blessed Assurance." Mark sings along, following the lyrics as they appear on the screen, but I know the words by heart.

"Welcome, all," begins the pastor, a large, middle-aged man with a full belly and a well-trimmed gray beard. He doesn't boom because he doesn't need to—he's wearing a small lapel microphone—and soon he's preaching about that morning's Scripture readings, the parable of the talents from Matthew, and about how we must use our God-given gifts to serve the Lord. I've heard it before, of course.

"We must ask ourselves," the pastor says, stepping out from behind the pulpit and walking among the congregation, "what are we doing with our precious gifts, with the gifts that

God has given us? Perhaps there's a young woman here who wants to study medicine, or a young man with a talent for teaching. How much God wants us to honor Him by using our talents. Our gifts."

My gifts—according to Pastor Garrett and Dad—are the gifts of the homemaker and nothing more. To raise up children for Christ and to be a good helpmeet. I try to picture Pastor Garrett preaching about girls becoming doctors, and it is so amusing to me, I have to watch that an inappropriate grin doesn't slip out during the sermon.

Later, there's communion with real wine, but Mark takes grape juice and so do I. And there's a big, resounding version of a more contemporary song I don't recognize, but I try to follow along. When the service ends, we file out into a room called the Parish Hall, where the excited chatter of so many people in such a small space hurts my ears and makes me want to leave. Mark and I get pushed along until we end up by a table with paper cups full of orange juice and boxes of glazed donuts.

"So what'd you think?" Mark asks, downing a tiny paper cup of orange juice in one gulp and starting on a donut.

"It was . . . nice. It was different."

"Better?" Mark asks. "Than your old church, I mean?"

I shrug. "Calmer," I say. "More . . . relaxed. But fancier, which felt strange. And I'm not sure if I liked that part or not."

"Fancier. You mean like the flat-screen for the song lyrics and stuff?"

"Yes," I say. "And the big band and the way the donation envelopes let you write down credit card information. At my church, everyone's encouraged to live without debt, so that sort of eliminates the credit card option."

"But what about the donuts?" Mark says, raising an eyebrow. "Don't the donuts sort of tip things in Peace Lutheran's favor?"

"Well, the donuts don't hurt," I say, grinning.

Mark smiles. "Yeah, the donuts aren't bad. And coming here isn't terrible. It'll be harder when school starts, though. On the weekends during the school year, I just want to sleep in."

"Until I moved in with Lauren, I'd never slept in," I say, helping myself to a cup of juice. "Not in my entire life. Except for when I was sick."

Mark's eyebrows dart up. "Really?"

"Yes, really," I tell him, taking a sip of juice. "I'd gladly get up early if I thought it would mean I could spend all day learning things."

Mark grimaces ever so slightly. "Rachel, do you know there's a chance I could have this dude named Mr. Taylor for U.S. Government class this year? The last time he gave an A to anyone, the U.S. government didn't actually exist. We were still a British colony. That's how ancient this guy is."

"Ancient?" I say. "You mean elderly."

"Vintage."

"Seasoned."

"Mature."

"Geriatric," I offer.

"Old," Mark responds. "And that's all I got."

I blush a little and look down into the bottom of my cup at the solitary swallow of juice I have left.

"Sorry," I say.

"For what?" Mark answers. "I think it's kind of cool you know so many words. But honestly, I wish I could get you to understand how freaking boring U.S. Government is."

I finish my juice and bite my bottom lip for a moment, trying to choose my words. "But you have . . . options," I finally begin. "I don't know that you totally understand that. Like what the pastor was saying in there. You can use your gifts any way you want to. It's not just that you can read Madeleine L'Engle books if you feel like it. It's more than that. It's like . . . a lifetime of possibilities."

Mark doesn't have a rapid-fire retort this time. He scratches at the back of his neck. "Yeah," he says. "You're probably right."

My cheeks are pinking up, but I look at Mark and ask, "Are you just saying that? Or do you really think I'm right?"

"No, I really think you're right," Mark insists. "I'm kind

of an ungrateful pain in the ass sometimes, if you want me to be honest."

"No, you're not," I say, shaking my head. "You're nice. And funny."

"Well," Mark says, like he's considering my words with care, "that is true. I am incredibly nice and funny."

"I never said incredibly."

Mark bursts out laughing, and then I'm laughing, too. It feels so easy to stand here and drink paper cups of juice and talk to Mark Treats. As if my brain has suddenly forgotten all the reasons why it was supposed to be difficult. Or wrong.

"Do you think you have options?" Mark says. "Like now? That you've left?"

Now that I've left. For good? Forever?

"Your mom says I'm a girl who knows what she wants and goes after it," I say. "I don't know. I'm still trying to figure it all out."

"I think my mom's right," Mark says, and his smile softens just a little and his brown eyes meet mine. "You're kind of tough as nails."

"Maybe," I answer, my heart pounding hard, insisting I pay attention to it.

"No, not maybe tough as nails," Mark says. "Definitely, absolutely, unequivocally tough as nails. I just listed antonyms for maybe. I thought I'd switch it up this time."

"Indubitably," I offer. "Decidedly."

"You're never going to let me win, are you?" Mark says, shaking his head.

"No," I tell him, smiling so hard my cheeks hurt.

⤬

When I get home from church, Lauren is busy in the bathroom coloring her hair a new shade of the rainbow.

"How'd it go?" she asks, carefully massaging a reddish-looking dye into her scalp, oversized plastic gloves on her hands.

"It was okay," I say, heading toward the couch. "It was nice in some ways." When I tell her about the big screen, Lauren steps outside of the bathroom to make sure she's heard me right.

"A flat-screen? Really?"

"Yeah," I say, grinning. "And you can make a donation to the church on a credit card!"

"But Psalms says the wicked borroweth and payeth not again," Lauren admonishes, mimicking Pastor Garrett, even waggling a dye-covered, gloved finger at me.

"I know," I answer. "But parts of the service I liked, actually. Like the sermon."

"That's nice," Lauren answers, heading back into the

bathroom. I hear the water turning on, like she doesn't want to talk about it anymore.

"Hey!" I shout. "Can I borrow your laptop?"

"You don't have to ask."

By the time Lauren has blow-dried her now burgundy hair and joined me on the couch, I have half a page of notes scribbled down. Phone numbers, addresses, a list of required documents.

"What's up?" she asks.

"I'm doing this research."

"Obviously. But for what?"

If I say it out loud to Lauren, it becomes real. It becomes something I'm doing instead of something I might do.

"I'm trying to figure out how to enroll. In school."

For once, Lauren is speechless. Her mouth actually opens and no sound comes out. She just peers at the computer screen, apparently looking for confirmation of my announcement.

"Clayton Independent School District Admissions and Withdrawals," she finally reads out loud, her voice quieter than normal. Maybe even in awe. "Really? Seriously?"

"When I turn eighteen, I can enroll myself."

Lauren opens her mouth and shuts it again. She looks carefully at the computer screen and then at me.

"You're smart," Lauren says. "You could probably enroll

as a senior and graduate with a real high school diploma, not just a GED like I have."

"Yeah. Maybe. It's probably stupid."

"No, it's not stupid," Lauren says slowly. Usually Lauren is ready with her opinions, but she seems to be carefully chewing over my idea. "I think it could be . . . really incredible for you. But . . ."

"But what?" I ask, frowning a little.

"It's going to be very different," Lauren says. "You'll be with worldly kids who don't know anything about your life and Calvary. It might feel a little overwhelming. Especially at first. I'm not trying to tell you what to do, but I remember what it was like when I first started hanging out with real worldly kids. I tried to be all tough, but they could be intimidating."

"Yeah, I know it would be strange at first," I say, running my finger along the bottom of the laptop. Lauren's words make me anxious, but they can't completely extinguish the idea of school from my mind. I think back to Mark's SAT prep and my curiosity over how I would do in such a class.

"If you go to high school, you can go to college, right?" I ask. Some of the boys from Calvary sometimes took a business class or two at the community college branch in Healy if it could help them get their own home-based businesses off the ground, but only with the permission of Pastor

Garrett. Girls were never allowed. And I'd never known anyone who'd gone to an actual four-year university.

"Yeah, if you finish high school you could go to college," says Lauren. "I bet Clayton High has full-time counselors and everything. They could help you figure out how to apply. And maybe get financial aid. College is really expensive, you know."

"I know," I say, and my cheeks pink up. "Lauren, I can't believe I didn't first say that I would still keep my job at the Treats. Or get another one. I mean, even if I went to school I would still be working. I wouldn't want you to think that I . . ."

"Stop," Lauren says, waving her hand at me. "We'll figure that part out."

"Really?"

"Yeah," she says. "I think school could be really good for you. I bet you spend hours just reading. And learning."

Hours spent reading and learning. Every single day.

I keep staring at the Clayton Independent School District website. *The adult student . . . may enroll without parental involvement.* I'm still amazed the words exist.

"I think I'm going to call them," I say, my stomach fluttering. "The school district, I mean."

"When?" Lauren asks.

"I was thinking Tuesday," I say.

"Why Tuesday?" Lauren questions. Then she claps

her hands together. "I know! It's your birthday. You turn eighteen."

I nod. Eighteen. A legal adult.

"So you're sure you're ready for this?" she asks.

"I think so," I say, not at all sure and just overwhelmed enough to want to change the topic. To my ears, it still sounds like I'm announcing that I'm going to swim the English Channel.

That night after Lauren heads to bed, I curl up on the couch and think of Ruth. Lately, I only let my mind venture to thoughts of her when I'm alone in the dark of the evening and there's no one to see me crying. Only at night do I allow myself to remember our cuddles and late night whispers. What would she think if I told her I was thinking of enrolling in school? Would she say I was committing a terrible sin? Or would she want to try and understand me?

Is she thinking of me right now just a few miles away? Or is she so exhausted by the work she's had to take on since I left that she's been dead asleep for hours, my empty bed next to her a morning reminder of all the endless tasks she must try to accomplish that day?

Oh, baby sister, I'm sorry.

And I miss you so much.

I swallow the lump in my throat and take a deep breath. And then another.

God, help me to do what's right. Help me figure out how to live this life. To be a good person. To honor you.

It feels like years since Lauren emailed me the Mary Oliver poem—the one that's become a touchstone for my heart. My everyday prayer. My true north. Even if I haven't always understood exactly what it means.

Tell me, what is it you plan to do with your one wild and precious life?

Lauren once said that the speaker in the poem was me—that I was supposed to ask myself that question.

But now I wonder, what if the speaker is God?

What if God is saying, *Rachel, what is it you plan on doing now that I've gifted you with this mind and this heart and this itch to know about the deepest parts of the ocean and the highest crests of the mountains and the darkest edges of space?*

What is it you plan to do, Rachel Walker, with this one life I've given you?

I take a breath and feel my rib cage expanding, my heart pulsing, each beat moving me forward through time.

I have this one life that's mine, stretching out before me like the smooth, dark water of the sea, and God is inviting me to hold my breath and slide through the waves, my arms outstretched, my feet kicking, my soul headed for points unknown.

Rachel, he tells me, *dive in.*

21

I think I'm working my way out of a job. When I get to Diane's this morning, she tells me I've done so much in the past few weeks she only has a little filing for me to finish.

"Come September, you could still help me out once a week if you'd like," she asks from the love seat where she sits examining her list of appointments for the day. "Until everything starts to fall apart again. Then you can come more often."

"That sounds good," I say, organizing the paper on the desk into small piles.

There's a pause, and I sense Diane's eyes on me. "You look so cute today," she says.

I blush just a bit and touch the nape of my neck. "I put my hair up like you said."

"Yes, you have your hair up, and I can see your lovely face," Diane says, peering at me. "But there's something else." She purses her lips, thinking. "Wait. I know. I see your shoulders."

Diane's right. I'm wearing one of Lauren's sleeveless tops—a light blue color—along with a knee-length denim skirt. The fit of the top is fairly loose, the straps are wide, and the scoop neck cuts just under my collarbone—it's not exactly scandalous by Diane's standards. But it's like nothing I've ever worn before. When I walked up the steps to the Treatses' house, it felt like the sun was kissing my skin.

"I borrowed this top from Lauren," I say.

"I like it," Diane tells me. "It's very becoming."

"Really?"

"Oh, most definitely."

I grin so hard I'm afraid I look silly, and I refocus my gaze on the papers in front of me. Diane gathers her belongings and makes her way to the front door. Before she gets there, I stop her.

"Diane?"

"Yes, honey?"

I take a moment to collect the right words and put them in order.

"I just want to tell you that I really want to thank you," I say. "For this job. For taking me to church. For everything." I want to say more—I should say more. But if I do, I'm afraid I might lose the sureness in my voice.

I expect a rapid-fire response, a typical Diane pep talk. But she just nods and smiles at me. "You're going to be just fine," she says, blinking twice, her voice barely audible.

And she slips out the front door.

I get to work on the filing, and after about an hour, the door opens again. For a moment I wonder why Diane is back early, but it's Mark, wearing dark blue, knee-length swim trunks and a gray T-shirt. His hair is still wet, he has a towel slung over his shoulder, and he smells of chlorine.

"Hey," I say. "How are you?" I'm nervous. Not awful, I've-been-caught-on-the-computer nervous, but what-did-I-get-for-Christmas nervous. Fluttery nervous.

"Hey," he says as kicks off his flip-flops and sits down on the love seat. "What's happening?"

"Just working," I say, shrugging my shoulders. My bare shoulders.

"Dang, you've really made this place look better," Mark says, surveying the room. "My mom was lucky to find you."

"She might want me to come back in the fall," I tell him. "Once a week, I think."

"You mean when school starts?"

I nod. The word *school* makes me think about my birthday tomorrow and the number for the Clayton Independent School District's main office printed carefully on a piece of paper in my purse.

"So what's going to happen to you come fall?" Mark asks.

He leans back on the love seat. He's unusually still. For Mark, anyway. "Are you thinking about school?"

"Yeah," I answer. "I think so. But I'm going to wait until tomorrow to call about it because that's when I turn eighteen. I'll be a legal adult and allowed to enroll myself."

"Hey," Mark says, his face lighting up, "well, happy early birthday. I don't turn eighteen until October, so you'll have to give me the heads up on what to expect."

"I promise to reveal all," I say. "You have my word."

"Excellent," Mark replies. "Thank you."

"You're welcome."

We sit in silence for a moment, and I expect Mark to get up and go upstairs, but he doesn't. Finally, he looks at me and asks, "If you go to school, your family won't be too happy about it, will they?"

I shake my head no. "It's so . . . I mean . . . you'd think I of all people would be good at coming up with words to describe my situation, but all I can come up with is *complicated*, and I'm so tired of using that word. But no. They won't be happy about it."

"They still want you to go to that church camp?"

"I think so, but I haven't spoken to them since I left."

"That still kind of, like, blows my mind that they want you to go there," Mark says.

I offer a rueful smile. "The longer I'm here and not there, the more it amazes me, too, but I still miss them," I say.

"Especially my little sister Ruth. But at the same time, if I was with them, I couldn't be here. I couldn't be thinking about enrolling in classes and earning my own money and visiting a new church and all of these things that are pretty exciting for me, even if they make me nervous, you know? So I go back and forth. My whole life is this mix of . . . mournfulness and euphoria." Wow. I think that's the most I've ever said to Mark in one sitting.

"Mournphia," Mark says, nodding.

"Yes, mournphia. I'm in a constant state of mournphia."

It's quiet again. Mark's dark eyes focus on me, his gaze is steady. My cheeks feel warm, but I don't want to look away. I don't want him to look away either.

"I meant to bring those Madeleine L'Engle books, but I can't stop rereading them," I say, when the silence becomes too much. But Mark shakes his head.

"You keep them. Consider them a birthday gift."

"Really?" I ask. My own copy of *A Wrinkle in Time* for all time.

"Really. I've got too much to read right now anyway."

"Like what? SAT prep stuff?"

"God, no." Mark shudders. "No, I'm reading these comics by this guy named Harvey Pekar and the third book in the *Game of Thrones* series and this other book called *Slaughterhouse-Five*."

"Wait, but which one are you reading right now?" I ask, confused.

"Well," Mark says, "I do this thing where I, like, read three or four books at once. Like switch on and off? My mom thinks it shows lack of focus. But I finish most of them."

"Oh," I say. "Wow."

"You could do it, too," he says. "You're smarter than me, and I can do it."

"I need more books first," I tell him, my heart picking up speed just a bit. "I've read almost every book Lauren owns, but she doesn't own that many."

"You can borrow some of mine whenever," he says, and finally he stands up and wiggles his back a bit, cracking his spine. Then he looks at me again.

"Don't take this the wrong way," he say, frowning slightly, "but you look different or something. You look nice." He groans, flustered. "Not that you didn't look nice before. Oh, hell, that sounded awful. Forget it, you must think I sound like a jerk."

"I put my hair up," I manage, despite the fact that my mouth suddenly seems to have gone dry. "And you don't sound like a jerk."

"No, I kind of do," he says, dragging a hand through his own hair so I can see all of his face. His forehead is lighter than the rest of him, evidence of his hours in the sun. His eyes seem darker than ever. More beautiful than ever, if you can call a boy's eyes beautiful.

"You really didn't sound like a jerk, I promise," I insist.

"Okay, fine," he says. "But just so we're clear and everything, you always looked nice, okay? Just today you look, like, extra nice. All right, I'm going to stop now."

"Okay," I say, failing to suppress a giggle.

"I'm glad my idiocy humors you," he responds, one eyebrow jumping. "Listen, do you want something to eat?"

"Yeah," I say. "That would be nice."

"Cool," he says, scooting off to the kitchen. A few moments later I hear his voice. "Hey, why don't you come in here and keep me company?" he offers. "I can continue to amuse you while I make nachos."

I look at the work Diane has left me. I've managed to get most of it done. There wasn't that much to begin with today, anyway. And I'm sure I'll have a little more time before she gets back.

"I'll be right there!" I shout. And I get up and head for the kitchen.

☙ ❧

I feel a gentle push on my shoulders.

"Wake up, legal adult."

I struggle to open my eyes. Sometimes I think I'm still

making up for the years of sleep deprivation back home. When I finally sit up, I find Lauren perching on the back of the couch holding a small package wrapped in yellow paper.

"Happy birthday!" she says, tossing me my present.

"You didn't have to get me anything, Lauren," I say, surprised.

"Well, I did, so open it," she says, jumping over the couch and sitting at my feet. She wiggles in excitement.

I unwrap the paper. Lauren's given me a small, black cell phone. Not one of those fancy ones with the touch screen like she has, but a phone just the same.

"It doesn't have the Internet or anything," she says, "but you can call and text. I put you on my plan and we can share the bill."

"Wow," I say, turning it over in my hand. "I have my own number?"

"Yes!" she says. "It's all yours."

I lean over and hug Lauren hard, and she kisses me on the top of my head.

"Thanks, Lauren," I say. "This is so nice."

"I was happy to do it," she says, sliding over the back of the couch and heading for the door. "I'm going to work, so don't call Europe or anything. Domestic calls only."

I roll my eyes at her and fall back onto the couch where I spend a good twenty minutes fiddling around with my present, trying to make sure I understand how it works.

Eventually, I shower and get dressed, stopping to look at myself in the bathroom mirror, checking for any sign I seem older. As a little girl, eighteen sounded hopelessly far away, as foreign as thirty or forty. Eighteen meant adult. When I was younger, I thought I might be married by now, or even pregnant.

On my birthdays back home, my mom would always make me silver dollar pancakes for breakfast, and Faith or Ruth would bake me a chocolate cake for after supper. There wasn't enough money for big gifts, but sometimes my mother would sew me a new blouse or my siblings would give me the gift of taking on my chores for a full week. There was only one birthday when I'd received a present of any financial importance.

I glance at the Titus 2 bracelet my father gave me the year I turned twelve. *To be discreet, chaste, keepers at home, good, obedient to their own husbands, that the word of God be not blasphemed.* Those are the words inscribed on this piece of jewelry I've worn for so long. One evening not long after I arrived at Lauren's, I took it off and looked at my empty wrist, and it looked so thin and strange without it, I put the bracelet back on again.

I touch it gently now, sliding the cool metal around and around on my wrist. I let my thumb skate over the inscription on the inside.

No matter how much love may have been behind this bracelet, I know I can't wear it anymore.

I make my way to the dresser and open the drawer where I've been keeping my clothes. I slide off the bracelet and place it toward the back, tucking it under my nightgown. My eyes sting a bit, and I blink back some tears, but I don't cry.

And then, as quickly as I can, so I don't lose my nerve, I find my purse and fish out the number for the Clayton Independent School District, which is silly since I know the number by heart.

I take my new phone and sit down on the couch. But I'm too nervous to sit, so I stand. Finally, I walk outside to the top of the metal stairs leading into the apartment courtyard and shut the front door behind me.

I'll count to ten and then I'll call.

I take a breath.

One, two, three.

God, I know I can do this.

Four, five, six.

By seven I decide I'm ready. I dial the number and hold the phone up to my ear. I listen to the tinny ring, picturing some phone on some desk in some office, waiting for someone to pick it up. Finally, a woman's voice answers.

"Clayton Independent School District, may I help you?"

"Yes," I answer. "I'm calling about enrolling in school." I

look out past the courtyard at the bright blue August sky. The morning sun is shining hard, so hard that as I keep talking, I have to shield my eyes from the brightness.

Clutching a bag of groceries and a very full purse, I barely make it to the front door of the apartment building without dropping everything. I've spent the better part of the morning at the school district's offices with two middle-aged women named Mrs. Murphy and Mrs. Sweeney, sitting with them at their desks as I filled out countless forms and scheduled something called a placement test, so the high school would be able to put me in the right classes. When I parked Lauren's Honda at the two-story brick building next door to Clayton Primary School and gazed at the main doors, I heard my father's voice in my head for the first time in months, stern and clipped in its delivery.

Render therefore unto Caesar the things which are Caesar's and unto God the things that are God's.

We had always been told we were children of God and not of the government, so the government should have no business raising us.

But still I opened the car door, got out, and headed inside, my father's words leaving me as quickly as they'd come, slipping through my mind like water through my fingers.

"I'm trying to remember the last time we had a student enroll herself," Mrs. Murphy said to Mrs. Sweeney after I explained my situation.

"It's been ages," Mrs. Sweeney said to Mrs. Murphy, popping open a can of Diet Dr Pepper. "Mostly they're trying to figure out how to get out of school, not get into it." She winks at me.

"I'm impressed with you," Mrs. Murphy added, pointing at me for emphasis, her neon-pink fingernails impossible to miss.

"So am I," said Mrs. Sweeney.

"Thank you," I said. I waited to feel myself blush, but I didn't. I was impressed with me, too, but the complicated process of simply enrolling reminded me once more how big and unknowable and strange this school experiment was going to be for me.

But by the time I've gone to the grocery store and made it back home, I'm also tired. I fish through my purse and find my keys, finally pushing open the front door with my hip and setting everything down before my arms fall off. The mail's here by now, but I'll have to make a second trip for that.

When I do, I briefly imagine a soft, pastel-colored envelope waiting for me—a birthday card from my parents or maybe from Ruth. But I know that's impossible, and I know that no matter how impossible it is, I still wish the impossibility of it didn't sting so much. I fight off the feelings of sadness, and when I make it to the mailboxes at the bottom of the stairs, I see ours is so full the mailman couldn't close it. Struggling, I pull out a stack of envelopes that look like bills or junk, and then I see what's been taking up the space. A thick, worn paperback novel with a white envelope slipped inside.

The book is called *The Hobbit*, and on the outside of the white envelope it says *Rachel* in a tiny, barely readable print. Next to my name are scribbled the words *Hey, I tried to stop by but you weren't here so here you go—Mark*

I immediately dump all the junk mail and the bills on the grass by my feet and rip open the envelope—but carefully, so I don't destroy the note on the outside.

The card inside the envelope has a picture of a dog on it wearing a funny hat and sunglasses. It says *Hope You Have a Doggone Happy Birthday!*

Inside Mark has printed—more neatly this time, in black ballpoint pen.

Rachel,

Hey, just wanted to give you a book I thought you might like. There's books by the same guy that come after too so if you like it tell me and I'll loan you the other ones. And if you end up at school let me know and I can give you some tips. Like don't take Taylor for U.S. Government. I'm serious. Okay, hope this is a happy birthday for you. And by happy I mean stupendous, amazing, ecstatic, thrilling, epic, and dynamic.

Later,
Mark
PS I win this round.

I read the card over and over, and I keep rereading it as I gather the mail on the ground and head up the stairs and bump a shoulder hard into the doorframe as I head into the apartment. But it doesn't hurt.

When I've read the card at least twenty times, I tuck it into my purse. I'll show it to Lauren eventually, but for right now, I want to keep it just for me. I examine *The Hobbit*—its cover has been taped back on more than once—and I run my fingers down the creased spine. It feels like a really good book.

By the time Lauren gets home for lunch, I'm thirty pages in and I already know I'll be asking Mark for whatever comes after.

"Hey, birthday lady," Lauren says, heading for the kitchen. "Man, I'm starving."

"So," I mention, trying to keep my voice casual, "I enrolled in school today."

"You did?" Lauren responds, stepping out from the kitchen.

"I really did," I say.

"Wow," Lauren answers, and she pulls me in for a hug. When she lets go, she puts her hands on her hips and grins. "Look at you," she says. "I'm making us lunch and we can talk about it."

When we sit down at the table to eat, Lauren starts asking me questions like how will I know what courses to take and when is the first day, each one coming on the heels of the next. I know she's curious as well as worried about me taking on such a big change, but her questions start to feel suffocating somehow. Suddenly, without any notice, all the excitement from the morning—my own phone, school, Mark's card and gift—collides with what I've been trying to ignore all day. I push my sandwich away.

"What's wrong?" Lauren asks.

I remember Mark's word. *Mournphia.* My life is full of mournphia.

"It's just that . . ." I start, my voice soft. I remember my last birthday. How Ruth used strips of bacon to make a smiley face on one of the pancakes my mother made for me. How Sarah scribbled me a picture of flowers for my present. "It's my first birthday without my family."

"Oh, Rachel," she says. "Yeah. Of course."

"Do you think they're thinking of me?" I ask, trying to swallow the lump in my throat.

"I'm sure they are," Lauren answers, and she reaches out

her hand for mine and squeezes it. Her hand is small, soft, but her grip is tight and reassuring. "I know they are."

I shut my eyes and hot tears spill out.

"But Lauren, they never came to look for me."

I'm crying hard now, and Lauren's eyes are reddening. She scoots her chair over and wraps her arms around me, letting me fold myself into her. Letting me cry and cry. Finally, I'm all cried out, and I dry my eyes with one of the paper towels Lauren set out on the table for lunch.

Then Lauren asks me, "Do you wish they'd come to find you?"

I sniffle a little and shrug. "I don't know," I say. "I guess . . . I guess the answer is yes. I mean, if my dad came here right now and demanded I go home and live under his rules, I wouldn't go. I couldn't. But that they never came to look for me? That they never wanted to see if I was all right? How could they not even try?" I feel the ache in my throat building up again.

Lauren nods at my answer, and I prepare myself for a long speech about the ridiculousness of the church and its rules. But she doesn't deliver one. She just rubs my back and keeps nodding.

"Everything feels good and then sometimes it feels so sad," I continue, choking my way through the words. "When is it just going to be okay?"

"I wish I knew," Lauren answers. "But I think you need

to just let them go, Rachel. I know it hurts, but I think you need to just focus on what's in front of you, you know?"

I don't answer. Instead, I take a few deep breaths, and we sit in silence for a while, Lauren's hand still resting on my back. An idea begins to burrow even deeper into my mind.

"I think there's something I need to do before I start school," I say. And I'm pretty sure Lauren's not going to agree with me about it.

"What?" Lauren asks, her forehead wrinkling in confusion.

"I think I want to go back," I tell her. "I want to see them, even if it's for the last time. I owe it to Ruth at the very least. I need to say goodbye to my family. I don't think I can just cut them off or let them go. I think I need to at least say goodbye." The thought of driving back there makes my stomach knot up. But the idea that Ruth may be waiting for me to show up back home at any moment, repentant, makes my heart hurt.

"Rachel, are you sure that's what you should do?" Lauren asks. She frowns, and the creases in her brow deepen. "I mean, if you think it's what you need to do then I guess you should. I just don't want . . ." It's clear she's holding back, fighting the urge to talk me out of it. "No, it's your decision. You have to do what you think is right."

I nod firmly. "Yes, I think it's what I have to do. I'll go tomorrow. And get it over with."

Lauren gives my back a final pat and pushes a small smile onto her face.

"You can borrow the car if you want," she says.

"Thanks," I tell her, and we sit there together not speaking, our lunch left uneaten on the table in front of us.

22

I pull into the yard in front of my house just before supper-time.

I stare at the house for a moment. Up until I moved to Lauren's apartment, it's the only home I've ever lived in. Honestly, it was the only place I really knew in the world outside of Calvary Christian Church. And I know it as well as I know my own reflection.

The small plaque with John 3:16 inscribed on it hanging over the open entryway into the family room.

The hall closet downstairs where Mom always hides the Christmas presents even though she knows we'll peek.

The wall of Sheetrock in the garage where Sarah and Isaac like to color with crayons, and Ruth and I always let them because it's just the garage.

The rich scent of fresh mud coming from the work boots lined up by the back door after my dad and brothers come home from a job.

The sounds of Sunday mornings, when Mom wakes us up by singing "To God Be the Glory" or some other favorite hymn.

To God be the glory
For the things He has done
With His blood, He has saved me
With His power, He has raised me

I know every bit of this place. Every square inch.

I cut the engine and when my heart speeds up so fast it hurts I turn it on again and shift the car back into drive.

It doesn't have to be today. I can come back.

But I know—as intimately as I know every bit of my family's house—that my heart won't let me. I need to make it clear to them that I've changed. That I'm glad I've changed.

I knock on the front door. Little Sarah opens it, and I wait for her to run to me, to grab me around the knees. But she doesn't. She just looks at me, her expression forlorn. Her gaze measured.

"She's here," she says over her shoulder. "It is Rachel. Ruth was right."

The door opens wider, and my father is standing there, my mother close behind him. The other little ones are gathering around their knees.

And Ruth is there, too, her face still, her eyes wide with surprise.

"Rachel," my father says in a neutral voice that reveals nothing. "Come in."

At this, my mother steps up and hugs me, my throat seizes, and I'm taken aback at how much I want to cry at her touch. Her hug is tight but quick, just like always, and she releases me as soon as she's taken me into her arms.

"It's good to see you, Rachel," she says. She sounds like she's speaking to a stranger, and I guess she may as well be.

And I know she allowed my father to send me out of the house, and I know she lives in fear for my eternal soul. But the truth is you only get one mother in your life, and she's mine.

And you always want the mom you've been given.

I swallow my tears back—tears I swore I would not shed—and look toward Ruth. My little Ruth. She's watching the exchange with careful eyes, and I can tell from the tiny red hives spreading up her neck that she's anxious. I give her a kind look, and she nods at me, but she doesn't smile.

"Rachel, we were sitting down to supper," my father says. "Why don't you join us."

I remember the parable of the prodigal son from the Bible. What happens after the prodigal son returns? Does he have to go to Journey of Faith? Can he read Madeleine L'Engle books? Is he allowed to go to school and talk to kids his own age without a chaperone?

Is he allowed to ask questions, seek knowledge, find answers?

No. Of course not.

At my father's words, I nod and head toward the table, then my body remembers that my father and brothers sit down first—I'm supposed to help bring in the food—and I make an awkward move toward the kitchen counter where I see stacked plates and a big pot of macaroni and cheese.

"Thank you for helping," my mother says, smoothing things over, and soon Ruth joins me as I scoop the food out onto the plates and she carries them to the table.

After she's taken in a few plates, I manage to reach over and squeeze her shoulders. She gives me a wary smile but doesn't say anything.

Once everyone is served, I take a seat at the table. I've chosen my outfit carefully—an ankle-length skirt and loose, three-quarter-sleeved blouse. Faith's boots are tied tight around my ankles. My hair is down. In the weeks I've been gone, I haven't gone so far as to wear pants, but I've certainly relaxed my understanding of modesty. Still, I don't want my clothes to be a reason for my father to send me away without getting a chance to speak for myself first.

"Father God, thank you for your love and favor," my

father begins, and I bow my head instinctively. "Bless this food and drink we pray, and thank you for all who share with us today, especially your servant, Rachel."

After a few bites in silence, Jeremiah can't help himself. "Where have you been?" he asks, wiping his chin with a paper napkin. "You just left all of a sudden and we weren't supposed to talk about it. Only pray for your soul."

Mom's face tightens, and Dad shoots him a look. My heart breaks for Jeremiah. He's forgotten that in this family asking questions that make people uncomfortable is inappropriate. Better to stay sweet and just smile. Better to stick with the carefully practiced words and routines, with everything everyone wants to say sitting just under the surface, like a ticking bomb we've all chosen to ignore.

"I've been staying with a friend," I finally answer. My mother looks down at her plate. I can feel my older brothers staring at me while I chew.

Jezebel. Salome. Lot's wife. Eve.

"Faith's doing really well," Ruth announces loudly, trying to change the topic. "Her morning sickness isn't as bad this time as it was with Caleb."

"That's good," I say. "I'm glad." I don't care if I see Faith. Does this make me a bad person? I know Faith is my sister and I should care, but if I don't see her while I'm here, I won't mind. I don't know what to say to her. And she must think I'm nothing but doomed for hell now anyway. The sense of not needing to see her eats away at me a little, but I can't deny it's truth.

We finish supper, and I help Ruth clear. Dad takes Mom into their bedroom, and I hear my father's muffled voice behind the shut door. My older brothers move into the family room, and Ruth and I are alone for a moment, washing the supper dishes. I collect my words to try and find the right thing to say. But Ruth speaks first.

"Rachel," she whispers, scrubbing at a dirty plate, not looking at me, "you only brought your purse. Please say you're not leaving again, Rachel. Please say you're going to stay."

My heart crumples. "Oh, Ruth," I say, "I've missed you so much. I want you to know how much I've missed you."

She turns to me, her eyes full of tears. "Rachel, you said in that note you left that you would get in touch with me and you didn't."

I put down my plate and take her into my arms for a hug, soapy hands and all. "Ruth," I whisper into her ear, "I did try to write you a letter. Lots of them. But I wasn't sure how I could get them to you without Mom and Dad reading them first. Same with calling. I know you're never alone. I'm so sorry I broke my promise to you."

Ruth pulls away suddenly and nods, wiping at a few tears with the back of her hand.

"I know," she whispers, shaking her head. "It's nothing."

"Ruth, it's not nothing," I insist, but there isn't anything more I can say because my parents walk out of their room, and despite the fact that there are still dishes left to do, my father asks that we join him in the family room.

We go, and I take my usual seat on the couch. Back here in this room where Pastor Garrett and my parents told me I was no longer welcome, I can't help but feel that the walls are caving in on me. That my breath is harder to catch. My father walks over to me and presses his heavy, rough hands on my head and starts mumbling, whispering words of thanksgiving and requests for redemption. "Father God, let us pray for your servant, Rachel . . ." I want to squirm out from under him and race into the backyard to fill my lungs with fresh air. I want to pray to God the way I know works best for me—alone with my own thoughts. With my own steady breaths.

But Dad's words continue. "Father God, we bow on our knees before you, from whom every family in Heaven and on earth is named. Heavenly Father, we know you protect us from your enemies and we know you are our everlasting shield. Strengthen us, Father God, for the challenges of this day, and help us apply our hearts toward wisdom. In Jesus's name we pray."

"Amen," my family responds.

"Amen," I say, not quite as loud.

My father sits back into his recliner. His large, calloused

hands are wrapped around his Bible, his face still. I remember when I was a little girl, how much I loved evening time with Dad. It was the only time we ever really saw him, and his words were everything to us. When he prayed, I was sure he had a direct connection to God that was better than any other father's. I used to imagine some bolt of lightning coming down from Heaven, making him a strong and faithful servant of the Lord. He was my provider and my guardian. He was my whole world.

The last time he saw me, I was sobbing and running from his home. I wanted to blame Pastor Garrett, and I wanted to blame him.

But I know now that my father did set the rules as he believed they must be according to God's word. And when I left I was scared into leaving because I was afraid of those rules; the possibility of Journey of Faith was a fate that terrified me. Now I know I haven't just left because I was afraid. I've chosen—with my whole heart—not to follow the rules anymore.

That's why I'm not coming back. That's the truth of all of this.

"Rachel," he begins, "your mother and I want to talk with you about what your being here means."

My mother squeezes her hands together tightly. I know she won't speak during this entire conversation. She won't say one word.

"Rachel, why have you come here tonight?" he asks. Not accusatorily, not even angrily. Just directly.

For a moment I'm caught off guard. I expected a speech, more Scripture. I didn't expect the chance to speak first. But I look at my father, at my family, and I speak in a clear voice. A voice I've been given by God.

"Mom and Dad, everyone," I begin, speaking the words I practiced over and over in the car on the way here, "I came here because I wanted to see you. I wanted to tell you, Mom and Dad, that I know you've always done what you believe to be right and guided by God. You raised me to be a follower of Christ, and I still believe I am one. A follower of Christ."

Ruth looks at me when I say that. A quick glance, just barely. But I notice it. I glance back, but she hides her face behind Isaac, who's sitting in her lap.

"I believe that God has given me gifts, and I want to use them," I continue. "I want to learn, and I want to go to school. I've been staying with Lauren Sullivan in town. I know you know that. But because I've turned eighteen, I'm legally allowed to enroll myself in school. I'll be starting next week."

I hear a huff of disbelief from one of my older brothers, but my father's face is emotionless. As if he's expected as much from me and isn't surprised. "Rachel," he answers, "this family has been built on Biblical principles. We tried to protect you from a God-hating culture, we tried to protect you from those who would turn you away from the Lord. This is not what God wants for your mission on this Earth."

"Yes, Dad, but . . ." I begin, and I can hear my voice starting to waver, not quite so clear anymore. "I understand that, but I want to believe that I can still . . . I was thinking that maybe . . ." I look at Ruth again, but she is still looking away from me. I can't even see if she is crying.

"I want you to know that I still love God," I try again. "And I still pray to Him, and I still have a relationship with Him . . ."

"God is not your buddy, Rachel," my father interrupts. "He's not some pal you can be friends with on your terms. Your soul should proclaim the greatness of the Lord Jesus. Your spirit should rejoice in God as your savior, not your friend." I finally hear an edge creep into his voice.

"Yes, Dad, I know that's what you believe," I say. My heart is pounding and my face is hot. Tears are seconds away and my body is numb. "But are you saying that I can't . . . that I can't even visit?" My voice breaks as I manage the words.

"If this is how you've chosen to live your life, you cannot live here and you cannot visit," he continues. "You can't be a halfway part of this family. Rachel, my daughter and child, I will keep praying that you will be led back to Christ. When you are ready to return home and live as the Lord God intended, you are welcome here. But not until then."

At that my father stands up from his chair, turns around, and walks away from me, out to the backyard where he'll stay until I leave. I know he hopes this denial of affection will snap me into compliance. And I know that it's the only way he has left to tell me he loves me.

My older brothers get up and leave, too, and the twins follow, but Jeremiah looks over his shoulder once before he goes. Tears are running down my face now, but I give him a hopeful half smile. He only glances back, confused. Heartbroken. I want so much to make him understand, but I know he doesn't and he probably never will.

"Oh, Rachel," my mother quietly manages from her chair on the other side of Dad's seat, her own tears rolling down her face. Sarah stands uncertainly by my mother before climbing into her lap.

"Mom, I just wish . . ." I say, barely able to get the words out through the tears that are flowing in earnest now. "I wish you could understand. I'm not a bad person, Mom. I'm not a bad person for wanting something else. I'm not."

My mother squeezes her eyes shut and shakes her head—she can't bear to listen to me.

"Rachel, you have to go now," she says. "You have to leave." She kisses Sarah on the head and puts her on the couch, then stands up and pulls me up from the chair into a tight embrace. "I'm praying for you, Rachel," she whispers into my ear. "I'll never, ever stop praying for you to return to Christ. But Rachel, you have to go."

Quick, like the strike of a match. That's how fast I'm cut out of my family.

I stand there, crying. Stunned.

When I told Lauren I wanted to come back to my family to say goodbye so I could move on, what I didn't want to tell her is that I thought my family was different from hers. My father had never beaten me or left marks on me. And that had to make my family different. That had to mean he would at least let me visit. He would at least give me that much.

But now I know that my family is not that different from Lauren's. Not in the ways that really matter.

And it breaks my heart so much.

My mother turns and heads toward the hallway and down to her bedroom. I hear her shut her door behind her.

Ruth is still holding Isaac who's tugging on her blouse— one of my old blouses that belonged to Faith before me. The pink fabric is soft and threadbare now after so many washings.

"Rachel go?" Isaac says. "Rachel go?"

"Yes, Rachel goes," Ruth answers, sniffling and looking away.

"Ruth . . ." I start.

"No, Rachel, you heard them." Her voice is deflated. Resigned.

"Ruth," I plead.

"Rachel. You heard them."

I nod and wipe at my running nose. I leave Ruth behind and turn and head toward the door—not taking in any of it. I want to miss this house, somehow, and all the knowledge I hold about it. But I won't miss this building. This space. I'll only miss that brief, precious time of childhood certainty. That sense of belonging to a family that seemed blessed beyond measure.

I walk, still sobbing, toward the car, and I'm about to get in when I hear Ruth's voice behind me.

"Rachel, wait. Wait!"

I turn and there she appears, alone, standing in front of me, her eyes red. Her face wet.

"Ruth!"

I grab her and hug her so hard. So hard so she knows I'll never ever let go of her in my heart.

"Rachel," she says into my ear, sobbing. "I don't understand. I don't."

"Ruth, I'm so sorry. I don't know how to make you understand. I don't think I can."

Ruth lets go of me. Her body is shaking from crying. She keeps glancing back at the house. The risk she's taken by following me out here is enormous. I haven't been gone so long that I don't know that.

Finally, she's able to speak again. "Did you really try to write me letters?"

I nod, emphatic. "Yes, Ruth, I did. I really did. Lots of them."

"What did they say?"

"I tried to tell you what was going on in my life," I tell her, "but that doesn't matter now. If I could write you a letter right here, right now, I would tell you all the wonderful things about you. I would remind you of what a smart and caring and generous person you are. You're all of those things, Ruth. All of those things and more."

I take her hands in mine, and we stand there by the car, surrounded by the thick August humidity and the rumblings of trucks off the nearby county road and the love that we have for each other.

"Rachel," Ruth asks, tears sliding down her cheeks, "do you know what scares me the most?"

I shake my head.

"That I won't see you in Heaven one day." Her voice cracks when she says it, and she starts crying harder.

"Ruth," I say, squeezing her hands hard. "I promise you that I'll see you in Heaven."

Ruth nods. "Okay," she whispers, but I know she isn't sure.

"Look," I say, letting go of her and managing to collect myself enough to find a pen and scrap of paper in my purse. I scribble down my phone number. "This is how you can get in touch with me, Ruth. Anytime. Day or night. Only I answer this number, okay? So you never have to be afraid to call me. Memorize it, okay?"

Ruth works the scrap of paper over in her hands and glances back at the house again. "I will," she says. "But Rachel, I have to get back inside."

"I know, Ruth, but Ruth," I choke, barely able to speak, "Ruth, I love you." I hug her again as hard as I can. "I love you so much. You have to promise me that you'll never forget that, no matter what you may hear about me. I love you, and I'll never stop loving you, Ruth."

I feel her little head nodding against me. I think of all our late night snuggles. All our whispered conversations.

"I love you, too, Rachel," Ruth says.

I don't know if I can drive with so many tears in my eyes. Wiping at my face, I get back into the car, start up the engine, and touch my hand to the car window in a final goodbye. Ruth raises hers in farewell.

And when I pull away, my little sister is still standing there, clutching my phone number, watching me until I disappear from sight.

I make it back to Lauren's apartment, and as soon as I pull in and park, I let myself collapse into tears, crying so hard

I can barely breathe. After a few moments I hear a tap on the car window, and I look up and it's Lauren. I open the door.

"I saw you drive up," she says. She reaches for me, takes my hand in hers, and leads me wordlessly back up the stairs into her apartment where we sit on the couch and I cry and I talk and she listens.

"I shouldn't have gone," I tell her.

"If you hadn't, you would have always wondered," Lauren answers. "Sometimes I wonder if I shouldn't have done the same thing myself, to be honest. To get real closure or something."

I nod, wiping away my tears. I know she's right. I'll never regret going back even though it hurt to do it.

"You know," Lauren continues, "I was scared when you went back this morning because I didn't want you to get hurt. But also because . . ." Her voice slips a bit, loses its steadiness. "I was scared that I wouldn't see you again. That you'd end up staying."

Tears well up in her eyes. She shrugs and breaks eye contact.

And before I can even think, I reach out and hug her. I can tell she's surprised by my embrace because for a moment she's stiff in my arms, but then with a great sob she squeezes me tight. I lean in and rest my head in the crook of her neck, her newly red hair tickling my nose.

The truth is, returning to Lauren's apartment felt more

like coming home than driving up to my house this afternoon. I've found a new home with Lauren. And I know that I don't want to ever leave it.

We sit on the couch, crying in each other's arms for a long time until our tears leave us and our breaths come and go at the same, quiet pace.

23

I pick at some nonexistent fuzz on my shirt and inspect my reflection with care. My heart is thumping so fast I wonder for a moment how fast it can thump before I pass out. I force myself to take several deep breaths, but my heart doesn't slow down much.

"You look nice, Rachel," Lauren tells me from her spot next to me in the bathroom. "Really nice."

We're in the bathroom finishing getting ready. I'm wearing a denim skirt that stops at the knees—one of mine that I've hemmed—and one of Lauren's scoop-neck T-shirts in bright red. I have my hair pinned up the way I like it.

Favor is deceitful, and beauty is vain, but a woman that feareth the Lord, she shall be praised.

The verse taps me on the shoulder. Frowns sternly at me and shakes its head in disappointment. Dad quoted that verse the night I went to the modesty fellowship. The night I cried in the bathroom because Faith told everyone my bra straps were visible through my shirt. My reflection sours at the memory.

I take a breath and keep staring at myself until I remember another verse. *He hath made everything beautiful in his time.*

I like that verse better.

"Do you think the other kids will know I've never been to school before?" I ask, frowning at myself in the mirror.

"Rachel," Lauren says, turning me toward her by the shoulders. "It's going to be okay. But like I said, I can drive you there for this first day if you want me to."

I smooth my outfit down for the hundredth time and resist the urge to say yes. "This is something I want to do alone. It just is."

Lauren nods. "I get that."

I've practiced the five-minute walk to Clayton High half a dozen times, making sure I know where to find the front entrance. I could get there blindfolded, probably.

"Well, if you want me to take you after today, just let me know," Lauren says.

"Thanks, Lauren," I answer, glancing back to the mirror and offering my reflection an encouraging smile.

"We'd better go," Lauren says. "We're going to be late."

I take my green and blue backpack from the table in the front room—I picked it out at the resale shop a few days before—and check inside to make sure I've got my new spiral notebooks and my sack lunch and my printed schedule.

Honors English IV, Introduction to Math Concepts, French I, U.S. Government. My assigned teacher for U.S. Government is a woman named Mrs. Becker, not the dreaded Mr. Taylor. I wonder for a moment if Mark was so lucky. Maybe I'll see him today, and I can find out.

I walk Lauren to her car. As she gets in, she turns to look at me. Her eyes are red.

"Rachel, I'm so proud of you," she says. "I'm being cheesy, I know. But I don't care. Seriously. So proud."

She leans in and hugs me and plants a wet kiss on my cheek. Before I can say anything, she climbs in the car and starts the engine, waving at me before she pulls off.

I smile to myself and thank God again for Lauren.

But now I'm alone. No one to distract me or tell me I can do this. I take a breath and start walking, navigating through Clayton's streets until I reach the high school—an old, red brick building with steep, wide steps leading up to the main entrance. Temporary buildings in fading grays and greens dot the perimeter of the campus, and a big football field with bleachers sits on the edge of the campus. CLAYTON CAVALIERS reads the sign on the scoreboard.

I see dozens of pickups and cars already parked in the student lot and tiny clumps of kids standing together, talking and laughing like they know one another, which they probably do.

It would be so easy to turn around and go back. To hole up

in Lauren's apartment, hidden and safe, until she comes back home. For a moment the idea is incredibly appealing. But instead I clutch my backpack straps more tightly and keep walking. My throat dry and my palms sweaty, I set out for the main building, adjusting my face every few steps. Should I smile? Should I act bored, like I've seen this all before?

And then I imagine myself months ago, my world the size of my family's house. My mind begging for a breath. My heart longing for something I couldn't yet identify.

I smile.

The air smells like hair spray and fresh cut grass, and I carefully pick my way through the growing crowd. The buzz of teenage voices grows louder as I get closer. I catch snippets of conversation swirling around me.

"Emma, you will never even believe what he texted me last night."

"Hey, dumb ass, I thought you said we'd meet by the field."

"Please tell me this is all a nightmare and summer isn't actually over."

"If I get Taylor for Government I will jump out of a second-story window."

The last one catches my attention because I get the joke.

Finally, I make it to the steps leading into the school and take in the sea of people heading inside.

My heart hammering, I climb until I reach the top.

Acknowledgments

As an English teacher, I am careful in my use of the word *literally*, but this book literally would not exist without my editor, Katherine Jacobs, who believed in it when I was certain I could not write it. Without Kate's confidence in me, I wouldn't have been able to tell Rachel's story in the way it demanded to be told. Thank you for trusting me, for asking the best questions, and for making me a better writer.

Many thanks to those whose work and time proved valuable resources in my research, including Kathryn Joyce's work of nonfiction, *Quiverfull: Inside the Christian Patriarchy Movement* and Vyckie Garrison's "No Longer Quivering" blog. Emily Maynard was kind enough to spend time with me sharing her own experiences, and many other girls and women both in and out of the movement provided me with valuable insight through their articles, books, and blogs. James Nellis offered information about Diane Treats's profession as a realtor that proved valuable when writing Rachel's scenes at work.

Hännah Ettinger, a truly patient soul, answered every single one of my questions about what it's like to grow up Quiverfull—including the ones I know I asked twice—and in the process of my writing this book, she went from source to friend. Hännah, I respect you so much, and I'm so glad to know you.

A million thanks to everyone at Roaring Brook Press and Macmillan for continuing to make my childhood dreams come true, especially Mary Van Akin, a truly terrific publicist.

Dearest thanks to my agent, Sarah LaPolla, for never laughing at me or my e-mails—even the crazy ones that I write in the middle of the night. You always fight for what's best for me.

Thank you to Kate Sowa and Liz Peterson for always being willing to talk plot and to offer feedback, and thank you to all those who make up the tremendous community of young adult literature fans and writers in Texas, including the YAHous, the Lufkin 6, and my friends at Blue Willow Bookshop.

Thanks to the students, faculty, staff, and administration of The Awty International School for all their support.

And thanks to my family, especially my husband Kevin who, I am thankful to say, embraces a worldview that is the complete opposite of the one pictured in Rachel's universe. Kevin, you are always on my side. Texas-sized love to you and Elliott forever.